MODERN MADNESS 2 - SECOND EDITION

Modern Madness: Gateway to the Grotesque

Soul Traitor

Tim Chizmar Also Featured in:

18 Wheels of Horror

Hell Comes to Hollywood 2

Chicken Soup for the Soul: Random Acts of Kindness

Halloween Tales

A Valley of Light and Shadow: Las Vegas Writers on good and evil

It's Alive: Bringing your Nightmares to Life

MODERN MADNESS 2

THE SCREAMING VIRGINS

SECOND EDITION

Kevin Lahaie
Anthony Ray Bench
Carolyn Mansager
Will Khambatta
Thomas J. Misuraca
Stacey Smekofske
Chrisi Talyn Saje
Daniel Selleck
Ashley Green
Sinn Bodhi
Carol Kjar
Ame Winne
Dan Farren
Mike Duke
Matt Betts
Mercedes M. Yardley

CONTENTS

MURDER

MONSTERS

"Tim Chizmar has dedicated his life to the genre and exists for the love of all things horror."

— BLOODY DISGUSTING MAGAZINE

PUT THIS DOWN
THIS COLLECTION IS <u>NOT</u> FOR YOU
THIS WILL BE YOUR ONLY WARNING

"If you're going to be CRAZY,

You have to get paid for it or else you're going to be locked up."

— Hunter S. Thompson

INTRODUCTION

A RETURN TO MADNESS:

An Introduction to more of the macabre...

How important it is to see your words actually published, available in a store, available to be downloaded onto a kindle, or listened to as narrated by a sexy voice like my good friend, Michael Hacker?

A majority of these writers found within these pages are delivering brand new never before experienced tales and most have never been published before now. I dedicated the first *Modern Madness* collection to the owner of *Big Time Books* for allowing me to participate in his book *Hell Comes To Hollywood 2* which I needed for my self confidence as a struggling wannabe prose writer. Until that short story sale I'd only sold screenplays in Tinseltown. We all have a comfort zone, and traditional writing wasn't in mine, hell I pissed away a 3-book deal I signed with a traditional publisher because I wasn't mentally ready. Eric's confidence and acceptance helped me to believe in myself. Through that experience I met more writers and began to have a career. This was my driving force behind wanting to do the same for others.

Not that all of the writers included in here needed my help, some like Mike Duke and Mercedes M. Yardley I had been a fan of, previously. The most recent amazing mature dark fiction I've read in the last year has been *Apocalyptic Montessa and Nuclear Lulu: A Tale of Atomic Love* by Yardley and *Warm, Dark Places are Best* by Duke so I sought them out personally and tugged on their arms until they agreed to be these pages. I love that this collection offers poetry, prose, a weird pseudo-screenplay and yes even sample pages from a graphic novel by a former WWE professional wrestler- this ain't ya grandma's collection, this is pure *Madness* motherfuckers so buckle up.

I'm happy to show the world some of my favorite authors combined with the best up-and-coming writers of pure insanity...

I captured them all, they rattle in their cages, and if you listen closely you can still hear them scream...

— TIM CHIZMAR MAY 2018 LAS VEGAS, NEVADA

HELL

NO ONE CARPOOLS TO THE ABYSS
MATT BETTS

*The Road to Hell is paved with hair extensions, cigarette
    butts, and candy wrappers. It is built on all the little
    things that everyone casts off.*
*The Highway to Hell is littered with invisible promises and
    threats—the stench of conquests won and lost fresh in
    the air.*
*The Turnpike to Hell is gridlocked, bumper to bumper, with
    indecision and hem-hawing, held up by people who
    don't have exact change or an E-Z Pass.*

72 HOURS

KEVIN LAHAIE

The sirens sliced through the night air, like the blades that had sliced his wrists just moments earlier. This was all wrong. He wasn't supposed to be alive. He wasn't supposed to be here. As he laid there staring at the white ceiling of the ambulance, he pondered what he had done wrong to be punished this way. What had he done for God to force him to remain on this planet? Jim closed his eyes and wondered what would happen next as he drifted into unconsciousness.

Jim slowly opened his eyes, trying to gain his focus through the bright white light. He was lying in a bed, but it was not his own. His eyes shifting from side to side as he tried to figure out where he was. There was a table next to the bed separating him from another bed on his right. To his left was a restroom and a door leading into a hallway. Jim took a breath and slowly began to remember the previous night. *I'm in a hospital*, he thought to himself. He recalled attempting to take his own life. He recalled flashes of blood, lying in an ambulance, and being pushed through the hospital hallways. No memory was clear. He felt as if he had lost a night of his life with only glimpses of memories to try to fill in what happened. He sat up in the bed and glanced down at his bandage covered wrists. He noticed a packet of paperwork sitting on the table by the bed. Written on the cover of the packet was, "Understanding your 72-hour hold."

Knock, knock. A doctor smiled as he entered the room. The doctor was tall and lean. He had short blonde hair and bright blue eyes. His wide smile exposing slightly crooked teeth that were as white as the paint on the walls. "How are you feeling this morning?" he asked as he pulled a chair up towards the bed and sat down.

"I'm not sure," Jim attempted to answer, "Where am I?"

The doctor took a deep breath. "Jim, you have been placed on a 72-hour hold. Do you know what that means?" the doctor asked with a deep sincerity in his voice.

"No," Jim responded. He was confused and groggy.

The doctor continued to explain. "Jim, you are in a psychiatric hospital. You attempted to commit suicide last night, and because of that have been placed on a 72-hour hold. That means you will be here with us for observation for the next 72 hours to make sure you are no longer a threat to yourself or others. Do you understand?"

Jim understood. He was being held against his will in some sort of nut house. He wanted to yell, "Fuck you, I'm going home," but all that came out was, "Um...... okay."

The doctor continued to go over the rules of the hospital with Jim. He was in what they called the closed unit. This was a unit with more doctors on staff and fewer patients. This was the special unit for people considered to be a threat to themselves and others. The rules included no physical contact of any kind with fellow patients and mandatory group therapy twice a day. Jim stared intently at the doctor's face as the words flew through the fog in his head. Jim felt as if he was in a trance. He could hear the words but was not listening to any of the meaning behind them. His eyes slowly drifted towards the ground. On the ground, by the bed, he noticed his shoes had something missing. Bewildered, he asked "Where are my shoelaces?"

The doctor's white teeth shined through his big grin. "We take the shoes laces from all the patients," he explained. "We take away anything you can use to harm yourself. You will be given your shoelaces along with any other personal items you had during check in when you are released. You will also not be allowed to keep any shampoo or soaps in your room. If you would like to take a shower, the nurses' desk has shampoo and conditioner for the patients as well as soap and shaving cream and razors."

Jim stared back in disbelief. "This is ridiculous," he said as the doctor interjected.

"You attempted to take your own life," the doctor explained in a slightly angry voice. "We take your safety very seriously. We will do everything in our power to make sure you do not harm yourself or anyone else while you are with us." As the doctor stood to exit the room, he turned to Jim and said, "First group therapy is in thirty minutes. You may want to look around and maybe take a shower before then. Therapy will be in the large room across the hall. I can walk you over there, if you'd like."

"No!" A scream echoed down the hall. "It's coming! It's going to find me! You idiots!"

The doctor rushed out the door, towards the continued screaming. Jim stood and walked towards the door. He peaked around the corner to watch the commotion. What he saw was not what he expected. He saw a small, middle-aged man strapped into a wheelchair and screaming at doctors and security guards that stood around him, attempting to calm him down. The man seemed to be in his mid to late fifties with skin like the worn leather of an old belt that has passed its usefulness. The man was very thin but appeared stronger than he looked as he shook to break free of the restraints.

"Why hasn't this patient been sedated," one doctor exclaimed.

"We gave him four milligrams of Lorazepam, ten milligrams of Haloperidol, and fifty milligrams of Promethazine," another doctor answered.

"I'm going to die," the man in the wheelchair screamed, "and I'm taking all of you with me!"

Jim could not believe what he was seeing as the doctors struggled to wheel the man into a room and closed the door.

Jim slowly exited his room and began to walk towards the nurses' desk. As he approached, he could hear the man still screaming in the room. A large woman sat at the desk. She had short curly red hair and wore glasses with a thick black frame. The large woman peered through her glasses at Jim. "Yes?" She asked as if annoyed by his mere existence.

"I was told I could get bathroom supplies from you," Jim answered.

The hefty nurse inhaled deeply, expanding her chest to the point it nearly reached over the desk and bumped into Jim. She let out a long-exhausted exhale and asked very slowly, "What kind of supplies do you need? Everything is in separate containers, and I am not going to make multiple trips because you forgot to ask for shaving cream."

Jim was now getting annoyed and responded abruptly, "Shampoo and some soap so I can take a shower. Apparently, I have group therapy coming up. Hopefully the person conducting it is as charming as you are."

The nurse quickly stood up, the sound of her chair squeaking across the linoleum floor echoing through the hallway. She walked into a locked office behind the desk and returned with a miniature bottle of shampoo and miniature bar of soap. Jim speedily took them from her hand and walked back to his room to shower and prepare himself for group therapy.

After his shower, Jim felt a little more relaxed. He was still apprehensive about where he was at and the people he would be forced to interact with. However, he felt he could maneuver his way through the next three days. He stared at himself in the bathroom mirror. He stared into his own dark brown eyes. He stared in examination as if what went wrong was somewhere hidden in his face. He examined his thinning black hair. He examined his cleft chin. He looked over his brown skin, which he was told matched that of his father whom he had never met. His mustached face stared back at him through the mirror. He splashed water on his face one last time and walked out of the room towards his first group therapy meeting.

As Jim walked into the large meeting room, he saw four other patients and two doctors seated around the room. He entered the room and sat down on a couch next two a young woman with shoulder length dirty blonde hair. As he sat down the blonde woman locked eyes with Jim and smiled slightly then looked away uncomfortably. Jim smiled at tall blonde doctor that had been in his room earlier as they gave each other a knowing nod. As Jim looked around the room, he noticed something. These were not the type of people he was expecting to see. He had a preconceived idea of what crazy people looked like and how they acted. He had seen it on TV and in movies. Now that he sat in group therapy in an actual psychiatric facility, he noticed these were just regular people. Nobody was acting out are staring into space. They were just people sitting around a room.

"Good morning everybody," the blonde doctor began. "For our new members, I am Doctor Colvin. This is Doctor Walker. Let's begin by going around the room and introduce ourselves. Rachel, would you like to start us off?" Dr. Colvin motioned towards the young blonde woman sitting next to Jim.

Rachel let a shy smile pass her thin lips and began to introduce herself. "I'm Rachel. This is my second day here," Rachel crossed her fingers and held them in front of her as she said, "One more day to go." Everyone in the room, including Jim, began to laugh. Jim had only been conscious for slightly over and hour and was already looking forward to day three himself. Rachel continued, "I am here because I tried to kill myself. I found out my husband was cheating on me. I couldn't handle it. I felt like the last eight years of my life had been a lie. I was crippled inside. I didn't see the point of continuing. I felt completely worthless. I felt like I wasn't good enough. The pain in my heart was too much. I ended up taking a bottle of pills." She took a deep breath before finishing, "And I woke up here. My soon to be ex-husband is the one that found me and called 9-1-1."

A sadness filled the room as Dr. Walker said, "Thank you Rachel. Jim would you like to go next?"

Jim took a deep breath and began, "I'm Jim. I also tried to kill myself. I took pills as well. But I also cut my wrist to make sure I wouldn't make it. But I somehow did. I'm not sure what happened."

"Why did you try to kill yourself?" Dr. Walker asked as he leaned forward in his chair towards Jim.

"I don't know," Jim said as he looked down at the floor and began to shake his head slowly back and forth. This was not true. Jim knew exactly why he had attempted to end his life. He just was not ready to express it to himself or anyone else. He was uncomfortable with the confusion and the overwhelming feeling of never truly feeling at home in this world.

"It's okay," Dr. Colvin interrupted. "Most people are not ready to open up during their first meeting. You don't have to say anything you don't feel comfortable saying." As Dr. Colvin finished the sentence, the room went black.

"Someone forgot to pay the bill," a voice said in the darkness.

"Very funny, Manny," another voice said through the laughter of everyone else in the room, which could've been either of the doctors. Everyone sat silently in the pitch-black room for a moment as if not sure what to do next.

"I'm sure everything will come back on in a minute. Just give it a second everyone and we can continue," This voice was unmistakably that of Dr. Colvin. The lights then returned as quickly as they went out.

"Oh, my God!" Rachel screamed out while pointing frantically at Jim's arms. Jim glanced down towards where Rachel was pointing. His bandages were laying on the floor, at his feet. His wounds on his wrist open, as if freshly cut, and bleeding onto his lap. Jim's eyes grew wide with horror as the doctors jumped form their seats.

"Nurse Parker," Dr. Colvin shouted into the hall, "We have a situation."

Before Jim knew what was happening, he was rushed into his room. The rotund nurse from the front desk was analyzing his wrists. "What the hell were you thinking?" She asked as if annoyed that she had to leave her desk. "This is worse than when you came in here. What did you use to cut this deep? I don't understand how you could do this."

Jim spent the next several hours sitting alone in his room. He stared at the fresh bandages on his wrists. He was dumbfounded as to how the other bandages came off and why his wounds had opened back up. He had been scolded by the doctors and nurse as if he had somehow re-cut his wrists. They even searched his pockets and around the couch for a sharp object. There was nothing to find. Jim had not torn off his bandages. He was as shocked, if not more, than they were. Tears fell from his eyes. He sat in disbelief as he cried, overwhelmed by the past twenty-four hours of his life.

Jim walked into the bathroom to wash the tears from his face. He turned on the water and watched it flow for a moment before placing his hands under the stream. He cupped his hands, filling them with water. Jim splashed the cold water on his face and began to finger through his hair, pushing it back and off his forehead. He felt his hair sticking between his fingers. He brought his hands down toward the sink and saw that they were full of his hair. His eyes darted up towards the mirror. He immediately saw the bald patches in his head where he had pulled his hair out. He reached up to touch his hair again and more came out. Jim was pulling out hair by the handful. His heart raced in panic as his hair continued to be pulled from his head with ease.

Suddenly, blood poured from his mouth, which was agape with shock. He leaned forward into the sink to spit the blood out and along with in came a tooth. Jim began to spit out teeth as fast as his hair was falling from his head. His heart raced faster and faster. Panic overtook his body. His hands and arms tingled and went numb. He tried to cry out, but no sound would escape his lips. The lights then went out again. This time for a mere two seconds.

When they returned, Jim found himself staring at his reflection in the mirror. There was no blood. There were no missing teeth and no hair in the sink. All appeared normal, though Jim's hands still trembled. His heart still beat fast and the tingling and numbness had not subsided. The panic he felt overtook his body.

"Lunch time," a gruff male voice said as Jim looked up towards the door. Rachel stood in the doorway.

"What," Jim asked.

Rachel spoke again, in her soft feminine voice, "Lunch time, Jim."

Jim followed Rachel, past the meeting room where they sat hours earlier and into another large room with multiple tables. The table at the far end of the room had plates of food with name tags on each plate. The only people in the room were the people from the group therapy meeting earlier in the day.

"Where is everyone else?" Jim asked Rachel.

Rachel responded softly, "This is everybody. This is closed unit. Only the craziest of the crazies get to come here. You know, like you and me." Rachel laughed and smiled at Jim, letting him know that she was a friend. "Get your plate," she continued. "You can come sit with Lynn and me." Rachel pointed at a table near the door with a woman sitting at it, alone.

Jim instantly recognized her from the meeting earlier. She was very thin. She had long black hair and wrinkles around her wide brown eyes. Lynn wore a large gold cross necklace and a caring smile. These two were the only women in the unit. Jim looked at Lynn and smiled. He was relieved he had not scared everyone off during the group therapy incident. Jim found the plate with his name on it and sat with Lynn and Rachel.

As the three of the new friends talked about life outside the walls of the hospital, Lynn looked over Jim's shoulder and smiled. "Looks like the other new guy is finally out of his room," she stated, as her eyes reverted back to the other two at the table. Jim turned to see the man from earlier in the day. He was standing in the doorway, no longer strapped to the wheelchair. No longer in a state of panic and screaming. The older man's eyes searched intently around the room as if he was looking for someone.

"Ben," the nurse called out. "Ben!" She called again.

The man's head slowly turned to his left as he looked towards Nurse Walker. "Get your plate and sit down, Ben," Nurse Walker demanded as Ben stared intently in her direction without ever really looking directly at her.

Ben turned his gaze towards Jim who was still looking at the man.

As their eyes locked onto each other Ben snarled, "How's the grub, Jimbo?"

"It's great," Rachel answered. "You're welcomed to join us," she continued in what Jim had come to recognize as her usual cheerful voice.

Jim couldn't help but think to himself, *How could someone be so cheerful and friendly just days after trying to kill herself.* He was amazed by her positive outlook and hoped he too could come out of this situation with the same positive outlook.

Ben took his gaze from Jim and focused on Rachel. Ben looked at Lynn in utter disgust. "Go fuck yourself, bitch," he stated in his gruff deep voice, "Your life is a lie." Ben turned away from the trio and picked up his plate. He then sat at a table by himself and began to eat.

"That was weird," Jim whispered.

"It's rough the first day," Rachel said compassionately.

After lunch, Jim returned to his room to find a bag on the bed next to his. *Great*, he thought to himself, *I get a roommate!* Jim turned away form the beds and walked into the restroom to wash his hands. When he returned from the restroom, he saw Ben sitting on the bed next to his.

"Hi there, Jimbo," Ben loudly said, peering up through his brow. "Looks like you've got the worst room in the place, huh?" Ben asked in a mocking manner. Ben slightly lifted his head as he continued, "This is where we're all going to die. It's coming. The time is running out and you're about to suffer the pain of one thousand hells, Jimbo."

Jim walked towards Ben very slowly and deliberately. He leaned in towards him until they were nearly nose to nose. A grin stretched across Ben's face as his eyes lit up like the ball dropping at Times Square on New Year's Eve.

"What's going on in here?" A voice shouted from the doorway. Both men turned their heads to see Dr. Colvin standing in the entryway.

"My new roommate is threatening me," Jim said.

Dr. Colvin glared at Ben. "We don't threaten people here, Ben," the doctor stated firmly. "If you continue to act up", the doctor continued, "You will be separated. I can take you back to the room you were placed in when you arrived. You can spend your entire time with us in that room, all by yourself."

Jim glanced at Ben and noticed a panic in his eyes. Ben was visibly frightened by what the doctor had just said. Ben's eyes widened as he slowly backed away from Jim. He breathed heavier as he continued to create space between himself and Jim. "It's okay," Jim said, baffled by how quickly Bens demeanor had changed. Jim turned his attention to the doctoring saying, "We're all right. It's our first day and we're both just a little on edge. It's a lot to deal with and we just lost control a little for a minute. We're both okay now."

Doctor Colvin lifted his clipboard and began to write. After writing for a moment, he turned a few pages and wrote on a separate sheet. He glanced up at the two men with a look of suspicion. He scribbled down a few more notes and turned to walk away. As he turned, he pointed towards the two men with his pen and said in a firm tone, "Remember, there is no physical contact allowed between patients." With that statement, he turned into the hallway and disappeared.

"Listen," Jim whispered to Ben. "Neither of us want to be here. I don't know why you are here. I was told I was going to be here for 72 hours. I just want to make it through the next few days and go home. Maybe we started off on the wrong foot. I've had a rough night and a very strange day. You seem to be having a bad day, yourself. You don't seem to want to be alone. I'm the guy you're stuck with. Let's make the best of it and get through the next few days."

Ben stared at Jim intently for a moment. His eyes then darted to the door and back to Jim. "It's too late. It's here now and it knows I'm in the building."

"What is here?" Jim asked.

Before either man could continue, a woman's scream suddenly echoed through the hospital hallways. Jim leaped to his feet and sprang towards the door. Ben sat quietly on the corner of his bed.

"Everybody go into your rooms," Doctor Colvin's voice boomed from the hallway with authority. "We need to keep the halls empty.

We have a situation and need everyone to cooperate by staying in their rooms until further notice."

Jim returned to the middle of the room. A nurse walked by and closed the door. Jim turned to Ben and shrugged his shoulders. "This has got to be the weirdest day of my life," he muttered in disbelief.

Ben lifted his head and looked directly into Jim's eyes. "You could save us all," he said. "You can stop it right now. We don't have much time. This time tomorrow, it will all be over."

Jim shook his head in disbelief. "What the hell are you talking about?" he shouted. "There is nothing coming for us! We are not in danger! We are in a mental hospital. A mental hospital that you clearly belong in."

Ben stood and asked, "What if I told you, I know what your suicide note said?"

Jim sighed. He was at his wits end. He questioned, in his mind, why he thought he could reason with a man that was clearly insane. He saw this man being wheeled into the hospital screaming and yelling. He heard the man claiming something was coming to get him. And now, he was trapped in a room with the guy. He answered, "I didn't leave a suicide note".

"You didn't leave a note," Ben responded. "But you did write one. You write it and you saved it. You never showed it to anyone, but you saved it, secretly knowing that once you finally ended your life someone would eventually find it."

"I did, huh?" Jim responded mockingly. "And what did this note say?"

Ben opened his mouth and began to recite a poem.

I've been baptized in blood and piss

By a God that doesn't believe that I exist.

I don't walk in darkness or dance with death

I just live and die with every breath

Is my vision clouded by this anger in my head?

I feel alive, yet they proclaim me dead.

Tell my friends I said good bye.

I'll be sure to tell the reaper you said, "Hi."

We all wear a smile, we all wear a lie,
Let's gather in a circle join hands and die.

"Who the hell are you?" Jim screamed with a mixture of anger and confusion. He knew the poem. He knew it because he wrote it when he was nineteen. In that moment, Jim's childhood came rushing back to him. The cold nights sleeping under the broken streetlights. The family that never seemed to care if he came home at all. The loneliness. All the feelings of a mislead youth and the feelings that he had the previous night, when he attempted to end his own life, all came rushing back. He had never shown that poem to anyone. He had never shown any of his poetry to anyone. Not that he had anyone to show it to. Jim never had many friends and never thought his poetry about death and misery would help him get any. Jim was confused by how Ben would know this poem and be able to recite it from memory. The room suddenly felt much smaller, and Jim felt trapped and helpless. Jim's helplessness would grow immediately as the ground began to shake beneath them. Several screams could be heard outside the door of their room. Ben and Jim locked eyes as they both began to tremble in fear. Then, as soon as the shaking started, it came to an end.

"I'm the one it's coming for" Ben whispered as if afraid the thing he feared would hear him.

"How do you know so much about me?" Jim questioned, continuing to tremble.

"I'm the other one," Ben answered. "I'm the one that knows you exist."

Jim became more confused with every word muttered by Ben. "What are you talking about?" he screamed.

Ben slowly and deliberately said, "I'm the first. You would call me Satan."

Jim became quickly frustrated with this response. He wanted a serious answer. He wanted to know who Ben really was and how he had so much information about his life. What he got was a joke. The answer was clearly part of Ben's delusion and possibly the reason he was in the hospital to begin with. Jim knew there was something behind Ben knowing such personal information, but being the Devil was certainly not in the realm of possibilities.

"If you're Satan," Jim said, "Why can't you walk out of here? Did you fill in that part of the story in your head? Why are you so afraid to be alone? What could possibly be out there to scare the devil himself? We are clearly going to be stuck in the room for the rest of the day. Why don't you fill me in on what the thing is that is coming to get you? Is it God? Is God finally coming to send you back to Hell?"

"God?" Ben screamed out in disgust. "You really think she has something to do with this? Do you actually think she has any more power than I do? You've been lied to by that bullshit book of yours. That's her version of the story and trust me, if she were here, she'd be just as scared as I am."

Jim could not believe what he was hearing. He slowly sat on the corner of his bed. His head dropped into his cupped hands. He rubbed his palms on his forehead and shook his head from side to side. "Okay Ben," he finally said, with his head still buried in his hands. He was giving in to frustration and had given up on trying to rationalize anything that was happening. "What is it I can do to save us all? What do you need to feel safe? You said I could end it all. How?"

"I need your soul," Ben responded without hesitation.

Jim threw his hands in the air while exclaiming, "Of course! How could I be so stupid? You're Satan, and Satan buys souls. I sell you my soul and then spend an eternity suffering in Hell. That will save the world, right? Why didn't I think of it before? What about God? What if SHE needs my soul?"

"If I tell you the real story, will you agree to consider giving me your soul?" Ben pleaded.

"Sure," Jim exhaled in utter surrender. "Tell me your story and I'll think about it."

Jim had quickly come to the conclusion that if he just listen d to Ben's story maybe Ben would calm down. He himself had seen some strange things since arriving at the hospital. He knew what it was like to be in utter panic. If listening to Ben tell a story could prevent that feeling in Ben, Jim was willing to listen. He had 72 hours to kill, after all.

"Then," Ben began as he extended his open hand towards Jim. "We have a deal."

Jim and Ben shook hands as Jim reluctantly responded, "Sure. We have a deal."

"Thank you," Ben said with a smile. "First of all, the Bible is a lie. I was here before God. The story of Adam and Eve is the story of God and me. I was created first. God came later. She had her hands all over that bullshit book, and it was written in her favor."

Jim listened intently as Ben spoke. He began thinking to himself, either Ben is an amazing liar, or he is actually crazy enough to believe everything that he was saying.

Ben continued, "That which created us has no name. To be named, there must be something here to name you. I was named, much like God, by our creator. We were the first two. We were the only two created without the existence of a soul. God decided she wanted a soul once that slut Mary had my baby and it had..."

Jim interrupted Ben mid-sentence shouting, "What? Are you talking about the Virgin Mary?" Jim was in complete shock as Ben continued.

"Virgin my ass," Ben said. "She was a slut. Those with a soul did not mix with us. We were shunned. Who but a slut would sleep with one of the soulless? God was jealous. She went as far as to change the story in her book and refer to my son as hers and herself as a man. She invented sin to control those with the souls. She took everything I did that she did not like and call it sin. Jesus was born with sin because Jesus was born from the soulless. Cheating on a lover was a sin because I cheated on her with Mary. Getting the souled ones to write that book was brilliant on her behalf. It helped her collect souls. She somehow tricked them into writing it after the trouble began. It didn't like that I had a child that was born to both the souled and the soulless. It decided to eliminate those without a soul. My son was the first to go."

Another loud scream echoed throughout the hallway and into the room. The high-pitched squeal was followed by a loud banging sound and more screams from various voices. As the shrieks grew louder, so did the banging. The banging sounds rang in a rhythm of every three seconds while the screams never seemed to pause at all.

"What the hell is going on out there?" Jim questioned as his voice cracked from fear.

Jim rushed towards the door. Ben tacked him from behind and held him tightly to the ground. Ben felt extremely strong and heavy on top of Jim's body as he struggled to break free.

"Those people could be in danger," Jim shouted. "They might need our help, asshole!"

The screams suddenly stopped, as did the continuous banging sound. A deafening silence surrounded the two men. Jim stopped struggling as the shock of the immediate silence overtook him.

Bens gruff voice whispered in Jim's ear, "I have to finish the story first."

Jim struggled to break free, but his efforts were pointless. He was unable to move. For the first time he began to believe that Ben really was the Devil. That perhaps he was the one causing everything that was happening. He began to think that this was all a game that Satan had been playing with him. He began to think that maybe he had killed himself and was actually in Hell.

"We don't have much time," Ben whispered. "The deal was for you to listen to the whole story".

"Okay," Jim responded with a tear in his left eye.

Ben stood up and freed Jim to stand as well. The deafening silence continued to fill the hall and room. Jim slowly stood.

"Am I in Hell?" Jim asked as he stood up.

Ben laughed out loud. His laugh rang out loudly in the silence of the hospital. When his laugh subsided, he replied, "There is no Hell."

"Why is it so quiet," Jim's words echoed through the room.

"These are the final moments," Ben answered in a very calm and serious voice. "You made a deal to hear the whole story. It's time to finish before it finds us. As I said, my son was the first to go. We were the only three without souls. The only three immortals. Souls die.

They decay in your bodies. Souls drain you of life. That's Hell! The Hell of having a soul. The Hell that I am stuck in by having to fill myself with a new soul every thirty days. Souls can only last within me or God for thirty days. That's how long we have to find another soul and keep hidden from that which created us."

Ben stared at Jim intensely. Jim felt as if Ben was staring a hole through his soul. A queasy feeling overcame Jim. His stomach began to turn. He felt as if he was going to vomit. He let his eyes drift from Ben's and looked down at his hands. His hands appeared to be aging and becoming callous. He rubbed his hands together. They felt hard and rough. His skin was becoming as rough as leather. As he closed his hands to make fists, his knuckles cracked and began to bleed. He looked back at Ben, but Ben was no longer standing in front of him. What stood before him was a mirror reflection of himself.

"What the fuck is happening?" Jim screamed at the top of his lungs.

"We had a deal," The reply came back in Jim's voice. "You saved me. You gave me a soul."

Jim's eyes grew wide in panic and fear. "No! No! This is not real! I agreed to listen. I agreed to consider it. Well, I considered it. My answer is no." As Jim spoke his voice slowly morphed into that of Ben. They had completely changed places. Jim had become Ben, and Ben had become Jim. The new Ben was not happy about it.

"We had a deal." The new Jim stated. "Making a deal with the Devil is as good as selling your soul."

Cracks began to form in the walls. The ground shook beneath the feet of the two men. The cracks forming in the walls slowly took shape. They pulsated and pumped. These were not cracks, the original Jim discovered quickly. These were veins forming in the walls. The veins stretched across all four walls and pulsated in unison with the original Jim's heartbeat. The room grew very, very bright. As the men looked upwards, they could see that the ceiling was no longer there. What was above them was a bright red cave. A red cave that seemed to continue to go upward. The cave itself, pulsating with the veins and heartbeat. Fluid then dripped from the cavern above the men. The fluid was thick and fell in long strands. It fell upon the two men and wet their clothes.

Movement was suddenly seen in the cavern. As the movement increased, so did the fluid that fell from the depths of the cavern. The fluid was thick and sticky. The veins continued to grow from the walls. Now they were as thick as baseball bats. They were dark purple and signs of blood pumping through them was beginning to show. The veins pulsated as fluid could be seen flowing from the floor to the cavern that replaced the ceiling.

The movement in the cavern above them also increased. One side of the cavern seemed to remain still while the other took on a slight rolling motion that continued to produce more of the liquid that slowly dripped onto the two men. The side with movement began to stretch. Something was detaching form the side of the cavern. The cavern filled with the fluid. All side appeared moist. What appeared to be a large stalactite broke away from the moving side of the cavern and rubbed against the opposing side. As it rubbed the caverns walls, the cavern began to close. The sides of the cavern came together, and large teeth could be seen. The original Jim realized that what he was looking at was actually a large mouth. The fluid was saliva. The moving stalactite, a tongue. The teeth clinched together as saliva continued to drip from between the teeth on to the two men.

The teeth separated and a loud growling noise escaped the mouth above them. The tongue slowly escaped the mouth and lowered into the room. The original Jim stood paralyzed by what he was experiencing. The new Jim stood surprisingly relaxed, as if he knew what was coming and new; he was no longer in danger.

The tongue lowered itself to an inch above the original Jim's head. The veins pulsated faster, as the tongue grew closer. Saliva continued to drip from the tongue as it softly touched the top of the man's head and the veins pumped viciously along the walls. The tongue then slowly moved towards the new Jim. As it approached, another loud groan could be heard from deep within the cavern. The tongue then touched the flesh of the new Jim and quickly darted back into the mouth. The cavern slammed shut.

The mouth above the two men opened in a loud scream. A thick fluid poured form the sky and covered the two men. The pink fluid filled the room with a rancid scent. The two men stood, paralyzed in the rancid vile that fell upon them. The fluid began to eat through their clothes. The fluid began to eat through their flesh. The veins in the walls pumping with veracity, nearly exploded. The burning sensation overcame the original Jim. This was the worst pain he had ever felt. This burning sensation that engulfed his body must have been the pain of a thousand Hells, Ben was speaking of earlier. He felt as if he was trapped in a swimming pool, filled with acid. The skin melted form his face as he looked across the room to witness the skin melting from another face that was his mirror image.

The fluids then all flew towards the sky. The saliva and acid disappearing into the depths of the open mouth that loomed over their heads. Their skin returning to its original form. Their clothes taking shape again. Everything in the room, began happening in reverse. Everything done was becoming undone. The pain intensified as the effects of the burning liquid reversed. The tow men looked up as the fluid rushed upwards and off their bodies. The ceiling slammed shut with a loud thud. The thud was followed by a low rumbling sound that moved from wall to wall as if circling the two men.

The veins in the walls continued pumping violently. They continued to match the heartbeat of the original Jim. Those also, would begin to slowly disappear into the walls. The room slowly took its original form. The two men, still paralyzed, stared deeply into each other's now blood shot eyes.

A rumbling filled the room. The sound came from above the men. The rumbling grew louder, as if something drew closer. The rumbling grew into a growl. As the growl grew louder and angrier, the room quaked beneath the feet of the two men. The ceiling ripped open into sharp fangs and released a howl that blew downward, past the two men. The sharp, pointed teeth then slammed close once again.

The room had returned to normal. The new Jim smiled. His eyes lighting up like the eyes of a child on Christmas day. The old Jim stood in shock. He could not comprehend what he had just experienced. He could not comprehend how Ben had somehow switched bodies with him. He could not comprehend why Ben would be smiling after what had just transpired.

Jim's fingers began to twitch. He was slowly regaining his ability to move. He glanced around the room, still afraid to attempt to move. His heart was beating to the point where he could see his chest moving with each pulsation. He could feel the pumping of his blood in every part of his body.

"It doesn't want me," Jim heard his own voice say from the lips of his mirror image that stood across from him. "It tasted me, and it tasted a soul. Congratulations, Jimbo! We did it! I have a soul now. I have your disgusting soul to keep me hidden for another thirty days."

The old Jim turned and ran from the room. He threw the door open to see that the hall was completely normal. There was no sign of the chaos he had heard from the other side of the door. The silence was gone. It had been replaced by sounds of random conversations taking place throughout the hall and various rooms. At the end of the hall, he saw a gurney being pushed through the main doors that exit the unit. As Doctor Colvin walked past, Jim grabbed his arm.

"What happened?" Jim asked, still confused by hearing the sound of Bens voice exit his lips.

"Well, Ben," Doctor Colvin replied. "There was a situation with Lynn. That scream you heard earlier was her. I'm afraid she has passed away. That's why we closed the halls. We needed to make sure the halls were clear for easier removal of the body."

"What about the other screams?" Jim asked in his new gruff sounding voice. These were his words, but the voice was that of Ben.

"What other screams? There was just one scream. Rachel screamed when she found Lynn on the floor. Once we cleared her from the room, there were no other screams." The doctor looked into his eyes with concern. "Are you okay, Ben?"

As the question left the doctors lips, a strong wind swept through the hallway. The wind circled the newly transformed man. The wind blew fiercely as it circled him again and again. The wind engulfed him in a tornado. As the wind closed around his body, he found it harder and harder to breath. With every exhale, the wind closed a tighter and tighter grip on his body. This made it impossible to inhale and he was quickly running out of air. His eyes widened one last time as a lone tear escaped his left eye and rolled down his cheek. He collapsed to the floor, dead.

"Nurse!" Doctor Colvin screamed for help.

The doctors and nurses all rushed to Doctor Colvin's aid. Ben's body, the body that once belonged to Jim, lay soulless on the floor.

"I'll call 9-1-1," Nurse Walker exclaimed, rushing towards the front desk.

"Oh my God!" Rachels voice echoed through the hallway. "Is Ben okay? What happened?"

Rachel stood in the doorway of her room. He right hand clasped tightly to her chest. He brown eyes slowly moving form the lifeless body of Ben to the eyes of Jim. As their eyes locked, a smile formed on her red lips. Her hand slowly left her chest to expose the golden cross that had earlier been worn by Lynn.

"Are you all right, Jim?" Rachel asked. Her eyes never leaving his and the smile never leaving her lips.

"Yeah," Jim replied. "I'm good for at least another thirty days."

THE TRIP

ANTHONY RAY BENCH

"What can I get you?" Sheryl, the waitress, asked. Sheryl was a kind woman in her early 40s, but years of drug abuse gave her the wrinkles of an 80-year-old. She'd since kicked her more dangerous habits; however, life had already passed her by and here she was, making penance for all of her past sins here in the hellish diner.

"The usual, Sheryl." Brad said with a smile, "But would you mind making sure the hash browns are extra crispy?" Brad replied. Brad had been a trucker for nearly 25 years, and aside from being away from his family, he was enamored by life on the road. He loved stopping by this diner. It felt like home because Sheryl wasn't a hollowed-out husk of a human being simply feigning interest in his life and business for a slightly larger tip. Sheryl cared, and that's why she deserved that slightly larger tip every single time.

"Absolutely," Sheryl responded, writing his order down on her notepad. "I'll have Earl deep fry the hell out of your hash browns. How have you been, hon?"

"Been good, darling." Brad replied, "I'm just on my way to California. I'm heading out there to pick up my daughter, Erica, and take her to the Grand Canyon just like I used to when she was a kid."

"That'll be so much fun! How old is she now?" Sheryl asked as she poured Brad a fresh cup of coffee.

"She's 19, but she'll always be my little girl. You know?" Brad said as his eyes subtlety began to tear up.

"Well, I hope you two have a great time." Sheryl said as she gently gave his back a quick and friendly rub. "I'll go put your order in."

As Sheryl walked away from Brad's table, his eyes filled with tears. He'd had a rough go at being a father, but this trip was going to finally reunite him with his little girl. He wiped his tears away and smiled, drinking his coffee and waiting for his food to arrive. The smell of grilled breakfast meats, grease, body odor, and strong coffee always stunk of places like this, but Brad felt a sense of community not unlike a church setting; the breakfast meats and strong coffee were for people living their lives just like him, and the grease and body odor belonged to his fellow brethren trekking from one side of the country to the other. He was in love with this lifestyle, but he was fully capable of admitting to his inability to balance his home life with his career on the road.

Sheryl brought him his food, and he dove in. First, he attacked his bacon, then he stabbed at his eggs, and lastly, he showered his hash browns in ketchup. They were crispy just like he liked them, so Sheryl would get a little extra on her tip. When he had scraped the plate clean and downed the last bit of his coffee, he stood up, took a notch off his belt to let his belly sit a little more freely, and he walked out the door.

"What a fucking creep," Sheryl said, scrapping her coin heavy tip from the table. She had expertly faked an interest in Brad's life and even touched the dirty bastard only to get a measly $2.15. She felt like a whore who'd been stiffed by her john after doing disgusting acts for the duration of 27 minutes. "How am I supposed to score a fix on this?" she thought as she mentally damned such scanty gratuity

After a six-hour drive, Brad finally arrived at his destination. He climbed out of his big rig into the cold wind and rain stretching his muscles and cracking his bones. He reached for his shovel and began digging into the wet dirt. A blister formed on his right palm and sweat drenched his brow and stung his eyes. He swelled with relief when his shovel slammed into something hard. He used his dirty, calloused hands to separate the dirt from the wood surface. He walked back to his truck and pulled out a small axe so he could chop into the buried crate. Thunder banged against the distance, and lightning lit up the darkness as Brad pulled his haul out from the mud and carried it to his truck.

"Sweetheart?" Brad whispered at his beautiful daughter. "You awake? I can't believe this. I drive all the way out to California and steal you away from your mother and you fall asleep on me before we can even talk." Brad said in disbelief. "I even bought you some beef jerky from that place we used to stop at. It's buffalo teriyaki, that's your favorite!"

Still no response from the mound of blankets Erica was wrapped up in, and Brad let out a loud sigh of exasperation.

"Okay, sleepyhead." Brad finally surrendered. "I guess I'll leave you alone. Anything to get out of spending time with your old man, huh?" He said, under his breath.

They'd driven for nearly seven hours, and finally Brad and Erica arrived at their favorite spot at the Grand Canyon. It was a place only truckers knew about, and there was no damned tourists that could ruin the nice and quiet times, as well as the sometimes not-so-nice quiet times. It was well known that this was a great place for weary truckers to take their truck stop whores, or for seedy criminals to dump their victim's bodies. But Brad always loved taking Erica there because of the beautiful view and the quiet nature of the place. They parked on the edge of the canyon and watched the sun slip away behind the horizon.

"I used to love your mother," Brad said, breaking the prolonged hush. "I still do, but when she took you away from me that was unforgiveable."

Erica still said nothing. The silence was stabbing Brad's heart like a billion pin needles; his throat choked on the words he had hoped to speak clearly.

"I know I wasn't the best father, Erica, and you'll never see me pretend to be." Brad said as his eyes flooded with tears he'd been trying to hold back, "But I did love you more than anything, and I would have done anything for you."

Brad could have sworn he had heard Erica crying, and he felt like he was actually reaching her. This was his chance to make amends, and he wiped his tears away and continued on with his impassioned speech that he'd rehearsed for years and years in the hopes that someday, somehow, he'd have the chance to actually say it to her in person.

"I wanted to make peace with you, and take you on one last father-daughter road trip just like the ones we used to take, remember?" Brad paused. His hand was trembling on the steering wheel. "I just wanted to hear you say 'Daddy, I love you' one more time before I die." Brad paused, allowing the words to sink into Erica's heart, "That's all I want."

"We used to be so close before your stupid mother stole you away from me like the selfish piece of—" Brad trailed off. "No, there's no reason for me to speak badly about her. It's hard not to call her every bad word in the book, but she's still your mother." Brad's grip on the steering wheel tightened, "She probably told you things about me, huh? She probably told you I was a bad man that did bad things with you, but I didn't!" Brad shouted, slamming his fist into the top of his dashboard, "I didn't! I'd never do anything like that to you...I didn't. I'd never..."

Brad reached his arm out to touch his daughter, but all he could feel was bone and dirt. He caressed her inner femur making a note that Erica was showing no resistance. He began to slobber and think impure thoughts as he went higher and higher, reaching her ischium...

...And then he stopped himself.

"No, never again." Brad said, shaking himself from his disturbing stupor, "I am a good Christian man and those kinds of desires are behind me. I'm cured by God's grace now." He began to sob uncontrollably, "I'm sorry baby, I'm so sorry."

He uncovered the blanket from her face and Erica's brittle skull detached from her clavicle and rolled onto the floor. Brad reached down and picked it up, placing it safely on Erica's boney lap.

"Look at this!" Brad roared in fury, "Look what your mother did to you! She said it was all my fault, and that I had done things to you... She said that you were no longer pure and then she took you away from me!" Brad shouted, "My little girl...my sweet little baby girl."

I'm sorry...I'm so sorry, all I wanted to do was hear you say 'Daddy, I love you' one more time. That's all I want."

Brad put his forehead against the steering wheel for a few seconds in an attempt to regain his composure. He wiped the tears from his face and snorted out some snot from his left nostril onto the floor of his truck. Without saying a word, he turned his key in the ignition and his truck roared to life. He slammed his foot hard on the gas pedal and headed towards the edge of the canyon. Ericka's skeleton slammed hard into the dashboard and broke into several pieces, but Brad didn't care at this point. This was just one last father daughter road trip before they'd be together forever.

Brad woke up covered in stress sweat. He used his arms and hands to confirm that his body was still completely intact. He dropped down the sun visor so he could look at himself in the mirror and nothing seemed to be out of place. He looked to his right and there was no trace of Ericka. He wondered if this had all been a dream, and if it had been, where in the hell was he now? He didn't recognize this place from any of his travels throughout his 25-year career. He opened the door and climbed down from his seat; he inspected the truck and noticed nothing was completely out of the ordinary aside from some fresh scorch on his grill and outer cab. The outside of his truck was hot to the touch, and the bright yellow sun had turned to a blood-red ball of fire.

He walked in one direction for miles, it seemed; at no point did the scenery give him any indication as to his whereabouts. The red sun began to blister his skin, and suddenly he'd remembered his daughter, Ericka. Brad's returning memories of his last moments with her filled him with horror and dread. Where was she? Where was his little girl?

He saw a figure walking towards him from the distance; it was a female by the looks of it. She wore a white dress, and her face was very skeletal. As he moved closer, her features became fuller and plainer; it was Ericka! She was as beautiful as she was the day before she died. Brad ran towards her and held her close. He pushed away the hair from her face and stared deep into her blue eyes. He leaned down, pulled her face to his, and kissed her on the lips; he could feel her tongue part his teeth. Brad knew what they were doing was incredibly wrong, but there was no one around to judge him, and she was doing it just like how he'd taught her. He reached under her dress and he felt cold bone and rotted flesh; she forced her tongue down his throat and was choking him. He tried pushing her away, but she wouldn't budge. Finally, he summoned all his strength left and he bit down, severing Ericka's tongue. He could feel it turn to ash in his mouth, and he spit out what he'd avoided swallowing.

Ericka was on the ground; her white dress was dirty. She sobbed loudly; something compelled Brad to pause for an instant instead of fleeing. Ericka rose to her feet, her bones cracking and contorting. Her head raised and she stared deep into Brad's fearful eyes...

"Daddy, I love you." Ericka said sweetly.

"I love you too, baby." Brad said.

Ericka smiled. In an instant her face became twisted and demonic, and her teeth became razor sharp fangs. She lunged at her father, knocking him to the dirt and dust; she bit into his right arm first, as he desperately flailed in an attempt to escape she bit down even harder, snapping through his bone and severing his arm. Next, she went for his face, tearing the flesh and chewing loudly while he watched in agony and fear. As soon as she swallowed the bits and pieces, she went for his eyes, gouging them out and popped them between her fingers. His screams for mercy became inaudible gurgles of blood.

"Together forever." Ericka said balefully, "We're going to do this forever."

HELL IS A CALL CENTER
CAROLYN MANSAGER

The office of the DAMNED, which is an acronym for Dear Association Making New Employment Deals, was on the 20th floor of a skyscraper that looked like a ringer for Nakatomi Plaza, but in Century City, California. The interior was as mundane as a John Grisham novel, beige walls and matching industrial carpeting with crimson threads woven through the rough fabric. Windows of the corporate tower stayed wired shut and alarmed but kept plenty clean by the spit and terror of the window washers terrified of heights, whose placement in their profession was also chosen by the DAMNED corporate office flunkies far flung away in their cubicles in Detroit.

It was a neat trick, black magic, really. Nobody on the 20th floor knew how the Beast Under the Floor managed to live underneath them in the hidden realm of terror. It was a dark secret that even the boss K.T. hid from the Membership Coordinators dialing as trained in hell and then working here, hell on Earth, between parallel worlds.

The parallel universe that existed among them somehow opened up every Friday at 3 p.m. and claimed the life of a membership coordinator with the lowest commissions. The numbers showed the membership coordinator in trouble today was Vallerie. The rest of the women eyed her with pity. Vallerie eyed the leader boards and The Watchers watched Vallerie, and she dug deep within her soulless body and dialed, dialed, dialed as directed.

The clock ticked and the second hand reached closer- closer- and then there was the rebellious voice. "K.T!" and the Devil floated to the cubicle of DAMNED Membership Coordinator Ally Bruener, the funny girl in the wheelchair, who struck a deal for standup comedy and the release from the body cursed with muscular dystrophy.

"Yes?" K.T. hissed like a viper. Her lifeless eyes trained on Ally.

Ally asked K.T., "What was your greatest moment in life?" and the rest of the Membership Coordinators paused on their dialers and waited for the boss's narcissism to give them reprieve. Those dead eyes glimmered for a moment.

"Why, it was when I was televised being presented with a sales award." K.T. flashed her canines wide.

"Tell me about it," Ally said, and she added, "Vallerie needs numbers and let's give her more time." They were in competition to avoid their next after life, through the gaping maw of the Beast. "Yvette has been here longest and is second in line for Fluffy."

"Fluffy?" K.T. asked.

"Fluffy is my pet nickname for the beast. We all know you are an animal lover. I thought you wouldn't mind." Ally squeaked out through labored breaths. She smiled at K.T. that upset the balance in the room. Nobody ever did that before. K.T. was not easy to knock from her perch of power in an easy reveal.

K.T. paused and said, "Very well. My televised awards ceremony for sales, they gave me a plaque that is still in my office to this day. I will even indulge you and get it. What the heck? It's Friday at almost 3 o'clock. I am in a good mood. Someone is going to be sacrificed." She floated to her office and patted Valerie on the head, who would cry tears like she did the first time she downed a shot of corn whiskey at her sweet 16 if she could, and then K.T. returned to Ally's cubicle that barely fit her wheelchair underneath her desk. The wheelchair had returned to her frail body and carried her to the office of the DAMNED.

KT lifted above her head an elegant, glass plaque that read, "The DAMED honors the membership of Kleopatria Turia for outstanding excellence and dedication to her profession and the achievement of women." She added, "See? Beautiful. I won this award, this elegant glass plaque for my sales prowess. It shows concrete evidence of my power. It also came with the beast you called Fluffy." She flashed her canines around the office.

"Seriously?" Ally challenged, and added, "I hope that you did not give up your soul for that glass plaque." Every dialer in the room held their collective breaths.

K.T. bristled. She defended, "It was an esteemed award, televised, with a surprise flash mob, and Jeff, my first kiss in the living room of his mother's condo was watching me. I know he was watching me, and he loved me, too. I could feel it. The Psychic Network told me so for only $4.99 a minute. I was in control then and now. That was what I gave my soul for. Power and control." I mean, Jeff now lives with his husband, John, but that doesn't matter. It didn't at the

Time. He was so competitive, and I won! I won!" She held up the plaque again and everyone gaped. Vallerie was busy dialing for souls to increase her numbers on the leader board.

Ally couldn't contain herself, "Pppppbbbttt that is the saddest." Ally said, and then added, I can't work for you, that are just too sad. Once I find a way out of these chains? I might find a way out of here and away from you.

K.T. the boss yelled and clapped her hands. "Dial! Let's make money!" Her eyes were lifeless like a shark with the difference that sharks are still alive. In truth, the beast had help. K.T. assisted in the sacrifice. The leaderboard and clock were her favorite objects, besides her award. There was a collective exhale in the room of the membership coordinators, and they kept dialing to stay ahead of Vallerie, although a few of them turned to mouth, "I'm sorry," in Vallerie's direction, whenever they made a sale and raised their names higher and away from being the Friday afternoon sacrifice.

In fairness, the clock was second most frightening object after the beast under the floor for all of the 30 women chained to chairs and cubicles. The sacrifice to the beast was only one option, the worst and most painful option that resulted in death and the unknown. Low enough numbers meant the end of the road, but some salvation occurred with reincarnation and a place in the DAMNED organization, where they became corporate executives and famous women and keynote speakers. That was how K.T. acquired her position in the first place.

Among the roomful of women in forced hell, was a mass biting of lower lips and free flowing tears. Trained speeches simultaneously stated to the outside world. They used subliminal speeches to pitch sisterhood memberships and cull from the masses the gullible seeking vanity, attention and employment. Some new members would fill their vacant seats in the 20th floor office of the "Dear Association Making New Employment Deals." (DAMNED) Their national events and conferences were given by celebrities like Arianna Huffington and Ivana Trump, who had been reincarnated from the bodies of prior membership coordinators and were now reincarnated fodder from the fecal matter of the Beast of Terror. They had dead eyes, but great outfits and hair. Top salespeople dreamed of joining them one day in acquiring new membership coordinators at malls and maybe white power rallies?

The beast defied physical logic living under the office floor. The ever-present low rumble under everyone's feet, the constant chill in the air suspended within a reasonable circumference, and the fact a membership coordinator watched a co-worker being sacrificed every Friday at 3 o'clock for work performance meant that ominous creature remained ever-present. Except, its roar was covered by piped in to help subliminally relax the staff. Currently, The Offspring played throughout the office music piped in, "Lean back and just enjoy the melodies, after all music soothes the savage beast." However, the focus group missed their mark on the music. It did not anesthetize them to the threat of the sacrifice, and the possibility any one of them could be next. The music was ironically unsuccessful in relaxing the staff.

During the sacrifice, staff speculated what the beast looked like.

The most vocal was Vallerie, in aisle six, row three of cubicles. She sat adjacent to the empty desk of the last membership coordinator sacrificed last Friday. Still fresh in everyone else's mind was the last sacrifice to the beast under the floor. Vallerie was recruited the following Monday and didn't remember the sacrifice or former membership coordinator that became the demonic beast's dinner.

The Sacrifice last Friday was Amy Burassa. The buzz about the Sacrifice still made it around the office. Sure, Amy had committed a large amount of credit card fraud, defaulted repeatedly on her student loans and ghosted many hopeful romantics at restaurants. However, Amy had rehabilitated herself before attracted to the Demons that led her here and the DAMNED. She followed K.T. here from the Peloton Bike store at the Mall, because it seemed like a better option than exercising.

Before this iteration of her existence, Amy repented by working for Jimmy Carter and built houses around the country for the poor and donated all her money to education and animals. Her attempts had not been enough. The Devil in K.T.'s form had found her and promised erasure of student loans, writing apology letters and helping Puerto Rico for her service.

Yet, as a result of Amy's penance, last Friday the membership coordinator's collective memories of Amy's descent through the floor disappearing and opening into the hellfire and gaping maw of the beast haunted the rest of the DAMNED employees. There had been a miscalculation that piped in Lady Gaga music could not distract them from nor erase their memories of this event, as was decided would be both possible and effective by a local focus group, by the DAMNED corporate entities. They corrected this error by offering a $50 gift card to Target for their remaining membership. Vallerie joined them before the terrorizing or the Target gift card. She had never met Amy.

Vallerie, a wide-eyed brunette who moved to Los Angeles from rural Illinois, met the Devil at the Westfield Mall outside Yogurtland and believing her promises of fortune whispered in her ear, while she waited on being called for either fame or a job as a server again at

Buffalo Wild Wings. She whispered pretty promises in her ear, as she had with the rest of the employees of DAMNED. Naive and full of Angry Orchard hard cider, Vallerie accepted the deal from the Devil. At the other, adjacent desk to Vallerie sat Ally, in her wheelchair also chained to her desk. Between dialings, and between Ally's last pre-approved responses, Vallerie first looked around for K.T. She volunteered a whispered guess about the beast under the floor.

"Hey, Ally? I think the beast has obsidian skin dark enough to swallow shadows and eyes the color of boiled cochineal beetles, which matched the licking fire in the gaping maw. It was the gargantuan and canine pet of demons used to motivate membership sales. What do you think it looks like?" She chewed on her lip and waited. Ally stayed on her dialer; she knew she did not have a chance to respond right then. She was the only one without eyes trained on the leaderboard.

The devil was the boss, who was who they knew as K.T. in business casual. She was blonde, leggy, not unattractive, but not Lola from Damn Yankees hot. She did have a bit of the nerdy girl wearing glasses in a library appeal to some. K.T. was not the type you would ever find at NASCAR events or a monster truck rally. She might find Dollywood quaint. The aerial view of the neighborhood she grew up in was full of manicured lawns, swimming pools and debutantes. K.T. is too young to reside in the retirement community of Pigeon Forge by her looks, which do not look a day over her 1,800 years or 40 human years old in Hollywood.

K.T.'s personal and repetitive mantra is "Don't give away your personal power," which is ironic, since she relies on the terror of the beast under the floor. K.T. was the master of double speak which also landed the membership coordinators in the call center of Hell. The office of the DAMNED was purgatory stop between the last life and the next one. There were whispers, "She's not smart enough to be the Devil." K.T. floated over to Vallerie's cubicle. She huffed, "The walls have ears, and the call center has a beast under the Floor. The Devil is not fond of being the smart girl left out of the popular, gossipy girls' table."

Ally interrupted the dressing down by K.T. and drew attention to her by shouting "Oops! [Mute] Caller! [Unmute] Hi! I am calling you from the office of the DAMNED and want to congratulate you on being accepted into our membership! [Pause] Yes! It's great!"

Vallerie watched Ally as she demonstrated why she remained at the top of the leaderboard as she turned that call into a sale into the DAMNED. K.T. studied her supposed protégé and likely planned the day that top writer (sales) membership coordinator, Ally, might join her as a keynote speaker someday, or recruits naïve girls from the Century City Mall. K.T. floated away to watch the leaderboard turning instead. She floated and watched the names roll with lifeless eyes and smirking.

The ethereal and improbable nature of such a beast served to make such a creature more repugnant. Air chilled within a wide circumference of its existence. It lived to eat terrified cursed, female flunkies chained to their desks. DAMNED membership Coordinators sported a fichus plant on their desk, which was the only gift or break given to them. Vallerie chewed on her bottom lip and raised her eyes to the Leaderboard, "o" and the number had not moved all day.

Membership coordinators were all female and focused on subliminal membership coordination pitched in modern English and practiced monotone. They only allowed pre-approved only responses to the outside called, "Indeed. Certainly. Understood. Very Well. And All Right." However, their limited response to the called on the other end of the telephone is not an excuse for low, sales numbers. There were more eyes on the leaderboard on Fridays than a sack full of Idaho potatoes, and just as fixed as on their rankings while speaking on the telephone in a carefully scripted and practice. They knew there would be a sacrifice. "Who?" The question always asked on Fridays before 3 p.m. the cutoff for dodging being the last name on the spinning sales board.

Amy wasn't a stranger to sales or soul stealing her. Other women on the 20th floor treated her as a mentor in how to keep their sales numbers high enough to avoid being eliminated. Amy had rehabilitated after a stint in jail following a large amount of credit card fraud and had ripped the tag off her mattress, which came out in discovery and added to her sentence. Amy initially attracted the recruiting demons at the mall while dressing down a food court employee. Never dress down a food court employee in a mall. They're connected. It was also a known secret that K.T. had high hopes in shopping for great outfits one day with Amy and now Ally, but she held no love for the hopeless Vallerie, whose sales number for the week read "0" and she never even drew her name for the lucky raffle.

It was almost 3 o'clock. There was no telling if they were fair or were following the rules. Vallerie was clearly in line for the great sacrifice. But Ally kind of liked the naïve country girl, and the wheelchair made her all crampy and sore. "Spare Vallerie, take me. I cannot stand anymore of a tale so sad."

Vallerie jerked her head up and said, "Well, I know have a lot to learn, but it's mean to call me sad, Ally."

Ally rolled her eyes harder than her chair, "No, Ally, I am talking about K.T.! Selling your soul for some sales plaque? Oh, please. I am tired of being in pain. That was supposed to go away with this sales agreement. I do not want to continue in this life. I am not letting someone take away my personal power."

K.T. yelled. "You are not in charge, I am! That came with the plaque! I have the power! I am in control!"

Ally said, "Thanks for the lesson in personal power! Open the floor, let Fluffy out. I cannot take living through this pathetic display of histrionics. I will take my chances with the next afterlife. It cannot possibly be this pathetic. Besides, shouldn't I be rewarded for self-sacrifice? Open the floor! Let out the beast."

Ally wheeled herself to the middle of the floor, to the place where Amy Burassa disappeared last Friday at 3 o'clock. "Get away from me. This is my last hurrah!" Ally rolled back and forth over where Fluffy should live. Something rumbled in the parallel universe and the floor opened. "Goodbye to this world!" Ally wheeled backwards and fell into the gaping hole in the floor and the ubiquitous rumble, and each dialer tossed their fichus plant from their desks as a tribute, before getting back to work. When the floor closed again, Lady Gaga music started piping through the office and membership coordinators started to dial with their eyes on the leaderboard, wondering who might next to be an invited key note speaker and recruiter someday. As for Vallerie? She winked at the window washers, hoping one day, one of them would be brave enough to break inside from their own hell on the outside of the 20th floor and release her from her chains.

The food court mall employees summoned another wide-eyed candidate for the Devil in business casual and shining her plaque.

ALWAYS WITH HER LEFT FOOT IN THE GRASS

WILL KHAMBATTA

Shouldn't let myself get jealous. Not of the whispers.

It always begins with the two of them whispering. Can't pick any words out; the walls are too thick for that. So, all I get's a stream of burbling, faded language with the kind of volume you hear in a dream. She mumbles something to him here; he gives a washed-out giggle there and I get to follow none of it.

It's not long before the chat subsides. They never talk for long, but then, he's not there to talk, is he? The pause here's the worst bit, because of what it means is happening. There might be the occasional mumble, but mostly they're silent at this point. Probably worried about what'll happen if they're too loud.

You know, in case I hear.

If there is a noise, it's usually the faintest hint of a gasp, the kind that's squeezed from behind a hand, or pushed through sealed lips. Still subdued of course, not much louder than their whispering, to be honest.

Eventually, I'll have to lie here and listen as the whispers give way to other sounds. Ironic that they're quieter now, when you think they'd be louder. The wooden bedframe betrays only the faintest moan as it bows while their weight shifts. Breathing turns heavy, but never hard. Bedsprings ache in rhythm to their movements.

And I have to lie there in the dark and listen to it, because there's no way I'm going to be able to sleep while they're going at it. Most nights, I don't have to put up with it. I'll already be asleep, but on a night like tonight, one where I've had just the wrong amount of coffee. Christ... there's no way I'm dropping off. No matter how quiet the pair of them are, you can still hear everything. Frankly, they might as well just go for it, just go all-out with the screaming and moaning, make it the Hollywood scene it clearly is in their heads.

Well, not their heads. Mostly his head, probably. To be fair, I'm not sure what she must think of it all. I'm sure she must like it. She lets him into her bed enough nights.

Rolling over, away from the sounds, I try to distract myself by thinking of everything I've got to do tomorrow. The spreadsheets I need to get done. The meetings I'm leading on. The things I'm going to say to management. But it's no good. The silence from the next room overpowers everything else, and so I lie there with eyes closed, teeth gritted, waiting for it to be over.

Christ, I want to be asleep.

There's been a year of this now. The first time I heard them together, I was disgusted. Well, who wouldn't be? Couldn't confront him about it, though. I mean, how do you even bring something like that up over tea?

Then – perversely I suppose, because you're not supposed to admit this – I was jealous. It took a while, but now... Now I can admit that. Probably because I'm not really jealous anymore. With the workload I've got? These days, all I want is to get to sleep as quickly as possible, and if the fun next door makes that impossible to do, well, rather her than me. Marriage isn't everything I thought it'd be.

It's not that I don't *like* sex. When it's done well, it's perfectly satisfactory. I think it's just... well, who's got time for it? And he's not exactly the gentlest lover, is he? No matter how handsome the stubble might be, it irritates my skin something fierce whilst he's... doing his business. And having to clean up afterwards; Christ, who wants to deal with all that? I mean, I know I *should* try harder – wifely duty and all that – but these days, it's just more effort than I can bear. So, if he's found someone else to satisfy those unpleasant needs of his, honestly, the happier I am.

Took me a while to admit that. I felt so guilty at first, but really, things are so much better without him slobbering into *my* ear at one in the morning anymore. If they want each other, more power to them, that's what I think.

I check the clock. Two forty-seven. God, I've got to be up in less than five hours. Come on you two, just hurry up and finish.

Ah, thank goodness: there he goes. You can always tell when he's finished. It's always with the same, whimpered, whining note. The kind of sound that's unexpected; one that's higher than you'd think a man of his size would make. Only a little bit longer and I'll finally be resting.

There's a bit more of his giggling. Bit more of his mumbling. Finally, able to get settled, I snuggle myself deeper into my duvet and close my eyes properly. David will be leaving her room and coming back to me any moment, and I can't let him know I've been listening. Shouldn't have to wait long, though. He's never been longer than ten minutes before.

There's someone in my room.

I know this in the way I know things when I dream; with the cast-iron certainty that only dream brings. And I also know that this person? Is not my David. They don't even feel like a person. They feel like… Like… I don't know. Not a person. My skin prickles the same as it does when there's one of those horrible huge spiders on the lounge floor, crouched and staring at me, ready to scuttle.

Wanting to move, paralysed by fear, I feel like a kiddie, hiding behind my duvet, eyes wide over its pink lace edge.

There's a woman.

She's old – ancient – her skin dark and gnarled like the wood of a long-dead tree, her hair done up in the kind of frizzy natural my crazy auntie used to favour. Her knotted hands aren't quite claws, but they're not exactly claws, either. She carries her age heavily, bowed beneath its weight. Ferocious eyes glitter from inside the shadows that hide her features, and something in that look makes my insides loosen. They feel the way they did back when I was a little girl in Trinidad, and Uncle Kendon's dog snarled at me. It had just killed our cat, and the poor, dead thing hung from its teeth, neck swinging like a worn rope. The dog's teeth glistened red without a single fleck of bone-white in there, and I knew, *knew*, that it would come for me next.

I wish my Uncle Kendon was here now, here with his loud voice and strong hands, ready to shoo this woman away like he shooed that dog.

She says nothing, makes no move. Staring imperiously, her eyes are heavy with hate.

As the moments pass, turning into first seconds, and then, nearly half a minute, fear mixes with a queasy embarrassment. I wish she would say something, do something, do *anything*... Anything except look at me with those awful eyes of hers. I want to say something, to demand she speak, but the thought that David will hear me? That he will hear me, and then we have to talk about what he's been doing, out of our bed tonight?

No. No, to speak would be far more terrifying than to stay silent.

"It's not there anymore, but time was, at the end of Cadogan Street, right on the Eastern edge of Point Forin, The Dancing Room was the place for people to be. Beautiful place it was. Beautiful. Every kind of young girl used to go; every kind of young man too, and all of them looking for love. Well, some perhaps a more *physical* kind of love than others, but that's by the by."

Her voice is deep with age. She's got the same thick Trini accent my grandmother had. Pulling herself upright with clear discomfort, she stands, her eyes blazing. I recoil into the yielding lace layers of my pink pillow.

"Who are you?" I ask, the words gulped out from behind the bedclothes.

She takes a step towards me.

"Your great-great-great-great-uncle had gone there. A huge,

barrel-chested boy, with hands like spades and the most beautiful curly hair you ever did see. He was desperately lonely, and so he had gone to meet a young woman in the hopes that his woman that night might one day be his wife."

"You know my family?"

I don't know why I asked the question, but now it's out, it sits there, ugly between the two of us. For a moment, I'm sure she must lash out at me, but she doesn't. Instead, her face twists into a craggy smile.

"I had waited outside. I had seen your great-great-great-great-uncle days before, and I knew I would make him mine. When he left that place angry and without company, his manhood aching with frustration... *that* was when I appeared to him.

"I didn't need to make myself pretty, so thick was his need, but I did. Seemed important to me then. Taking his hand, I whispered to him, whispered the sweetest things a man can hear, that I was lost, and scared, and vulnerable. What man can resist the chance to play the hero when a pretty woman reveals herself to him? I needn't have bothered; when a man's blood is up, he'll rut with the hole in a fence.

"Of course, there was one thing that mattered."

"What?" I ask.

She smiles, a slow, sadistic smirk.

"I made sure to keep my left foot in the long grass. No need to panic him."

From where I'm lying, I can't see her left foot. I don't know if I want to.

"So, we walked together, he and I, walked all the way. By the time he realised where the way led him, it was too late of course. We were where I wanted by then. Most of Point Fortin is flat, you see, so it took a while to walk him carefully out to somewhere high, my foot always in the long, long grass. Of course, whilst we walked, I spoke the things he wanted to hear, of my loneliness and my ache for masculine company, of my admiration for his fine features and chiselled body."

Laughing once, softly, she looks away from me. For the first time, her expression shifts. Something that looks like regret seeps into her eyes.

"That boy would've accompanied me into Hell."

Settling down onto the side of the bed nearest me, she sits, and the sheets don't give even a little. Her left foot lies, hidden in shadow.

"By the time we reached the cliff, he was so besotted with me that there was no room left in his world, not for anything but me. Wind whirled around us, and the hungry waters cried out from around the rocks below us. And as he leaned in for that first, gentle kiss... the first kiss he would ever receive instead of taking... *That* is when I pushed him over the edge."

She leans towards me.

"He screamed all the way down. Sounded *just* like a little boy. His head came apart and the water feasted on the dreams inside. You've seen films where people fall, I am sure. The way their bodies lie, splayed in awkward positions at the bottom?"

Her face close enough to mine that I can smell the ashes on her breath, I nod.

"Well, real-life is *nothing* like that."

She closes her eyes, looks away, her face lost in darkness.

"You people are mostly water, you see. When a body hits the ground from that kind of height, it just... *pops*. Your great-great-great-great-uncle, his body *popped*, like a great red flower, the petals of him unfurled across the jagged teeth of the great water-stones. The wind carried the smell of him up to me, all salt and metal and shit."

She comes back from the memory, the glittering dark of her eyes falling on me.

"What do you want?" I ask, small, afraid, child again

"To change," she replies, and moves to sit on the edge of the bed.

"What?"

"His girl's name was Faith. She was seven months younger than he, and she had thought that they loved one another. But Faith was well named. A dutiful girl. Believed in the words of her God, and her duty to him meant she moved too slowly for your uncle. She demanded they wait until marriage, but she might as well have asked her God to delay the day of judgement. So, your uncle took her, and once he was done, her pain called out. It called out..."

– her voice drops a full five octaves –

"*...and I answered.*"

She smiles, and for the first time, I see her mouth is filled with at least three rows of extra teeth.

I want to scream, but no part of me will so much as move.

Suddenly, the old woman pulls away, sits up, her manner is easy-going, conversational. She could be an old friend talking about weather, or the washing.

"She cried at his funeral. They always did, all the other girls whose pain was just as fine as hers, if not perhaps so recent. I'd stand there, watching each and every one of them, at every one of the five hundred or so funerals I've been responsible for over these long centuries, and I'd think the same thing every time: good riddance to bad rubbish."

She pauses, staring at me thoughtfully.

"Bad rubbish," she repeats, without taking her eyes off me. "Your 'man', this David? He is bad rubbish too."

"What do – "

"*Shhhhh,*" she says. "Please do not say anything. If you say something? Then I will go, and I will act. And you will not thank me for that."

Sighing, she folds her hands in front of her. She looks the way a little girl does, as though caught calling other girls names.

"I am trying very, very hard here. I do not think you appreciate how hard I am trying. When I left Trini, I made myself a promise: that I would leave those ways, The Old Ways, behind. That I would forge a new life for myself, one without purpose, but with possibility."

"Possibility?" I ask.

"Of hope. Of happiness. Of freedom from who and what I was. In that regard, I flatter myself that I am doing very well. I have a stall on Castle Market where I sell plantain. My grandson lives with me, and I recently adopted a daughter. If you can believe it, I even have a boyfriend. An *English* boyfriend. Me with a white boy, eh?"

Turning to me again, her face is normal again. It's lost its horrible aspect, her mouth filled with only the normal number of teeth now. She smiles, and it's not malevolent, but sad. Sad, and sincere.

"So, you can see, I *am* trying.

"That is why I am here, doing not what I *should*, but what I want. For the sake of my change, I will not appear to your David in a shape he finds pleasing. For the sake of my change, I will not walk with him, always with my left foot in the long, long grass. For the sake of my change, I will not stand with him as he leans in for that first perfect kiss, only to crash into the rocks. I will not do these things, because I am trying to be better; trying to be less angry."

"I don't understand," I say.

"Understanding is not necessary for compliance."

She leans in, close. Far too close.

"Your daughter calls to me as she lies in her pain. Not every night, but most nights. For a year and a day, I have ignored her call. For a year and a day, I have forgone my duty. But your daughter's blood is your blood, which is the blood of Trinidad...

"Which means it is *my* blood. I must answer it."

"But she *enjoys* it," I say, not knowing why I'm trying to argue, my voice small, hollow.

"And those are the nights she is in the most pain of all. But you look away. You lie to yourself. *While he is with my daughter*, you say, *well, at least he's not with prostitutes or other women, is he?*"

She makes an angry, tutting sound with her teeth.

"Your vanity is disgraceful; his violations flatter you, because when he's with her, it's almost like he is with *you*. Because what is she, if not a younger version of you? That's what you tell yourself. So, you don't have to be jealous, and you don't have to go through a messy divorce, and he takes care of you and her. If you're happy, what's the problem, isn't that how you think?"

Her silent roar shakes the edges of the world, her mouth impossibly large, filled with row upon row of triangular teeth like a shark's.

She leans back, takes a moment.

"No," she says, composed again, talking now more to herself than me. "Come on, old girl. You can do this. You are changing, and change is hard. You knew this sort of thing would happen when you began, Lajables, you knew. Come on. *You can do this.*"

She stands.

"I leave the decision to you."

"Decision?"

"Rise above yourself and help both your daughter and I... or don't."

There's a sudden crackling, and I'm alone again.

Diving beneath the covers, I lie there shivering, waiting for David's arrival. I've no idea what I'm going to do when he gets in.

What I'm going to say.

Then I realise how much time's past. He's been in Janelle's room for ages now. Ages.

Oh God. Something's happened. Oh God in heaven, what do I do, what do I -

The door opens. David sneaks in. I'm so shocked, I can't help myself.

"Honey?"

"Oh, hiya," he replies, giving a sheepish smile. "Sorry babes, didn't mean to wake you."

Turning around, I look at him. My husband. The man I love. The man who takes care of my daughter and I. His strong, muscled arms, so tender when they hold me. Tattoos of a Union Jack on one arm, his regiment's insignia on the other. My husband, the twenty-year veteran, the war hero who pulled five men out of a minefield under fire. Who delivered food to orphans in Kosovo and built schools in Syria? Who cooks the best barbecue I've ever eaten, who runs marathons for charity, and who leaves our bed three nights a week to have sex with my nine-year-old daughter?

I want to say something. I want to confront him. To take control of the situation.

Then David smiles at me, the shy smile of a little boy... just like it always is. Not wanting to, I can't help myself from smiling at the sight of it, and the moment I smile, I know I can't say anything right now. The timing's not right.

So, I lie.

"No, love," I say. "I only heard the door go as you came in, that's all. Were it your insomnia again?"

"Yeah," he says, nodding. "I just needed the toilet, and then I couldn't sleep. I was downstairs, watching the TV. Didn't disturb you, did I?"

The excuses and lies fall from him with such ease, I could almost allow myself to believe they were true.

"No," I say, reassuring him. "I was asleep the whole time."

And he kisses me, and we roll over together, and I decide that we'll talk about it tomorrow over breakfast. That I'll confront him then, get everything out in the open. That I won't go to the police, because he doesn't deserve that. Because he *has* looked after us, and he *has* protected us, and he *is* a good man. He *is*. I've allowed him to go on, that's the problem. It's my fault. So, I won't go to the police, but he has to go. Maybe he'll be able to come back after a while. Maybe. But there are going to have to be some big changes.

Breakfast. I'll talk to him over breakfast

The timing isn't right.

Munching through my Special K, I don't feel right. That dream I had last night, about the old monster-woman, it still has me feeling weird. I'm not usually one for nightmares, so it's properly got me going. Left me... I don't know, not scared exactly. More sort of... disquieted, maybe?

David's in the kitchen, frying up the bacon for his morning sandwich, the glass of protein shake already poured. Janelle sits next to me, eyes lowered, eating Rice Krispies as she watches the television. It's some local news story or other about Park Hill flats, and for the life of me, I've no idea why she should care, but those eyes of hers are fixed on the telly, studiously avoiding mine.

After my dream of last night, I feel like I should say something.

"Janelle?"

She doesn't look over.

"Did you sleep well last night? Lots of pleasant dreams?"

She doesn't say anything, pointedly choosing to spoon more cereal into her mouth instead. I wonder if other little girls behave so rudely, or if it's just mine.

"Janelle? I asked you a question."

"Answer your mother, little boo boo," comes David's voice from the other room.

"It was fine," she says, without looking over.

Taking a mouthful of my own cereal, I wonder what to do. None of this is my fault; I mean, I haven't done anything. Still, last night's dream has me wondering. It's just so hard. I've no idea what I can say. With the truth too impossibly big to mention, I try to force a little small talk.

Only how do you make small talk with a child? Do I mention the weather? Ask about school? Compliment her cornrows?

Of course, there is only one real choice of topic, isn't there?

"I dreamed about a witch," I say.

This makes her turn. Smiling, I nod.

"She was old, had crazy hair and gnarled fingers. It was ever so weird."

Janelle stares at me. Her eyes, usually emotionless as a doll's, suddenly give the slightest of shivers. I don't think I like it.

"Did she say something?" asks Janelle.

For a moment, I feel utterly dislocated. Like I'm not talking to my daughter, but like I'm still in last night's dream, watching myself talk to her.

"She told me about Trinidad," I say.

Janelle doesn't say a thing, but just stares. The lower lids of her eyes quiver, and for a moment, it looks like she's about to cry.

"Who told you about Trinidad?" asks David, coming in and sitting down heavily, his teeth ripping a huge hunk of bacon sandwich out as he does so.

"No-one," I say, insides curling for reasons I can't explain. "I was just telling Janelle about the dream I had last night."

"Oh yeah? Sexy one, were it?" he asks, smirking with cheeky good humour.

I force a smile.

"No, nothing like that. It was about…"

He smiles at me.

Janelle's looking at the television.

He smiles at me.

He smiles at me.

He smiles at me.

"… can't remember," I lie.

He raises his eyebrows, shrugs, and takes another bite of his sandwich.

"You know how you forget a dream once you wake? It's like that," I lie.

"Yeah," he says. "Happens to me too."

We laugh in the way of a gentle, domesticated couple. Janelle watches the television.

"Right, better get going," says David. "Don't want to be late for my big speech."

"Yeah," I nod. "When are you on?"

"Assembly starts at nine, but I'll need to be at the school for eight thirty so they can sign me in."

"You doing the meet and greet afterwards?"

"Yeah. They're calling it '*Speed Dating with Industry.*' Lieutenant Bill and I get to talk to all the spotty oiks, get all those teenage lads to see how a real man acts. Maybe pull me a sexy schoolgirl."

He laughs, nudging me to show he's only joking.

"Nah, you know I'm kidding. I'm just gonna show 'em what a great career option the army is."

"Well, you'll want to do the regiment proud," I say.

"Forget the regiment; I've got a fiver bet says I can get more signed up than Billy."

We laugh.

"Okay then. Well, best be off," he says, grabbing his protein shake and slurping. "I'll see you both tonight. Love you."

"Love you," I reply.

"Bye," says Janelle with her eyes fixed on the television.

As I clear away the breakfast things, watch David pull the car out of the driveway, my dream comes back to me again. The old woman's words.

I should've said something. Should've spoken up. Asked where he was last night. Where he *really* was. Made him say it out loud. Made him confess.

Watching Janelle as she finishes her cereal, I wonder what she's thinking. Why she's so quiet. So rude. Maybe... maybe if I say something, she'll...

No. Not now. Now you need to get to work. You don't need to think about this now. You could've said something, but you didn't. But that doesn't mean you won't later.

The timing wasn't right.

"Come on Janelle. Don't want you being late to school."

"Mrs. Cameron?"

I stood amongst the huddle of mothers outside school, waiting to make the pickup. I'm surprised by the sight of one of the teachers coming my way. It's Mrs. Wilcox, a year five teacher, her large frame bright in summery clothes, stark against the grey concrete around her.

"Mrs. Wilcox?" I ask, confused.

"Hello there. I'm so sorry to bother you. Actually, I was hoping we might be able to have a bit of a talk. Is there any chance you could come inside?"

"I need to meet my husband at four-thirty," I reply.

"Oh, this won't take long at all. It's just about Janelle," she says, her face cloudy with concern.

"Okay," I say, a little worried, but following her inside.

She leads me into a small side office, decorated with a huge calendar, reams of folders, and a patchwork collage of photos of her children, all round-faced and smiling like her.

"How can I help?" I ask.

"Well," she says, biting her bottom lip a little. "As you know, Janelle's just come into year five. And while she's always been a quiet girl – I taught her in year two and three, as you know – but since coming back to our form, I've noticed... Well. I'm sure you'll agree, she's changed *a lot* in the last year, hasn't she?"

"Has she? I haven't noticed," I reply.

"Oh," Wilcox returns, a little downcast. "I mean, it might just be me, but she seems much more... clingy than she used to be. In year three, she was quite happy, sat off to one side, doing the work, but now, it seems as though she's always finding excuses to come over and see me. She'll need me to check her work, she'll want me to look at something. It's like she's scared all the time. The poor thing won't even leave my side at break times."

"Well, that's probably annoying for you," I laugh genially, "but little girls are just like that, aren't they? Probably just shy, but that'll change. I don't see that it's a problem."

She makes a tutting sound with her teeth.

"On its own, I'd agree with you. But it's not on its own; there are other changes too. You say she's shy, but when I taught her, she used to have lots of friends. Now? Well, now she's become... I don't want to say shy; it's nothing as simple as nervousness or introversion. No, Mrs. Cameron, I'd say she seems *secretive*. A couple of times, I've seen her with girls who used to be her friend, and while she talks to them, she's different to how she was before. I've asked her if there's any problems, you know, with other girls, but she just won't say. So, I was wondering if you might have noticed anything?"

Tell her.

Tell her what's been happening. You don't have to say you know;

you could just say you're *concerned*. That you have *suspicions*. She doesn't need to know what you know.

Tell her, and then it's her problem, not yours.

"Well..." I press.

"I mean, I don't mean to suggest anything," she says. "It's just... well, you're her mother. No-one's going to know her better than you."

Tell her.

"No-one's going to love her harder than you."

"Honestly..."

TELL HER.

But if I do...

...if I do, they'll take him away. And then I'll lose him, to say nothing of his income, pension, possibly the house.

I want to tell her.

I really, really want to tell her.

I breathe in, and then

"No," I say. "I've not seen anything that makes me worried."

"Oh," she replies, clearly disappointed. "Because I have to admit, I've been very uneasy. Actually, I've been meaning to broach this with you since last week."

"Last week?"

"There was an incident."

"Did she hit someone?"

"No, no. Nothing like that. No, we were doing a geography lesson. About Trinidad, actually," she smiles. "Well, the Caribbean in general, but we were looking at things like traditional industries, culture, foods, all that sort of thing. Anyway, I'd bought in some Trinidadian food from Castle Market for them to all look at, and while we were handing them round, she refused to touch the sweet potato. Everything else she was fine with, but the sweet potato? She wouldn't have a thing to do with it. Wouldn't even touch it. So, I went and asked why."

"What did she say?"

"She said, '*It's veiny like a cock.*'"

I have to fight to suppress a smile. Wilcox shoots me a disapproving look, and I quickly regain control of myself.

"That's not really appropriate for classroom," I say.

"No," she says. "But that wasn't the issue. I mean, yes, there was a lot of giggles at that, and I sent her outside, logged it as a behaviour point... but I find that comment worrying."

"Why?" I ask.

"Because taken individually, none of the things she's done are terribly significant. But taken together, well."

She looks like she's trying to say something but can't quite get the words out.

"Look," she says finally, "I should probably report this all, but I wanted to talk. To you. You know, before I get anyone more senior involved. I mean, if you've not noticed anything, I might be making a mountain out of a molehill is all."

"No, I see where you're coming from," I say, nodding and smiling. "But I don't think there's anything to worry about. It's probably just the start of puberty. I'll have a word with Janelle tonight, find out if there's anything going on you or I should know about."

"I'd appreciate that. Like I say, I don't want to create any problems for you."

"That's very good of you; I really am thankful to you for that."

We shake hands and say goodbye. As I walk out, Janelle looks up from where she's been sat outside. Taking her hand, I smile at her. She stays silent, but that's fine.

Because I've made up my mind.

I'm going to have a word with David tonight, like I should've done months ago. The timing wasn't right, but I'll talk to him the moment he gets home. We'll finally have this all out and over once and for all. I'll do what I should've done and sort this. Even if I *do* end up losing the house, I really have to put my daughter first. Stepping out of the school building, for the first time since last night, I start to feel good about myself again.

Then I see her.

Stood outside the school gates, across the road. She's in the same old dress she wore last night, the wind lashing at her frizzy puff of hair. In the light, her face only looks older; more worn, like fabric made thin by the years.

Her eyes, though. They glitter with cold fury, abject and terrible.

But my chest grows taut at the sight; after a day of feeling strange, I'm going to have it out with her. Taking a step forwards, fists clenching, I start to prepare the tirade of abuse I'm going to give her.

My cell phone rings. Stopping my advance, I fumble in my handbag for it. Despite this, I never take my eyes off the hag across the road.

"Mrs. Cameron?"

"Yes. Who is this?"

"This is South Yorkshire Police, Mrs. Cameron. Are you alright to talk?"

"Yes," I say.

My insides loosen.

The old woman's look grows righteous.

"I'm very sorry to be calling you, but there's been an accident, Mrs. Cameron. I'm very sorry, but we'd like you to come into the station."

"What?"

"Is your husband's name David?"

Looking away from the old witch for a moment, I flinch at the sound of his name.

"Yes. Why?"

"I'm afraid he's– "

"*What*?" I snap, interrupting. "He's *what*?"

"He was crossing the road outside Westfield School, Mrs. Cameron."

I try to swallow, but there's no saliva in my mouth.

"He was giving a talk there today."

"Yes, his regiment explained as much. Apparently, after he left, he ended up in conversation with a young woman. When they reached the road, he wasn't paying attention. I'm terribly sorry, Mrs. Cameron; there's no easy way to say this. There's been a crash. He's been– "

The phone clatters as it hits the floor.

Ancient eyes stare across the road at me. Withered, oaken skin twists into a smile.

A sudden wind catches at my hair, at my coat. The old woman's long dress lifts just slightly, just enough, just barely exposing the bottom of her left leg.

No.

Oh God, no.

My own legs become unsteady. For a moment, my head swims, and I'm sure I must collapse. How I remain standing at the sight of that awful revelation is beyond me.

A car drives past.

When it's gone, so is the old woman. The only sign she was ever there is a scorch mark on the pavement, the left footprint burned in the shape of a single cloven hoof.

GHOSTS

THAT HOURGLASS, THO

MATT BETTS

Restless in my early grave, I think of
you and your bright colors that
hypnotize me into that dull smile.
I feel your limbs enfold.

Your poison in my veins sizzles.

Restless in my early grave, I dream of
you and your long legs
spinning some web around me.
Encasing me. Holding me.

I need you
You spin me
You knead me

You save me for later

Restless in my early grave, I think of
how you and your silk whispers
punctured me. *Ecstasy now.*
I feel my life's meaning.

Your poison in my veins
boils and churns.

THE GHOST IN THE DEVICE
THOMAS J. MISURACA

I'm not scared, Emma Fisher told herself. *It's just a house. People lived here once. A long, long time ago.*

"I knew you were chicken," her best friend Cindy taunted her. It were days like this that Emma reconsider that title. But Cindy was the only girl on the field hockey team who wasn't a total bitch.

"I'm not scared," Emma spoke aloud the mantra in her head.

"Then what're you waiting for?"

"To make sure nobody sees me go inside."

"Here?" Cindy laughed.

Emma knew nobody was watching them. The end of Martin Street was deserted. The old Hodges' place was so aged, it looked like it could fade into the past at any moment. Emma had no idea how long the house had been abandoned. It was already dilapidated when Emma and her family moved into the neighborhood over a year ago. The place itself was a legend. It was the setting of sexual triumphs, wild parties and the occasional ghost story.

Most importantly, it was a rite of passage. You weren't anybody in school until you ran through the halls of the old Hodges' place. Everybody in school had the selfies to prove it.

Emma wasn't worried about ghosts, or even the derelicts that lived there. She doubted either of them would come out by day. What worried her were the germ-filled horrors she'd find inside.

Repeating her mantra, Emma summoned her courage and climbed the steps.

"Don't die," Cindy called after her.

Emma knew the entrance had been forced open years ago. But the idea of touching the door turned he stomach. Upon closer inspection, she noticed it was ajar. Her thin frame was able to slip inside without having to touch anything.

Inside, the smell was beyond disgusting: dust, mold, garbage and… yeah… urine and feces. Emma hoped those were from stray animals but remembered how drunk boys and homeless people acted. She covered her nose as she surveyed the room.

The floor was littered with broken and whole bottles, cans, food wrappers and other unrecognizable, deteriorated garbage. Graffiti both professional and amateur covered the walls. The home may have been abandoned, but this house had been used and abused by the kids and vagrants of the town.

There was some torn up and decrepit furniture in the former living room. Emma wondered if the previous owners left it behind, or if people thought this would be a great place to dump their unwanted chairs and couches. The cinder blocks and milk crates were certainly additions from the weekend night partiers.

Emma took a selfie in what she assumed was the living room, then turned to walk down the hall. Her phone transformed from a camera to a flashlight. Plenty of light shone through the broken windows, but she wanted to make sure she didn't step on anything gross.

At the end of the hall was a large room Emma assumed was the master bedroom. Somebody had thrown a mattress in there. Emma didn't want to think about what disgusting things happened on that filthy object, and what creatures were living inside it. She took a quick selfie and got out of there.

A few more rooms were connected to the hallway, but there was even less to see in those. She crossed through the living room again and into the kitchen. Nature had conquered in there. Dirt and splotches of grass covered the floor, some of it bursting through the tiles. The sink was rusted and filled with leaves; from it came the sound of movement. Emma's heart pounded like a baseline. How many germ carrying creatures were in there?

One quick picture and she was done. There was no need to go upstairs. Most were smart enough to realize using the stairs in a corroded house could be deadly. And if anybody were living (or hiding) in the house, they'd most likely be up there.

Emma emerged victorious into the afternoon light.

"You survived," Cindy joked.

"It was nothing," Emma replied.

"How many pictures?"

"Three."

"Show 'em."

Emma held the phone up for Cindy to flip through the images.

"There's four," Cindy said.

"What?" Emma was sure Cindy was teasing her again.

Cindy flipped back a couple. "Who's that guy?"

"What guy?"

"Right there!" Cindy pointed to the phone, even though Emma couldn't see it.

Emma pulled the phone away from Cindy and glanced at the photo. It was not one of the three selfies she took, but a shot of the living room.

"I didn't–"

Emma froze when she noticed the shadow. Instinct told her that it had to be hers, or something outside the window. But it looked like a man. Most of him was dark, yet she could make out some of his features: a large nose, squinted eyes, and a curved mouth, opened ever so slightly.

"Let's get out here," Cindy's voice snapped Emma out of thoughts. "We don't want that guy coming after us."

"There was nobody in there," Emma was certain. She would have known if there were a man that close to her. Wouldn't she?

"He must've been hiding in the shadows."

Emma tried to protest, but knew it was pointless to argue with her friend, especially when she was bolting up Martin Street. Emma hurried to catch up to her.

"You should post that one to Instagram, too," Cindy suggested. "It'll get tons of responses."

"We'll see," Emma said. She made it a point of not turning back to look at the house, afraid of what she'd see.

Emma sat on her bed and flipped automatically through the four pictures. She was trying to figure out what that shadow was, and why she hadn't seen it standing right next to her. Did she narrowly escape an attack? Or was this just a glitch on her phone?

She was almost startled by the text from Cindy asking her why she hadn't posted her pictures to Instagram. Emma ignored it. In fact, she wanted to delete all the pictures from the Hodges' place, but hesitated. Maybe things would make sense in the morning.

Emma turned off her phone and crawled into bed. As she closed her eyes, the image of the shadow man floated in the darkness. It took her longer than usual to fall asleep.

A scream pulled Emma out of her sleep.

Not a scream. An alarm. Was there a fire? No. It was her phone. It wasn't her usual alarm, but the one that rang for Amber Alerts and tornado warnings. She grabbed her phone to silence it.

The image on her screen had changed from Hello Kitty to a close up of the face of the shadow man. His white flesh twisted into a horrible scream, as if in synch with the screeching alarm.

Emma's shaking hands fumbled with the phone until she turned it off. A moment of silence was broken by a pounding on her bedroom door. The shadow man!

"What the Hell's going on in there?" It was her brother, David.

"Nothing," she lied, her phone jerking and wriggling in her hands as if it were alive.

David threw open her bedroom door. He held his cell phone before him like a shield.

"Get out of here!" Emma shouted at him automatically. But in truth, she felt safer with him there. "You're not supposed to come in without knocking."

"Not when you're sending me creepy shit."

"What're you talking about?"

David showed her the image of the shadow man on his phone.

"How'd you get that?"

"You texted it to me just now, you idiot."

Emma knew she didn't.

"What the Hell is it?"

"Nothing."

"Sure looks like something."

"I know it's not the dick pics you're used to receiving."

"Shut up," David yelled at her and left her room.

Emma wanted him to stay.

She looked at her phone. The notes app had opened on its own. Random letters and characters were appearing quickly on the screen as if somebody were typing furiously.

Emma threw it across the room, not caring if it smashed to bits. The alarm returned, louder than before. For the rest of the night, Emma battled various alarms and reminder sounds chiming loudly just when she though she might fall asleep.

Emma's mother observed her daughter wasn't speaking during break-fast. After her divorce, Mrs. Fisher found her children to be more brooding than usual. She found it best to leave them alone until they were ready to talk.

When David came downstairs, he practically attacked his sister. "Thanks for fucking up my phone."

"Davey!" Mrs. Fisher scolded. Though after the divorce, she knew trying to get her son to stop swearing was a lost cause.

"What'd I do?" Emma was on the defensive.

"After you sent me that pic, my phone went haywire. Kept opening apps and making weird sounds. And Google maps tried to send me to the old Hodges' place."

Emma's defenses dropped. "What?"

"I'm sure you're deaf from your alarm going off all night, so I'll repeat it." He raised his voice, "My maps keep routing to the old Hodges' place."

"Did Cindy put you up to this?"

"Cindy? What would I talk to that bitch for?"

"Davey! That's enough!" Mrs. Fisher tried in vain.

"You guys are playing some game with me after yesterday."

"I haven't played games with you since we were little kids," David said. "I got better things to do."

David realized that he'd left his sister wide open for a tease. But to his surprise, she asked again, "Are you sure?"

Mrs. Fisher had enough of being an observer. "What's going on?"

"Yeah, sis, you're acting nuttier than usual."

Emma though about lying, by couldn't. "Cindy dared me to go to the old Hodges' place yesterday. And take selfies."

"Alone?" Mrs. Fisher asked, shocked.

Emma nodded.

"Everybody in school's done it," David told his mother.

"Even you?"

"Yeah, like when we first moved here."

"That place is dangerous. Broken glass everywhere. And who knows what... dangerous men are living in there."

"I didn't see anybody," Emma said. "I wasn't there too long. But when I got outside, I found this strange image on my phone."

"The one you sent me?" David asked.

"Yeah."

David showed it to his mother.

"There was somebody there!" Horrible scenarios of what might have happened to her daughter flashed through Mrs. Fisher's mind.

"It's just a shadow," Emma defended. "I didn't see anybody else. I think... it was..."

"A ghost?" David finished for her.

"Go ahead, tell me I'm crazy."

David gave her a free pass.

"Maybe not," Mrs. Fisher consoled. She wanted to tell her daughter that when she was younger, she'd seen strange things that her friends and family couldn't. But she didn't. Instead, she rushed them to get ready for school.

Once they were gone, Mrs. Fisher checked her phone and found a text from her daughter of the shadow image. As she stared at it, she knew this wasn't a trick of the light or deviant of society. This was something worse.

Emma didn't want to look at her phone until the shadow figure was a distant memory. But to go without social media for so long was excruciating painful. She decided to check it on her laptop.

As she opened it, she thought she saw the image of the shadow figure flash on the screen for a moment. It couldn't be. Her paranoia was playing tricks on her.

The background screen was black. It was supposed to be a picture of the cast of *Riverdale*. David must have changed it to annoy her.

Emma needed some music to drown out the silence, so she opened iTunes and hit "shuffle." Creepy sounding tones echoed out of the speakers. It was like nothing she'd ever heard before. After a moment, Emma realized a song was playing backwards and slowly, turning a pop tune into a horror movie theme. She paused the music and again silently blamed her brother. Because the alternative was worse.

With a click on the icon for Safari, the screen flickered, and the innards began to grind noisily.

"David!" she called.

He came running as quickly as a teenage brother does: sauntering slowly into the room.

"Now what?"

The computer moaned as if in pain. The backwards music started again, even slower this time. David leaned over her shoulder.

"That's messed up," he said. "You brought a virus into this house."

"But I never connected my phone to my computer."

"It must have gotten into the network." That didn't sound logical to David, but he was at a loss for a better explanation. "Damnit, sis, this is going to mess up everything."

"Sorry."

"You will be if I lose any of my data."

David ran to turn on his mother's desktop, which the family shared. The start-up gong sounded more like a moan of agony. The screen never lit up, but like the laptop, it made cringe-worthy grinding sounds as if the machine was being torn apart from the inside.

David ran around the house and disconnected all the devices from their home network.

"I may have to take everything to the Genius Bar," he told his sister once he was done.

"No!" she snapped. "I don't want this to spread any further."

"They have the best virus protection."

"This isn't like any virus I've ever seen."

"Like you've ever seen a virus. If my phone continues to act all stupid, I'm bringing it."

What if that's what it wants? Emma asked herself.

That evening, Emma tried to forget the craziness of the past 24-hours by binge watching *Gossip Girls* on Netflix. She was so tired, she couldn't keep her eyes open. Just before she drifted off to sleep, the image of the shadow man fluttered over the screen. Emma cursed her imagination for continuing to frighten her.

The calming wind chime sound of The Ring filled the house. Emma looked up in surprise.

"Ignore it," David said. "Probably a truck."

David was busy gutting his own laptop, which was also malfunctioning and making painful sounding internal noises. He valiantly tried to salvage the information on his hard drive.

The Ring chimed again.

"Something's out there," Emma said.

"Let 'em stay there."

"What if it's mom?" Maybe she'd come home early from work.

"She has a key."

The chimes came continuously now. When David wasn't looking, Emma opened the iRing app on the family iPad. On the live view of their doorstep she saw the shadow man. "David . . ." Emma called her brother over.

He was furious when he saw she was looking on the iPad.

"What're you doing?" He snapped.

"He's out there."

"Better than in here."

The dark figure leaned closer to the camera. Blackness engulfed the screen.

"What's it doing?" David asked.

Bang!

They both jumped. Somebody pounded at the door.

"It's trying to get in!" Emma cried.

The banging came again; louder this time. The iPad shook with it. With one final bang, the screen of the iPad cracked.

Emma screamed.

"What the Hell did you do?" David shouted at her.

"Nothing. It just... cracked."

"That's the iPad I use for the sound system."

Emma hated hearing disappointment in David's voice. Everything he'd set up in their new home was being destroyed.

Whispered laughter echoed through the house.

"It's in the Bose system," David said, realizing how ridiculous that would have sounded to him if said out of context.

"How?" Emma asked.

"Like everything else," David explained, "it's connected to the network. I forgot about those."

"It'll harass us forever."

"Not if I turn off every device in this house."

David ran from speaker to speaker disconnecting them. The laughter grew louder. Emma could no longer tell if it were coming out of the speakers or the air around her.

The siblings were as happy to see their mother come home as they were when they were little kids. But the two made a mental pact not to mention any details of the afternoon's events.

Emma woke in the middle of the night with a feeling that something was wrong. She immediately checked her phone. It had been self-playing videos of horrendous accidents all night long, so she hid it in her drawer. A disgustingly bloody (yet unrecognizable) video was playing in slow-mo, but the device was silent.

That's when she realized her room was as hot as a sauna.

Emma got up to lower the thermostat. The blue glow of The Nest was like a beacon at the end of the hallway. It pulsed slowly, ocean waves of light washing up and down the walls. Did it always do that?

The heat was turned all the way up. It was currently 92 degrees. Emma placed her hand on the nob to turn it down.

A ripple of electricity shot up her arm. She was surprised her scream didn't wake the household.

Automatically, the thermostat lowered to the opposite end of the dial. The heat turned off and the air conditioning came on. Emma decided it was easier to let the house cool than to try to change the settings.

"Emma..." From the kitchen came a whispered voice.

Emma hoped it was her brother playing a trick on her, but she knew he wasn't.

"Emma..."

She reached the kitchen.

"Emma..." The Echo hissed.

David must have forgotten about disconnecting that one. They hardly used it once the novelty faded.

"Emma..."

"What do you want?" Emma asked softly.

The Echo remained silent, but Emma knew. This lost soul wanted to escape the darkness of being trapped between worlds. And it wanted Emma to help her. She was so warm and welcoming.

"No!"

If not Emma, then... her brother?

"Get out of my house!" Emma screamed to silence the voice in her head.

Then she laughed. She sounded like every horror movie she'd ever seen.

The Echo shrieked in response. A high-pitched tone pierced Emma's ear. It was relentless.

"What's going on?" Mrs. Fisher raced into the kitchen. David was quick on her heels.

"It's the virus," David explained.

"What virus?" Mrs. Fisher asked as she unplugged The Echo.

The deafening sound stopped.

"Emma's phone picked up a virus," David continued, "and it spread all over our network."

"It made The Echo do that?"

"It's torturing me," Emma said.

"Don't be so dramatic," David snapped.

"But..." Emma wanted to tell them the shadow man's intentions, but she knew they wouldn't believe her. Did she even believe it herself?

"There's a simple way to stop this," Mrs. Fisher said.

"An exorcist?" Emma asked.

"No." Mrs. Fisher unplugged The Echo. "Problem solved."

The ear-piercing tone burst again from The Echo.

"Stop it, mom," David begged as he blocked his ears.

"It's unplugged!" she replied, dumbfounded.

Mrs. Fisher grabbed The Echo, then screamed and jerked back her arm.

"It shocked me!" She exclaimed.

"But you unplugged it." David couldn't wrap his head around what was happening.

Mrs. Fisher pulled two oven mitts out of a drawer. She slipped them on, grabbed The Echo and threw it into the sink, stuffing the top of it into the garbage disposal. She started the blades and ran the water at the same time. The Echo screamed as if a living creature were being sliced to bits. Steam rose from where the water hit the plastic.

After that, the kids confessed the events of the afternoon.

"Let's turn off the network," Mrs. Fisher suggested. "Without that, this... thing will have nothing to cling to."

David wanted to kick himself. Why hadn't he thought of that? He ran to the den to disconnect the router. As he reached out to pull the plug he stopped. He could feel the heat emanating from the cord.

"It's going to fry me," he told the others who now stood behind him.

Mrs. Fisher still had on the oven mitts; she knelt beside her son.

"This one?" She pointed at the plug.

David nodded.

Mrs. Fisher reached out for it. The air around it crackled with electricity. If she got too close, it was going to shock her worse than The Echo.

"We need a plan B," she said.

"Get as far away from here as possible," Emma suggested.

"We're not leaving this house," Mrs. Fisher said. "We can't give in to this thing."

Mrs. Fisher recalled encountering these types of beings in her youth. Terrifying entities that wanted her to help them escape the darkness. But she knew if she let them in, they would never let her go. Back then, they were hidden in the shadows, easy to ignore. Now, one had attached itself to the unseen energy around them. And it wanted her children.

"I don't want to move again! The first time was bad enough."

"Then what are we going to do?" Emma asked.

"We're going to evict it!" Mrs. Fisher replied.

"How?" David asked. This wasn't like the time they had rats in the attic of their old home. Their mother wasn't going to solve this with traps and poisoned cheese.

Emma knew. She still didn't quite understand how, but she would do what she could to help her mother.

Mrs. Fisher concentrated. The lifetime of shields she put up slipped away with ease. She felt the dark presence in her home. It was everywhere, weighing heavy in the air. David was right, this thing had found its way into the energy emitted from their network. The ghost in the ether.

"You pissed off the wrong mother!" Her kids were shocked at her tone. "You can either go back to haunting that old house or stay here and be thrown out into nothingness."

Laughter burst from the disconnected Bose system. All three of their phones sounded the heart stopping alarm. The computers churned and moaned. The Ring chimed endlessly. The other motion detection cameras in the house sent messages of motion detected. The Nest blew the cold air stronger, plummeting the house into a deep chill. It was a demented electronic symphony.

Emma and her mother could feel the shadow man reaching out for them. One of them would weaken. One of them would allow him to escape.

David automatically picked up his phone and unlocked the screen. "Maybe I can turn off everything remotely."

"No, David!" Mrs. Fisher cried out to him.

David stared at the screen, hypnotized. His face draining of color

"Let him go!" Emma screamed.

Her command caused the unseen grip on her brother to weaken, but it had no intention of releasing him. Mrs. Fisher ran to her son and tried to pull the phone out of his hands. David wasn't giving it up without a struggle, and Mrs. Fisher feared she'd hurt her son.

It felt as if the noises around them were intensifying while Mrs. Fisher arm-wrestled with her son. But what if this were just a way to distract both of them while this thing went after...

"Emma!" Mrs. Fisher called out.

Emma was no longer in the room. Mrs. Fisher didn't know if she should go after her daughter or stay there and break the grip on her son.

"Emma," she called again.

"Right here, mom."

Emma returned to the room, wielding her field hockey stick. She swung it over her head.

"What're you doing?" he mother cried, fearing the worst.

Emma brought the stick down on the router. She continued to smash the plastic box until it cracked open and spilled its guts on the table.

One by one the sounds in the house ceased.

David's body crumpled; his phone fell to the ground. Luckily his mother was still close enough to catch him.

"Davey!"

"I . . . I couldn't help myself." David sounded on the verge of tears.

"Fuck it," Mrs. Fisher said. "Let's get out of here."

"And leave all our electronic devices," Emma added.

"No duh!" David appeared well enough to be his usual salty self to his sister.

His mother still had to help him to his feet. She led them to the door.

The pounding returned, even louder this time.

"It can't be," Emma cried. "It should have dissipated."

"It's one last effort to scare us," Mrs. Fisher guessed. There was no way of knowing for sure, but she wasn't taking any chances. She grabbed her kids and barrelled toward the door.

The knocking intensified.

Mrs. Fisher sensed the energy as she reached the door. But it was weaker. She pushed it open and pulled her children outside.

"Are we taking the car?" David asked.

"No," Mrs. Fisher feared it had attached itself to the Bluetooth in the car she won in the divorce. She had a few dollars and her ATM card in her back pocket.

"What're we going to do?" Emma asked.

"We'll figure that out when we can't walk anymore," her mother replied.

Emma Fisher and her family fled into the night.

Emma didn't care that all her electronic devices were left behind. She never wanted to see them, or that house, again.

I'm not scared, Bobby Whelton told himself. *It's just a house. People lived here once. A long, long time ago.*

"I knew you were a pussy," his best friend Steven taunted him.

"I'm not scared," Bobby spoke aloud the mantra in his head as he bravely ascended the stairs of the old Fisher's place . . .

IT'S NOT WARM WHEN SHE'S AWAY

STACEY SMEKOFSKE

Walking into the old house was a bit anticlimactic. Chris anticipated that she would feel a bit more excited, maybe anxious, but she only felt tired. The house was a white adobe style that had been constructed in the late 70s, and it was probably meant to resemble ancient homes built by skilled South American craftsman. The cast iron gate led to what was once a magnificent courtyard; all that was left was a pile of rocks in a massive hole. The former fountain might have once added a happy trickling sound to the environment; Chris paused imagining the ghostly splashes as they echoed off the walls of the courtyard. A set of large studded oak double doors stood open for the movers. She stepped inside and an air-conditioned blast hit her face as she gazed upon her new dwelling for the first time. It was naked. There was a couch in the sunken living room with a tv stand in the corner that looked miniature in the space. The kitchen was situated in the distance, furnished with a pile of dirty dishes in the sink and a mound of crumbs on the Spanish-tiled counter tops. On the opposite side of the living-room, a treadmill stood watch with a towel draped over it. There was nothing hanging on the walls; they were exposed for all the world to see, but upon closer inspection a tiny web with residents lurking were found in a corner or two. All the movers moving her stuff in and the existing furnishings looked small in the immense space. Chris thought that this was appropriate, a blank house for a blank slate. She gripped her baseball-sized stuffed poodle to her chest and sarcastically sighed, "I guess I can live with the lack of space."

"Hey, you must be Christine," a nerdy-chic guy came out of a hallway to Chris's right and reached out to shake hands.

"Yeah, you can call me Chris."

"Cool. I didn't think you would be so cute. Your pictures don't do you justice," nerdy man-boy was good at making a girl feel uncomfortable.

"Thanks, I guess," Chris didn't know how to take this frank manner. The guy was a little ragged. He looked like he hadn't bathed in a week, and yeah, the smell was a bit on the *pizza for breakfast and some beef jerky stuck between the cushions* aroma meter. He donned an open flannel and a dirty white t-shirt. He let out a little belch which he blew away from Chris's direction, thank heavens.

Chris quickly changed the subject from herself, "You must be Steven. It's nice to finally meet you in person." He may have been a bit rough around the edges, but Chris felt that there couldn't be much harm in sharing a place with a smart computer nerd that made tons of money programming security systems for the casinos. According to Steven, he inherited the house from his grandpa who happened to be some rich real estate tycoon, Ron Groodin. Chris met Steven online while searching for place to live in Vegas. He was friendly enough, and the place was more than over-sized; she figured she could avoid the stench if he neglected grooming for long stretches of time.

"Do you think you could show me where my bedroom is? I am so tired from the trip," Chris tried to seem nonchalant, and not too much like she was trying to get away from him. The smell was a bit harsh on the nose hairs, not that Chris had much of those. She was a well-groomed female after all.

"Oh, yeah. No problem. Follow me."

As Steven led the way, Chris hung back a few steps to avoid the scent heading downwind. She chuckled a little at the thought of Steven in a business meeting. The image of people fanning their faces and casually opening windows flooded her mind; he must be a genius for people to tolerate the stench.

From a room, ahead on the right, she heard the familiar voice of Bill Withers crooning about no sunshine when she goes away. The song haunted Chris's memories. It was one that her father always played on Saturday mornings before the frenzy of the day commenced. She quickly shoved the memory out of her mind just as the door swung wide open, and a dark-haired mass gruffly asked, "Is this the new roommate?"

Startled by this guy's size and lack of friendliness, Chris found herself instinctively reaching for Steven's sticky hand. Steven cheerfully replied, "Yes, Craig. This is Christine, oh wait, Chris."

Craig shrugged, his gray eyes examining Chris. She felt like he was staring right into her soul and it was unnerving. Chris felt like she was having that dream when you go to work naked. Craig's muscled bulged under his tight *Jaws* t-shirt. He looked pleasing, but that was terribly overshadowed by the intimidation that Chris felt from his unwelcoming intensity. Bill Withers purred, "this house just ain't no home anytime she goes away."

Chris tried to break free of the gaze, but luckily Craig did that for her. He closed the door, but as he did, she thought she heard him say, "Watch yourself, Chris."

Steven looked down at Chris, who was cowering close by and breathed, "Yeah, Craig is a little, strange. He just likes to keep mostly to himself. Don't worry about him, he'll stay out of your way."

They continued down the hall to a large door that faced their approach like a sentinel. It was arched on top and studded similar to the front entrance. As it opened and the hinges whined like they were protesting the weight.

Chris took in a breath when she observed the grandeur of the room. She was amazed that this was the room the others were willing to let her have. It was an amazing apartment, with a bathroom to the left and a reading nook nestled between built-in dark mahogany bookcases. The room framed a set of glass doors that led to an immense patio. It was all hers, a paradise set in a big city. This was completely different from the tight, ancient, and traditional brownstone that she escaped from in Boston. Chris was going to share this huge house with two other people, it felt like she had won the lottery. The rent was cheap, and she was living in a mansion that looked like a Spanish hacienda in Las Vegas; a new life. An exciting fresh start.

She thanked Stinky for showing her the way and gave the usual "catch you later." Steven told her to let him know if she needed anything and left her to enjoy her suite.

She slowly approached the glass doors to her balcony and then hesitated. She felt the black beady eyes before she saw them. She tried to shake off the ominous feeling of dread that the bird usually brings with it. She shivered, and then quickly opened the doors. The black feathers glistened in the sun as the winged menace sat staring at her. Chris returned its gaze as fear rose to her throat. She gulped it back down and yelled at the raven, but it sat still and cocked its head. She was taken aback a little by the audacity of such a bird. She turned her back on the stupid thing and on the hot afternoon and decided to escape back into her cool bedroom; as she turned to close the door, the bird that once sat impudently on her banister was gone. A cold chill raced down her spine. Why was she so creeped out by a bird? She decided she read way too much Poe.

Just then she got the urge to peek out her door and glance at the dwelling of the other menacing creature that had presented himself, Craig. She slowly turned the doorknob and peeked through the little gap between the door and the jam. A tingle crept up her spine and instantly tears stung her eyes; she was looking directly into Stinky Steven's brown eyes. He had an odd smile on his face. She quickly shut the door.

With her back against the door, she tried to catch her breath. Freaking bird! Stupid roommate! They were totally throwing her off balance. She didn't lie to Steve when she said she was tired; It had been a long day. When she finally started breathing normally, she took a look around her empty room. Boxes lined one of the walls and she wished it was all unpacked. Luckily the movers had done a great job at propping her mattress against the wall in her room, so all she had to do was pull on the edge a bit to get it to flop down on the ground. Good enough. She plopped her tired body down and didn't even think to get a pillow or blanket out. She clutched her ragged poodle; it didn't even resemble a dog anymore. She looked into the one marble eye that was left and pulled a little at the stitching that had unraveled years previously freeing all the stuffing from the little body. Chris felt a tinge of anxiety and thought of home. Fighting back a little sob, she whispered, "This is our new home," and fell into a quick and restless sleep.

Chris's eyes flew open. There was a scratching noise coming from the glass double-doors. That damn bird was back. She sat up and squinted toward her patio, expecting to see that raven, but nothing was there. The scratching persisted. She slowly got up and made her way toward the sound thinking there must be a cat. She looked out the glass and saw nothing. The scratching was still going on. The room wasn't pitch black; this was Vegas after all. An eerie neon glow filled the room, but she still couldn't see what was making the scratching noise. She moved quickly away from the door. The scratching continued; it sounded like nails against wood. Chris had the sudden feeling that she wasn't alone. Her heart was pounding against her ribs and she listened to her breath in the shadow drenched room. Her eyes glanced up at the large dark beams that crossed the ceiling, she thought they looked like gallows. Uneasiness had slipped into her psyche as she considered whether she made a good choice to come to the Vegas valley. Her throat was dry and though the room was cool from the air conditioning she felt as if she was being mummified alive, and all the moisture was being sucked from her skin. Chris raced toward her bedroom door. She felt eyes on her.

There must be someone there, but she couldn't see them; she

needed to escape this room. The scratching wouldn't stop but she really couldn't find the cause, so she chalked it up to new sounds in a new house. She decided to get a drink and shake off the anxiety that crept into her brain. Her bedroom door moaned as she opened it and then she crept into the hallway. The hallway seemed to stretch as she made her way along the dimly lit wall. As she passed Creepy Craig's door, she could swear she heard movement. She hurried her steps and quickly tip-toed across the sunken living room to the kitchen. She felt along the wall hoping to find a switch in what she would think is an obvious place. She was unable find it in what would be a normal place for a switch; she decided to follow her hands to another wall. She couldn't help but wonder if one of those little residents in the web might find her hand before she found a light. Suddenly a loud click and the lights were burning a hole into her brain. She turned and there was Craig.

His eyes looked even more menacing than before. He was ruggedly attractive with a scruffy 5 o'clock shadow and a prohibition hair cut that in its current state fell into his eyes. She awkwardly stared longer than was normal. How could his eyes be even greyer than earlier?

"I heard you get up. I decided to come see if you needed anything." He walked over to the sink and grabbed a dirty glass from the pile.

"Uh, no. I just needed a drink. My throat was dry is all," Chris started nervously opening cupboard doors trying to find a clean glass. She thought there had to be one somewhere. Craig didn't offer any help he just observed her as she fumbled along. Finally, she found a plastic cup that was obviously a 7-11 cup that had become part of the bachelor-pad-fine-China set. She looked inside the cup and blew out whatever might have been in there. Slowly she crept to the sink, hoping that her movement toward Craig would urge him to make room for her. He didn't.

Chris tried hard not to show fear. She remembered hearing that if you make eye contact with a predator that they will believe you are strong and not attack you. She looked straight into the stormy eyes and reached to turn on the sink, Craig just stared back; he was so close that she could count the faded freckles that marched across his nose. Chris's goosebumps caused her raised arm hairs to brush against Craig's flannel shirt. Maybe that advice was just crap.

Craig leaned down just a little to put his face closer to Chris's ear and whispered, "You're being watched."

Chris reared back almost spilling her water. Craig reached up and turned off the sink. He took a sip of his glass and then turned and dumped the rest out. He paused a moment, examining Chris and strode out of the kitchen. She shivered in the vacant room. Craig left, and it felt like the temperature dropped 50 degrees. She waited till she heard the latch of Craig's door lightly slide past the strike plate of his door frame as it closed. She breathed out a sigh of relief, but then sucked in a sharp breath when she heard a faint tune coming from his room. "Ain't no sunshine when she's gone, it's not warm when she's away,"

Chris stood frozen in the kitchen, wondering about what to do. Her insides screamed to get out, run, escape. She reminded her lungs to breathe. She knew she was being silly, but then after what seemed like hours, she realized she hadn't even taken a drink out of her Big Gulp cup. She felt nauseous and decided to just dump the water and run-walk back to her room and find a way to lock the door. Amazingly she did return to her room safely. The scratching had stopped, but as she stood with her back against the door contemplating her silliness, her eyes grew larger as she read a message scratched in the bottom of the beautiful door that led to her patio, "GET OUT NOW."

That did it. She forgot to breathe. She choked a bit when her body's survival systems kicked in. She coughed a bit, leaning forward and tried to come up with a logical explanation. There was nothing. Feeling her knees go weak, she wobbled to her mattress on the floor. While never taking her eyes off the message, she sat down hoping the letters would disappear in her shifting positions. They didn't go anywhere. A tear silently fell from Chris's eye; she decided to let it slide down her cheek, because the sensation made her feel alive.

It wasn't clear to Chris what time she fell asleep that night, but sunshine was now filling her room. The daylight brought with it a breath of life and hope that she previously hadn't felt in the darkness. She sat propped against the wall facing the patio; she must have stared at the carved message until her eyes gave up. She sat feeling the warmth of the sunlight through her closed eyelids and hoped that while she slept the words faded with the shadows, but her pulse quickened when she saw "GET OUT NOW" still carved into the wood doorframe. She forced herself to control her breathing and to slow her heart rate.

Chris edged along the wall, giving herself as much distance from the message as she could. When she moved past her bedroom door, a quick flick of her wrist locked the entrance. She made her way to the bathroom and closed and locked that door as well, "Breathe Christine, this is crazy." She tried to talk to herself the way her father would; his soothing voice echoed inside her memories. She never believed in the supernatural. Sure, every girl likes to hear ghost stories, but they never believe them. Deep down it is understood that it's all just for fun, but this wasn't fun at all.

Chris decided to have a shower to try and calm down. Luckily, she didn't have to start working till next week. She planned to give herself a full week to settle into her new dwelling. This haunted settlement was going to take all of that week to get used to. She turned on the shower to a nice hot temperature and starting undressing. The room quickly filled with a warm wet haze and she walked into her southwestern tiled shower that looked more like a stone sauna than a place to bathe. The hot water felt nice over her flesh, the goosebumps rose again on her body, but contrasted the cool fear that caused them to appear the night before. As her body temperature rose, she felt relaxation and normalcy return. She watched the steam swirl above her head and thought of her decision to move.

Boston was great. She loved the busy city and she hoped Las Vegas would grow on her the same way. Although Chris believed nothing would ever compare to the smell of Fenway Park, the feeling of cobblestone beneath your feet on Acorn Street, eating the best grits and Polish sausage at Mike and Patty's, or her Dad dancing with her on Saturday mornings. Her stomach began to rumble. Chris remembered that she hadn't eaten anything since that bag of pumpkin seeds yesterday afternoon. The shower was over, it was time for her to get something to eat.

She turned off the water and took in a cleansing breath of vapor. She stepped onto the tiled floor and remembered she hadn't unpacked a towel. She found a box labeled bathroom sitting in the Jacuzzi tub and luckily there was a towel wrapped around her bathroom accessories. She carefully unwrapped everything and then proceeded to dry off. Chris flipped her head over, wrapping her towel expertly around her long brown hair. She flipped her head back up and stood up straight looking at herself in the mirror. She could only see her outline since the fog had adequately coated her mirror. She admired her shape and then slowly she backed away as an invisible finger wrote in the foggy mirror, "DANGER." The letters dripped with the condensation like blood that drips from a wound. Chris believed she needed to finally *girl-up* and look closely to see if this was a trick. She leaned closer to the mirror examining the mirror's qualities. Her eyes shifted focus as she began to see a face looking back at her. Her thoughts were drowned out with a scream that failed to escape her throat. She was looking into the visage of a man. His eyes were the most prominent feature, they looked frightened and frightening at the same time. She fell backwards and slipped on the wet floor. Her hand reached up and caught the doorknob. She yanked the door open, stumbled into her bedroom, and then slammed the bathroom door. Her room echoed with the sudden exit.

The room was unoccupied. She looked around just to make sure. Chris stood frozen and naked, like the statue of Venus, except for the pink turban accessory that she was donning. She slowly eyed the first message and noticed some movement outside. She squealed and gasped at the same time, which sounded like a strange hiccup. The shape of a man standing at her window faded and she saw the raven was back and gawking at her.

"That's it," she said aloud, "I gotta get out of this room." She quickly found the box labeled clothes and put on the first thing she found, which happened to be a pair of striped shorts and a Boston Pops T-shirt.

Chris hustled out of the room, taking care to tip-toe past Craig's room, and headed straight for Steven's room. The long hallway was only shortened by her quickened pace. Just as she was about to raise her hand to knock, she heard a breath behind her.

"Hey, what's going on, you look wired," Steve looked a little wired himself. He had huge bags under his eyes and seemed a little out of breath.

"Steve! Shit, you scared me. I need to talk to you," Chris tried to sound a little less freaked out than she actually was. "I am sorry, did I interrupt your workout or something?"

"No, I was just, uh . . . working on something. Some big project for work has got me working late. What's up?"

Chris tried to slow her breathing, "I was wondering about this house. Um, has anything sort of. . ." she paused and tried to carefully choose her words, ". . .weird happened to you or anyone in this house before?"

Steve chuckled and combed his fingers through his greasy hair, "Weird? Do you mean something weirder than Craig? No. Why?"

Chris internally trembled at the thought of Creepy Craig but remembered that ghost faces are a bit stranger than a roommate's obsession with a Rock and Roll Hall of Famer's song. The same song that was coincidentally her father's favorite too. Eerie. But still not ghost eerie.

She decided she better just tell him. "Look, Steve I need you to come to my room. I need to show you something."

Steve smiled slyly, "Okay."

"No, it's nothing like that. Something strange is happening and I need to know if I am going crazy."

Steve started to look a little anxious, "Fine. Sure. I am right behind you."

She quickly spun on her heels and headed back to her room. As they passed Craig's room her father's song rang out louder than ever. The song filled the entire wing of the house. Steve shrugged, "He really likes that song, he's played it non-stop since you got here."

She puzzled over that a little but continued down the hall toward her room.

Steve stopped her before she opened her door, "I forgot to ask you, why did you decide to come to live in Vegas. Boston is a long way away."

Chris sucked in some cool dry air and rested her hand on the doorknob. *Hey, I oughtta leave this young thing alone, but ain't no sunshine when she's gone* rang in her head. She turned and said, "I have nothing left in Boston."

"Where's your family?"

"I'm an only child. My mom died when I was born."

Steve looked sympathetic, "Damn, I am sorry. What about your Dad?"

Chris turned back toward the door and slowly turned the knob, "He had a heart attack two months ago. He's gone."

She pushed against the door, and it protested with its pitiful moaning. Chris slowly lifted her eyes, "Daddy?"

Her father stood in the room. How could that be? He's dead. What the hell is going on, has she completely lost her mind? No, wait! Steve must see him. She quickly turned to see what Steve's reaction was and was met only by a strange smile, his eyes boring a hole into her, and his morning breath. She stepped back and then back around to see her father just as he faded away.

"What did you want to show me," Steve walked past her and plopped down on her mattress.

Chris was really uneasy with his familiarity in her room. She pointed to the patio doors without speaking; she hoped that she would look and see her dad again somewhere else in the room, but he didn't reappear. She must be really tired, or was she?

"Damn, Chris," Steve got up and inspected the door. He traced the words with his fingers and laughed, "You aren't supposed to ruin the house your first day here."

Her body stiffened, "I didn't do it! There was this scratching going on last night, and I didn't see anything. I have no idea how it happened." Chris felt her eyes begin to fill with tears.

"Hey, I was just kidding. I believe you. I have no clue what happened here. I really am stumped, maybe the movers did it," Steve replied as he ran his fingers through his lube-soaked hair.

Chris started moving toward the bathroom, and then hesitated a second. She silently debated whether or not she should tell him about the mirror. After seeing her dad, she began to think he may be haunting her. She forced the words out, "I think that I am being watched."

Steve looked concerned, "What do you mean?"

"Well, I feel like I have eyes on me. And then I saw a face in the mirror when I was taking a shower. I saw a guy standing on my . . ."

"Whoa, whoa, whoa. Are you sure? I mean come on, that's crazy. Some guy watching you through the mirror. Do you honestly think you have like a two-way mirror in your bathroom or something? You must be seriously tired," Steve shifted his weight and crossed his arms across his chest. He chuckled uncomfortably.

"Well, uhh, I don't know. I mean, you are right. I am tired. I guess I could be seeing things," Chris shrugged, "You are probably right. I guess it just weirded me out that the scratched words on the door appeared and then Craig was all creepy in the kitchen last night."

Steve suddenly looked alert, "What do you mean, Craig was 'creepy in the kitchen last night'?"

"I just went to get a drink and Craig came in and told me that I was being watched."

"Huh. That's weird," Steve let his eyes glance down the hall, "You don't think Craig is watching you, do you?"

"No, you are right. He could be just trying to scare me or something. Playground games, boys, that kind of thing," Chris sighed.

"Yeah. I think you are right. I am sorry about your door. Maybe some animal got into your room and scratched that on there," he shoved his hands in his pockets completely ignoring that the fact that the scratches spelled words. "I am sure you just need some rest and maybe some food after your long drive. Do you wanna go get something to eat with me, maybe?"

Chris was somewhat disturbed by his invitation, she couldn't put her finger on why, "No, thanks. I think you are right. I should just rest."

Steve seemed a bit perturbed, but turned to leave and said, "Okay. Well, if you change your mind, just let me know."

"Well, thanks for helping me feel a bit better," Chris walked to her bedroom door with the intention of closing and locking it behind him, but she was horrified to see Craig walking up the hallway toward them.

He had a vintage David Bowie concert t-shirt on which seemed strangely paradoxical to Chris; it clung closely to his chiseled chest. His features were agreeable, but his aggressive and somewhat combative demeanor left Chris feeling troubled. He pushed past Steve and walked into Chris's bedroom staring at her patio door. After an uncomfortable pause, he turned to look at the departing Steve and Chris.

Steve looked hesitant, but finally spoke up, "Well, I guess I will catch you guys later." He turned down the hall making the hike to his bedroom seem arduous.

Chris didn't like Steve's awkwardness, but she really missed it when she thought about what was now standing in her room glaring at her. She turned and asked Craig what he wanted without trying to sound too nervous.

"What happened last night?"

His abruptness made the hair on her neck stand up, "I just heard some scratching at the door. It spooked me. That coupled with my sleep depravity just made it an uncomfortable night is all. No biggie."

"Hmph," Craig looked unsatisfied with her response, "I guess." He slowly shifted his gaze to the corner of the room above her empty bookshelves. His inspection of this corner was a bit longer than casual.

Chris noticed his attention and expecting to see some ethereal presence when she looked up but was unable to see what captured Craig's focus. Craig suddenly pivoted and left the room shutting the door behind him.

Chris was dizzy. She had no clue what just spooked Craig, but felt she needed to inspect that corner a bit better. She grasped the chair that was in the opposite corner and dragged it to the suspect corner. While standing on the chair she could see the top of the shelves, and she then spotted a small hole that was drilled in the shelving. She moved in on her tiptoes and saw what looked like a shiny black lens of a camera peeking through the hole. She nearly fell off the chair when she tried to move back away from the peeper.

"I am being watched! What the freaking hell?" Her mind was scrambled. She had no idea who was watching her, and what was she going to do.

Chris felt more than ever that she needed to leave that room, but Craig was surely ready for her to leave. His creepy behavior made perfect sense now that she knew he was watching her. She tried to appear comfortable while she tried to figure out the camera's blind spots. Chris started to unpack her boxes, but to the observant it would be obvious she wasn't making any progress. Her mind was spinning. She whispered while she worked, "Daddy, what should I do? I miss you." She finally figured that she should go get Steve again and point out the camera so that he would kick out Craig. They could remove the camera and find a new roommate. Determined, she appeared to casually head toward Stinky's room; she hoped he was there.

As she moved stealthily past Craig's room, her dad's favorite song leaked out. The memories of dancing with her dad came flooding in. It was becoming painful to hear that song; now it was linked with a good-looking peeping tom.

After the long walk to Steve's room, she knocked lightly on the heavy door to Steve's burrow. Chris imagined a room full of wires and computer screens, and she wasn't too far off. Steve cracked the door open; he was holding a soldering iron, "Hey Chris, you hungry?"

"Uh, No. I found something in my room that you should see."

Steve looked worried, "Okay. He leaned over nervously to put the iron down, giving Chris a look over his shoulder into the dark room. There were computer screens lining the back wall. In just that quick glance Chris thought she saw one screen that made her shudder. There was a mattress on the floor and half unpacked boxes strewn about. Her room.

She turned suddenly and headed back toward her room, "Um, Steve. I am sorry to bug you. I think . . . I will show you later. I don't mean to interrupt. I will catch you later." She began a quick walk down the long hall toward her room, not sure that was the safest place, but positive she was going to get out of there.

She quickly opened her heavy door and again the aspect of her father stood before her.

She took a step forward and her father reached out, a look of horror raked across his face.

"Daddy?"

Just then Christ felt jerked back and Steven's arms wrapped around her with force that prevented her from moving, he yelled, "What the hell is going on."

She didn't dare scream; she was perplexed and too scared for it all. Her father was there, but yet he wasn't. His countenance was translucent and ghostly. Her father suddenly looked chilling when he smiled eerily. He faded. "Daddy, don't go."

"There ain't no sunshine when she's gone," sang out louder.

Chris looked into Steve's face over her shoulder, "Did you see that? You leave me alone." Steve looked demented and he grabbed her while holding a knife to her throat.

Chris didn't have any hope; she was wrapped up in the arms of a man who had clearly trapped her and she had misjudged him this whole time. This wasn't a harmless techy, he was crazy.

He pushed the knife through her soft fleshy neck. Chris felt the warmth of the blood as it oozed down her chest. Steve whispered, "I was just watching you, there's no harm in that," he sucked in some air between his teeth. With a soft whistled he spoke in her ear, "Now you go and get all freaky."

Just as suddenly as she was grabbed by Steve, a sudden jolt hit Steve and Chris from behind. It caused Steve to release her, but their weight shifted together and they both fell to the ground. She grabbed the side of her head. It was throbbing.

She turned to look up at the reason she and Steve became a heap on the floor. There stood Craig, with a baseball bat. His hair fell across his forehead and his gray eyes gazed into Chris's.

He tossed the bat on the ground and quickly picked up Chris. "You ok?"

Chris turned to glance at the foul-smelling form on the ground. Creepy Craig just knocked Steve to the floor, and a small pool of blood began to pool in the gaps between the tile. That grout was going to be hard to clean. Steve began to stir; Craig reacted by kicking Steve hard in the gut while shoving Chris toward the exit.

"Wait, what happened? Did you see my dad?" Chris's head spun and not just from the sudden jolt. Her hand reached up to her neck and pulled it away. There was a little blood that caked her fingers. She laughed to herself about her terrible judgment.

She escaped Craig's embrace for just a moment as she stepped over crazed computer guy's struggling frame and picked up her sorry excuse for a stuffed poodle. "My dad gave me this when I was a kid," Chris sniffed.

Craig ushered her back down the hall towards the front door, leaving Steve unconscious on the once stunning floor.

"This house is beautiful; I just don't know if it's right for me." Chris mumbled.

"Yeah, me either," Craig said with what Chris could only figure was a giggle. "The cops are coming."

As Craig lead her outside the blast of heat hit her, like that moment you first open an oven. She looked at the dry fountain and then up to the sky. She could still hear her dad's song.

Wonder if she's gone to stay
Ain't no sunshine when she's gone
And this house just ain't no home
Anytime she goes away

"I love you Dad." Chris walked out of the courtyard and decided she was ready to start again, just not in Vegas.

THE FRIGHT SHIFT

CHRISI TALYN SAJE

Darkness shrouded the grand theater, turning ornately carved figures into haunting shadows. The dirt strewn wooden floor caused his shoes to echo an eerie crunch into the rafters. His breathing grew heavy. It always grew heavy when he sensed a presence. This one felt near enough to touch, but veiled in the blackness, he suddenly felt confused and turned around. He no longer could tell where the wings were. He thought backstage was still behind him, but the heavy curtains that gave him his bearings were nowhere to be seen. Panic grew. He reminded himself she couldn't hurt him. She wouldn't. He was there to help. Quickly, he mustered courage and reached his arms out in front of him.

"White Lady of the theater," his voice bellowed in the emptiness. "I know you have suffered all these many years. But you need not be bound to this plane. Go, release yourself." A pale white hand appeared before his, its fingers reaching, trying to grasp his own. His strength grew and his voice burst through the darkness. "Find your loved ones on the other side and be free. Be free! Be _free_! Be--ah! _Fuck!_"

Instantly the lights clicked on, chasing away the shadows and revealing an entire film crew encircling him. A voice called, "Cut!"

and the crew, barely containing their frustration, reset their equipment. Beside him was an actress in a white gown and heavy pancake makeup who looked around in confusion, unclear why the scene had stopped.

"Dirk, what's the problem?" Karen stepped forward from behind the camera. She tried to hide her annoyance. Dirk was the talent and as the producer, she had to do a lot of ass kissing. But after twelve hours, a poorly catered lunch, and a deadline to move the crew out or pay the location penalties. Karen's patience had reached its limit.

"There! Right there! I tripped on one of their damn cables." Dirk adjusted his wig as he waved a dismissive gesture at the hapless crew. "How am I supposed to communicate with the afterlife under these circumstances?"

"You aren't communicating with the afterlife, Dirk." Karen gritted her teeth. "You're communicating with Lisa." She pointed to the young actress in white shoving a jelly donut in her mouth.

"That is for the reenactment. I still need to get into my trance."

"I thought you needed to cut off the head of a chicken for that." Jason, a camera atop his shoulder, stepped forward and boldly challenged Dirk. The medium happily accepted.

"I'll settle for the head of a cameraman."

The crew gave a forced laugh, the kind servants do for a king.

"How 'bout I just get some reaction shots of you." Jason went on as if nothing were at stake. "We'll eliminate camera two and keep the boom op behind me. Then you can move wherever you want, and we won't interfere with your trance."

The room fell silent, frozen with anticipation. The crew's exhausted eyes begged with anticipation. Karen chomped on her pen, adding to the grooves already embedded in the plastic cap. Jason stood firmly, fearlessly.

At long last Dirk released an agreeable sigh, "Fine. That'll work."

The tension of the room dropped. The crew hustled to reset. Lisa dabbed at the fresh jelly stain on her white dress and Jason adjusted his camera, sharing a smile with Karen.

"I never had this kind of problem on my web series." Dirk directed his contempt at Karen as he marched back into place.

"Web series?" Jason snarked under his breath to the producer. "He had one YouTube video he shot in his living room."

Karen stifled a snicker. Jason was her director of photography by title, but truly a mix between director, lead camera and Karen's sanity. Jason always had a light humor about him on set, no matter the length or grueling nature of their shoots.

"Are you saying Dirk isn't a genuine psychic?" Karen smiled through her own sarcasm.

"He's a genuine pain in the ass." Both shared a laugh until it was interrupted by Dirk's shrill demands.

"If we don't do this soon, I'll need another sushi break."

"Okay, everyone, back to one." Karen took her position as the lights went out.

Through the darkness the crew called the beginning of the roll and finally came, "Action!"

"White Lady of the Theater," Dirk's acting was that of summer stock Shakespearean actor, "I know you have suffered all these many years. But you need not be bound to this plane. Go, release yourself." The talent reached his hands before him, but Lisa's hands did not appear. He repeated himself with precision, "Release yourself!" Nothing. "Once more I say–release yourself!" The white, delicate hands emerged at last, dancing above Dirk. He continued, "Be free! Be–" Suddenly, the hands grabbed his wrists. He pulled back in shock against their surprisingly strong grip. "Cut! Cut!" He struggled to break free, but the hands held fast. "What the hell are you doing?"

"Soon." She whispered unseen, with a voice that stopped Dirk cold. "Soon."

Instantly the lights came on. She was gone.

"What the fuck was that?!" The psychic's anger boiled out of his ears.

Karen tried to calm him down. "Dirk, what are you talking about?"

"She's not supposed to grab me! And who gave her a fucking line?"

"Who, Lisa?"

Upon hearing her name, Lisa hurried onto the stage, a large wet spot on her gown where she'd smeared the fallen jelly. "I'm sorry I missed the shot. I was in the bathroom."

Seeing Lisa far across the room, the medium was taken aback. "Okay, then which one of you grabbed me? It wasn't funny!"

"Dirk, calm down. Let's just reset, alright?" Karen began to motion to the crew, but Dirk wasn't letting go.

"It was a woman! Who did it?" He whirled around looking for a female face in the crowd. A few makeup and hair girls turned away, trying to avoid his wrath.

"Dirk, nobody grabbed you." Karen's annoyance was getting hard to disguise. "I was watching the monitor the whole time."

"Play it back."

"Dirk–"

"Play it back!"

Karen reluctantly motioned to the assistant to play the footage on the monitor. There was Dirk, looking like a photographic negative of himself as the camera's night vision captured his every move. The scene played back exactly as he recalled, but there were no ghostly hands. Indeed, on tape, there was no evidence he had been grabbed at all.

The psychic, all of his pompousness drained from his face, spoke for the first time in a quiet, vulnerable voice. "I can't do this anymore today. I'm... I'm going home." The crew watched as, without a sound, Dirk shrunk away and left the theater.

Jason broke the silence, approaching Karen. "You're just going to let him go?"

"What is it they always say?" She sighed. "We'll 'fix it in post'?"

And with that, it was a wrap.

In the vast sea that is reality TV, *The Fright Shift* boasted a devout following of viewers who wanted to believe in spirits more than they cared about ruthless housewives or barbeque cook-offs. The first season launched with Dirk Stone channeling his spirit guide to explore the mysteries of ghosts in attics, ghosts in theaters, ghosts in churches and, on one occasion, a ghost in a butcher shop, which turned out to be a very pissed off cow.

"Every night around three a.m. I hear heavy footsteps–thump, thump, thump, like that–up in the attic." Sitting in her living room on a worn sofa, the chubby woman in her fifties clutched a throw pillow on her lap, as if it would protect her from the story she was telling. Dirk sat beside her, like a ghost therapist, carefully pulling out the tale of her encounter.

"Paula, do you know the history of this house?" His voice was calming, and she went on.

"When this first started happening I asked around." Her voice trembled, "I heard from one of the neighbors that about twenty years ago, the owner of the house died when he tripped down the stairs."

"Tripped down the stairs. Gotta love that one." Karen listened from the foyer, looking up at the typical suburban staircase. "The afterlife must be filled with clumsy ghosts." She mused to Jason as she kicked the bottom step with her Jimmy Choos.

"This place is pretty scary." Her partner in mockery sat on the stairs, examining the wall full of framed family photos. He pointed to one and whispered. "They drive a Windstar."

"I don't know if we can do another episode of a death-by-stairs. Who else are we meeting today?" Karen looked down at her tablet. "Ooo, a high school gym. A dead cheerleader would be good for ratings."

"What about that daycare that burned down in 1956?"

Karen matter-of-factly agreed. "There's always a good audience response to dead babies."

Dirk and Paula entered the foyer, catching Karen in mid-sentence. Dirk gave his producer a stern frown.

"Mrs. Duffy wishes to show me the staircase where the activity occurs." His disapproving gaze moved to Jason.

The cameraman stood up, "I should probably move, then." Jason and Karen quickly retreated to the living room, trying not to be heard as they stifled their giggling.

"Honestly, no matter how many of these people I meet, I just can't wrap my head around anyone who believes in ghosts." Karen flopped down on the Barcalounger.

"My grandmother believed there was a little girl in her basement who'd died when she slipped and drowned in a washing tub." Jason casually paced the living room, thoughtfully examining each knick-knack he spied. "She said she could see the girl reliving her last moments over and over again."

"If everyone repeats their last moments on earth for eternity, I want to make sure I die on a Carnival Cruise with a fresh Mai Tai in my hand."

"In middle school," Jason continued as he scrutinized a Precious Moments figurine, "I was into photography and used my grandparents' basement as a dark room."

With teasing sarcasm, Karen prodded her storyteller on. "So, did you ever see the ghost?"

Jason gave a weak chuckle. "I actually thought I did. I mean, her stories were really vivid, and I was like, twelve." Karen watched her friend's confidence fade as he fiddled with the fringe on a nearby lampshade. "I dunno. My grandmother always insisted she saw the girl. Couldn't convince her otherwise. So, you know, I let her think I saw the girl, too."

All ridicule gone from her voice; Karen replied thoughtfully. "I'm not saying your grandmother was like Dirk or anything. Trances, spirit guides, talking to the dead. His whole act is just to make money."

"So is this show." Jason grinned.

"Thank you, reality TV." Karen proudly smiled back.

Dirk burst into the room. "We absolutely must film in this location. Mrs. Duffy–" Dirk looked to her, eager in the doorway. He corrected himself. "Paula," the pudgy woman attempted a girlish blush, "has a very angry ghost here and I simply have to communicate with it. Schedule the shoot immediately."

Obeying, Karen grabbed her tablet. "How about the week of the twenty-second?"

"That far out?" Dirk was impatient. "My spirit guide wants me to look into this right away."

"Dirk, we're in Atlanta until the nineteenth, remember?" Karen's exhaustion with being his private secretary came through in her tone. "The Civil War battle site?"

"Can you calm the ghost down for now?" Jason suggested. "Comfort him that you'll be back?"

Dirk looked up at the ceiling as if pondering his next move. "Yes, I believe I can."

Karen gave Jason a relieved look and mouthed the words, "thank-you."

"Paula," Dirk continued, "let's do the twenty-second. But if you hear anything before then, I want you to call me." Paula looked giddy with the thought of being able to personally call the psychic. "Karen, give her your card." He turned back to Paula. "Karen can give me any messages." And with that, Dirk ceremoniously marched out.

Karen gave the now deflated woman her card and promised to call to set up the shoot. Outside, Karen lingered a bit. Jason stopped just before he got to the car.

"Something up?"

Karen was hesitant. "The rest of the crew isn't... um... upset they're not going to Atlanta, are they?" Karen asked with an anxiousness she normally would never display as the boss. "It's part of the tax incentives Georgia is giving us. We have to hire locally."

"Relax. No one takes it personally. And they know I'm the only one who–" Jason stopped himself before he went too far.

"The only one who can handle Dirk." Karen looked into the backseat of the car to see the talent on his Bluetooth talking animatedly. She sighed, "I don't know how you do it."

Jason tried to humble himself. "Well, Dirk pretends this whole ghost thing is real and I let him believe I believe him."

"Like you did your grandmother?"

"Someone had to believe her."

Arriving home late that Friday night before her Monday company move, Karen wearily stumbled into her immaculately decorated condo. She dropped her things on the kitchen table and shuffled towards the bathroom, not bothering to snap on lights as she moved about the apartment. She knew its layout well, and the light pollution of Los Angeles did the rest. But she did flip on the unforgiving bathroom light and sighed, taking a moment to observe her exhausted face in the mirror before opening the medicine cabinet for her toothbrush and toothpaste. Like a programmed robot, she went to work on the task of brushing her teeth.

As Karen bent over the sink to spit, the crown of her head still reflected in the mirror, a faint shadow of a woman filled the glass. The woman appeared to be standing directly behind her, an image barely more than a white silhouette. The apparition whispered one word, "Soon." Karen popped her head up instantly in response, toothpaste dribbling from the corner of her mouth. But just like that, the mirror woman was gone.

"I cannot believe I'm being denied peanuts. Is this first class or have they simply put leather chairs in the baggage hold?" Dirk stood over Karen in a huff, blocking the aisle in coach so an elderly woman behind him couldn't reach the lavatories.

Never looking up from her laptop, Karen replied in her usual placating way, "People have allergies to peanuts, Dirk. They give out pretzels now instead."

The elderly woman grunted a little, hoping to gain Dirk's attention, but her polite nature was not going to get her what she wanted.

"Do you remember in episode four that woman who died having sex because of an undetected latex allergy?" Dirk turned, at last, to take notice of the elderly woman. He directed his next comment to her. "If she'd only given him a BJ, she'd be alive today."

"Is that what it's going to take for you to let me use the restroom?" The old lady stood unflinching; her wrinkled lips pursed together in a geriatric duck face.

Dirk reluctantly gave way for the woman as an impossible to restrain snort came from Jason seated next to his producer.

"I remember episode four." Jason offered playfully. "We spent six days in a strip club for you to talk to a murdered stripper. And, as I recall, half the budget on dollar bills for you and the dancers."

"Don't question my methods for reaching the other side."

"A hundred dollars got you to the other side of that lap dance."

"Alright, enough." While Karen never muzzled Jason, right now she had a migraine and five more hours on the plane, so she wasn't going to indulge the two. "Dirk, we paid for your first-class seat, why don't you go up there and use it?"

"Sylvia Browne would've gotten a private jet." He chided.

"Sylvia Browne was out of our price range, so we went with you instead."

Another snort from Jason found Dirk stunned silent. He was used to his insult war waged willingly with Jason, but not Karen. Producers, Dirk imagined, were there to keep the talent happy and did little else of value. So, in a last-ditch effort to keep hold of his dignity, Dirk retorted, "We'll see what SAG has to say about the peanuts," and stormed off, flinging aside the curtains to first class.

Deeply amused, Jason glanced up to watch the psychic vanish behind the curtain to join the wealthy elite of the aircraft. Just as a smart-ass comment was about to pass his lips, he saw it. A wispy transparent woman in a white silk gown standing in the aisle, staring only at him.

"Soon," she said and raised her finger to her lips, shushing at the cameraman who was now pulling upwards against his seatbelt.

An accidental elbowing by Jason pulled Karen's attention away from her laptop. "What's going on? You need to get up?"

In a cloud, Jason looked to Karen, then back to the curtain. The woman was gone.

"I... I didn't get much sleep this weekend." He settled back into his seat.

Half focused on her computer screen; Karen gave a programmed response. "Who needs sleep? We'll sleep when we're dead."

Alarmed, Jason shot a look at her, then cautiously gazed up one last time at the first-class curtain. Trying to erase the moment, he folded up his jacket as a pillow and attempted to go to sleep.

The flight arrived well before dawn, with exhausted passengers trying to comprehend the time difference. As Jason gathered the gear, Dirk all the while treating him like his own personal porter, Karen stumbled into a Starbucks to refuel. Before long, the three were on the road in their rental van.

"Could the hotel be any further from the airport?" Karen sighed to Jason, irritated at herself for booking the accommodations.

"Right? Sherman's troops didn't have to march this far to reach Atlanta."

The darkness of rural Georgia spread out before them. This was real darkness. It made Karen smile to herself thinking of all of the Angelinos who turned on their high beams driving over Laurel Canyon Boulevard. Laurel Canyon was as dark as a football field with stadium lighting compared to this. Each Georgia mile threatened to be the end of the earth. Even if the moon were shining, the tall pine trees encroaching upon the road made sure no glimmer shone through. The houses, if there were any at all, sat far enough back that they gave no whisper to the traveler they existed.

"I hate all of these budget restrictions." Karen put her feet up on the dashboard, picking a piece of fuzz off of her pants' cuff.

"All shows have a tiny budget the first season," Jason offered. "I did this one cupcake baking competition show that brought in Albertson's cupcakes because they couldn't afford the ingredients to bake as many as they needed. We weren't even allowed to take any home because the PAs would have to wrap them up for the next day."

"And I thought <u>Dirk</u> was stale." Karen smiled proudly at her joke.

"Don't let him ruffle you." Jason reassured with his eyes fixated on the narrow road the headlights struggled to illuminate. "You're a good producer. And, come on, you know this show is going to make bank."

Karen smirked, "That's the only thing that makes it worth dealing with Dirk and 'ghosts.'"

Playfully Jason replied, "Boo!"

Suddenly a bump in the road sent a jolted shudder throughout the van, causing Karen to burst out with a surprised laugh. She was answered by Dirk popping his head up.

"Are we still in the van?" Dirk's wig sat askew atop his head, feeding Karen's giddiness.

"No," Jason never missed an opportunity to smack the psychic down, "actually, we've been teleported through time and space and are in a spa on Mars. Is the steam too hot for you?"

"There will come a time when you'll pay for mocking me."

"On the 'other side'?" Jason taunted.

A devilish grin primed Dirk's response. "When I get you fired from my second season."

Karen chuckled as she glanced out of the windshield but was quickly sobered. There she was again, the woman from Karen's mirror. The producer bolted up in her seat as the van barreled down upon the faint aberration.

"Stop the van! Stop the van!"

The woman vanished and was instantly replaced by a wandering deer crossing the road.

Disoriented, Jason slammed on the brakes, causing the van to skid as the tires tried desperately to grab a hold of the asphalt. The three lurched forwards, with Karen's screams filling the night's silence.

Then there was nothing but blackness.

"Could the hotel be any further from the airport?" Karen sighed to Jason with irritation.

The darkness of rural Georgia surrounded them as before, their lonely van continuing to venture forth through the night.

"Right? Sherman's troops didn't have to march this far to reach Atlanta."

Karen put her feet up on the dashboard and began to pick a piece of fuzz off of her pants when she stopped herself, turning quizzically to Jason. "That joke wasn't funny the first time."

"What? Who else has been using my hilarious Civil War humor?"

Karen pulled the piece of fuzz off and rolled it between her fingers. "I dunno. I thought I heard it before." She flicked the fuzz to the floor and proceeded without concern. "I hate all of these budget restrictions."

"All shows have a tiny budget the first season. I did this one cupcake baking competition show--"

"Where you had to use Albertson's cupcakes." Karen finished his thought, surprised at herself for knowing exactly what was coming next.

"Yeah. Did you work one of those shows, too? We weren't even allowed to take any home because the PAs would have to wrap them up for the next day."

Karen found the following words leaving her mouth without intending to speak them, "and I thought Dirk was stale."

"Don't let him ruffle you." Jason continued without a beat. "You're a good producer. And, come on, you know this show is going to make bank."

"Yeah, you said that before." Karen felt a heightened awareness of everything around her. Again, the van hit a bump, this time eliciting a startled gasp from Karen.

"Are we still in the van?" Dirk drooled with grogginess.

"No," Jason quipped, "actually, we've been teleported through time and space and are in a spa on Mars. Is the steam too hot for you?"

Karen became uneasy as the two men went on.

"There will come a time when you pay for mocking me."

"On the 'other side?'"

"When I get you fired–"

Karen quickly cut Dirk off. "Okay, I'm having some serious Déjà vu."

Dirk reveled at sharing his believed wealth of knowledge on all things spiritual and otherworldly. "Déjà vu is the spirit world letting you know you're on the right path."

Still trying to comprehend what was possibly going on, Karen glanced out of the windshield to see the female apparition again. "Stop the van! Stop the van!"

The woman vanished once more and was instantly replaced by a wandering deer crossing the road. Jason slammed on the brakes, the van skidded, and Karen screamed.

Then there was nothing but blackness.

"Could the hotel be any further from the... uh..." Karen trailed off as her eyes darted about the van.

"The airport?" Jason offered. "I know, right? Sherman's troops didn't have to march this far to reach Atlanta."

"How long have we been driving?" Karen demanded curtly with a nervous anxiousness that surprised Jason.

"Uh, I'm not sure. What time is it?"

Karen turned her attention to the van's dashboard clock, but it sat dark. "The clock isn't working."

Jason perceived fear mounting in Karen's voice. He attempted to calm her, "Look on my phone. It's in the cup holder."

Karen snatched his phone but it, too, was dark and lifeless. "It won't turn on. Is the battery charged?" She feverishly pushed the buttons, but the device wouldn't start.

"Yeah, I thought so." For no logical reason, Jason found himself changing the subject. "Ya know, I did this one cupcake baking competition show--"

"I know about the damn cupcakes!" Karen snapped just as the van hit the bump in the road, awaking Dirk. The psychic opened his mouth to speak, but Karen attacked him with his own words. "Yes, Dirk, we're still in the van. We haven't traveled through time and space and we're not on Mars! Stop the van!" She barked at Jason who immediately obeyed.

The producer hurried out of the vehicle, straining to see into the darkness surrounding them. She didn't know exactly what she was looking for, but she knew it was out there.

Jason got out of the van and joined her. "Karen, what's going on?" Her actions were making him uneasy.

"Shh!" She heard it, a rustling in the nearby bushes.

"You're tired." Her cameraman offered. "We need to get to the hotel--"

"No, wait!" Karen pointed into the headlights where a startled deer passed and quickly disappeared back into the darkness.

Suddenly, the van door burst open and Dirk, with little grace, stumbled out of it. "I need my rest. If I don't get enough time to sleep before the turnaround, my union rep is going to hear about it!"

Dirk's demands fell upon deaf ears as Karen cautiously inched towards the van's headlights, now spotted with insects dancing in the beams.

"Look at these skid marks." Karen pointed to the ground.

Jason tried to remain levelheaded. "Lots of roads have skid marks."

"Is anyone listening to me?!" Dirk bellowed like a bored child in a shopping mall.

"But these marks lead right to this tree." Karen investigated with more urgency. "Right here. The marks on the bark are fresh."

Jason looked at the panic in his friend's eyes. He spoke cautiously. "Karen, let's just get back in the van."

Karen whipped around, the vehicle's high beams highlighting her in an eerie spotlight. "No! We can't go back in the van!"

"Karen, come on. You're exhausted."

"I'm exhausted!" Dirk's tantrum grew, "and my eyes are going to be puffy for the shoot!"

"Seriously, Dirk. Shut up." Jason turned back to Karen. "Come on, let's go." His approach was backlit, giving him the appearance of a featureless silhouette and causing Karen to retreat slowly towards the tree.

"No, stay away from me." Karen's eyes looked wild in the head-lights, like a feral cat trapped in an alleyway.

Jason reached her and tried to put his hands on her shoulder. She violently pushed him backwards, causing him to stumble and momentarily lose his balance. Jason went down on one knee, his hand catching himself on the road in the center of the skid mark. The pavement felt like a hot stove, bolting Jason upwards. He stared at his hand in disbelief, and then locked eyes with Karen. They both understood.

"That's it. I need my sleep. Wake me when we reach the hotel." Dirk turned to climb back into the van.

Karen and Jason desperately pleaded with Dirk to stop, but it all happened faster than their voices could carry.

Then there was nothing but blackness.

The van sped down the empty rural Georgia road. Karen sat erect in the passenger seat, her breath shallow in a near pant. Jason clutched the steering wheel and stared straight ahead, afraid to twitch a muscle. Dirk snored from the backseat.

"What's going on?" Jason spoke, attempting to move as little of his face as possible.

"I don't know. But you should stop the van."

Jason slowed the van carefully. The squeaking brakes were the only sound for miles. Dirk popped his head up in a sleepy stupor.

"Are we still in the van?" Dirk looked to Karen, then Jason. Their attention focused unflinchingly out the windshield. "Why did we stop?" His pleas, unanswered, fueled his frustration. "We'll never make it to the hotel if we just sit here." Without prompting, Jason and Karen exited the van, leaving Dirk in utter confusion. "This isn't funny! I <u>am</u> the talent! You shouldn't treat me like this!" The psychic shifted to reach the van's sliding door. "I oughta report them to SAG," he muttered to himself as he stumbled into the Georgia night.

Outside the vehicle, Dirk found Jason in the van's headlights staring down at the road while Karen's gaze fixated on the woods around them.

"Did we hit something? What?" Dirk tried to maintain his composure. He was certain this was some sort of revenge joke being played upon him. "Alright, you've had your fun. Don't think my abilities haven't been the butt of many pranks in my day. So, ha, ha. You got me. Let's get back in the van and get going."

In unison, Karen and Jason turned towards the tree and walked, as if in a trance, over to it. Both brushed their hands against the bark.

"I thought you two were professionals." Dirk's pleading became more genuine. "Even if you don't respect my skills, at least be professionals and respect our shooting schedule." Fear mounted in the medium with every ignored demand. He moved towards them, cautious as he approached, looking to the ground and into the woods. What did they see that he didn't? "Please? Can't we get back in the van?"

All three stood before the tree, unsure why it had such control over them. Then a noise from the van made them swing around. The headlights grew painfully bright as the driverless vehicle kicked into gear and sped towards them. They leapt out of the way to watch the van skid and careen to its side, screeching upon the asphalt and coming to rest with an ear-piercing crash into the side of the tree. Then it was silent again, save the van's wheels creaking as they spun high over the road. Smoke rose from the hood, creating a haze in the never yielding headlights. The trio stood frozen, their mouths agape at the carnage before them. They only looked away once, as a shy deer tip-toed out onto the road, then, seeing them, scampered back into the safety of the darkness.

"What happened?" Dirk's voice squeaked out.

Jason uttered in quiet awe, "The van crashed."

"By itself?" Karen's eyes were locked upon the wreckage.

"It sure is a pity," began a soft feminine voice, "that it had to happen."

The three looked up to see their ghostly stalker standing before them as real and vivid as they laid witness to each other.

"What had to happen?" Karen looked at her with recognition from a dream.

"You living need to respect the other side."

Dirk immediately protested, "I respect the other side!"

The woman sharply pointed a long finger at Dirk, "The liar," she turned to Jason, "the denier," and then, with an angry scowl, pointed to Karen, "and the greedy. All of whom would happily make money off of what they do not believe." Her haunting laugh rose through the empty night, lingering after she vanished.

With anxious determination, Karen made a beeline towards the van.

"Karen, don't!" Jason reached to grab her arm, but she pulled away, unable to stop herself from approaching the wreck.

Karen circled to the front of the van. Her boots crunched the broken glass of the shattered windshield. She was hesitant, but knew she had to look inside. When she saw it, she burst out a terrified scream to which Jason hurried to her aid. She buried her face in his chest. He looked over the top of her head to see for himself.

"What?! What is it?!" Dirk ran up to the van before waiting for an answer.

There, inside the van and mangled in the glass and steel, were the bloody, lifeless bodies of the producer, the cameraman and the talent.

Then there was nothing but blackness.

"Could the hotel be any further from the airport?" Karen sighed to Jason, irritated at herself for booking the accommodations.

"Right? Sherman's troops didn't have to march this far to reach Atlanta."

Jason smiled at his joke. Karen picked a piece of fuzz from her pants' cuff. A snore bellowed from the backseat of the van. And the shrouded Georgia night stretched out in front of them...forever.

FRED THE POSSESSED FLOWER

FRED THE POSSESSED FLOWER
SINN BODHI

"Sinn Bodhi is ahead of his time."
   – WWE Hall of Famer, Jake 'The Snake' Roberts

"Sinn Bodhi is the evilest silliest man I know."
   – WWE Hall of Famer, Dusty Rhodes

"You passionate handsome lunatic, you!"
   – WWE Hall of Famer, Rowdy Roddy Piper

"Sinn and Freakshow Wrestling is not just out of the box but across the hall from the other room where they keep the box."
   – The Amazing Johnathan

THE SINNFUL MAN

S inn Bodhi, The Warlord of Weird, is the creator of Freakshow Wrestling ... He has traveled the world performing as a professional wrestler for TNA, WWE, and he has been a circus strongman. He is the puppet master of the most fun, most violently violent spectacle in the galaxy, a live show that sells out regularly in Las Vegas ... Freakshow Wrestling.

Now behold, from this warped, twisted mind ...

HAPPY
PREDATOR
PUBLICATIONS
HAPPY NICK'S
FRED
THE POSSESSED FLOWER
1
"THE PLANT BEHIND THE SCENES"
GUEST STARRING:
GOD & SATAN

FRED
The
POSSESSED
FLOWER
THE PLANT BEHIND THE SCENES
WHEN PEOPLE HEAR FAIRY TALES, TYPICAL, CANDY COATED IMAGES COME TO MIND. HOW IN FACT, DOES A JOLLY, FAT, MAN KNOW IF WE HAVE BEEN NAUGHTY OR NICE? WHY ARE TRIPPY, CHOCOLATE EGG LAYING RABBITS SO SOCIALLY ACCEPTABLE? WOULD YOU BE TOTALLY AT EASE KNOWING THAT SOMEONE HAS BROKEN INTO YOUR HOUSE AND HAD REPLACED YOUR CHILD'S TOOTH WITH SOME POCKET CHANGE? DO YOU REALLY WANT TO KNOW WHAT MYSTERIOUS SOUL WRITES THESE ANONYMOUS TALES?
HELL'S MOUNT RUSHMOORE...
HITLER
NIXON
SADAM
YOKO
CREATED, WRITTEN and ILLUSTRATED by: HAPPY
WELCOME TO HELL
POPULATION 666 ZILLION

HELL'S BREAK ROOM...
HEY CUPID, MY MAN, HOW WAS YOUR DAY?
FREAKIN' LONG, MY WINGS ARE READY TO FALL OFF. WHAT ABOUT YOU, BOOGIEMAN?
SAME JIVE, DIFFERENT DAY. WHAT ABOUT YOU, TOOTH FAIRY?

MY BACK IS SOAR AS HELL FROM LUGGING AROUND SACKS OF TEETH AND POCKET CHANGE ALL DAY.
I DON'T KNOW ABOUT YOU GUYS, BUT I THINK THAT IT'S ABOUT TIME THAT OUR WAGES AND BENEFITS WERE INCREASED!

AMEN!!!

THIS IS CRAZY, WE HAVE GOTTA TALK TO FRED.

I SAY THAT WE GO STRAIGHT TO THE TOP AND TALK TO LOUIE, IN PERSON.
TOOTH FAIRY, ARE YOU NUTS? FRED MANAGES EVERYTHING DOWN HERE. IF WE GO OVER HIS HEAD HE WILL INCINERATE US!

OUTSIDE FRED'S OFFICE...
IN RECEPTION...
EXCUSE ME, FRED... THE TOOTH FAIRY, THE BOOGIEMAN AND CUPID ARE HERE TO SEE YOU.
THANK YOU, GRETCHEN. SEND THEM IN.
FRED'S OFFICE...
WHAT CAN I DO FOR YOU BOYS?
WE WOULD AHH...
LIKE A LITTLE MORE AHH...
AHH... PAY.
SERIOUSLY?... WELL GUYS I'M SORRY, BUT THE COMPANY CAN'T AFFORD IT RIGHT NOW.
IN THAT CASE WE WOULD LIKE TO SPEAK WITH THE OWNER.

LOUIE IS UNAVAILABLE. AND IF YOU DON'T LIKE YOUR SITUATION WHY DON'T YOU GO WORK FOR THE BIG GUY? YOU KNOW?... LEAD YOURSELF OUT OF TEMPTATION AND DELIVER YOURSELVES FROM EVIL.
WE USED TO WORK FOR HIM BUT HE WAS REALLY CHEAP. ALL THAT WE GOT PAID WAS OUR OWN SELF-FULFILLMENT. WHO CAN LIVE ON THAT?
YA, THAT IS WHY WE STARTED FREELANCING FOR LOUIE IN THE FIRST PLACE. BUT NOW THAT WE ARE UNION, WE WILL STRIKE IF WE DON'T GET WHAT WE WANT.
I DON'T KNOW HOW SANTA AND THE EASTER BUNNY STILL DO IT, ESPECIALLY WITH ALL OF THEIR OVERHEAD COSTS.
STRIKE!
HAPPY 1

HELL'S SPA...
LOOK LOUIE, WE CAN'T AFFORD TO PAY OUR EMPLOYEES MORE, EVER SINCE PURGATORY STARTED OFFERING LOWER HOLY REDEMPTION RATES ON HEAVENLY ADMITTANCE.
THE BIG GUY IS USING A LOST LEADER TO PUT ME OUT OF BUSINESS?
EXACTLY! ONCE YOU ARE OUT OF THE PICTURE THE BIG GUY CAN MAKE UP HIS MINOR LOSSES AND OVER FILL HIS QUOTA DUE TO HIS NEWLY ACQUIRED MONOPOLY.
WHILE WE ARE TEMPORARILY WITHOUT STAFF I WILL NEED YOU TO DO MORE FIELD WORK AND TO SPEND LESS TIME IN THE OFFICE.
YOU WANT ME TO GO PUBLIC? BUT I AM A BEHIND THE SCENES GUY. I RUN EVERYTHING FROM AN EXECUTIVE, INTERNAL LEVEL. BESIDES, I HATE PEOPLE, THAT IS WHY I WORK FOR YOU.
THOSE ARE THE EXACT REASONS I NEED YOU TO BE MY NEW FIELD AGENT.

IF I WERE TO FILL IN, I WOULD BE A SCAB.
WHY CAN'T I HEAD UP THE SEARCH FOR REPLACEMENT WORKERS AND JUST TEACH SOME SEMINARS, OR SOMETHING?
THERE IS NO TIME. YOU KNOW ALL OF THE INS AND OUTS OF ALL THE DIFFERENT FIELD AGENTS JOBS. THIS IS ONLY A TEMPORARY ASSIGNMENT. THE BIG GUY CAN'T KEEP UP THESE LOW RATE DEALS FOR LONG. WE JUST HAVE TO SURVIVE LONG ENOUGH FOR HIM TO EXHAUST HIS LOST LEADER PROMOTION.
YOU ARE THE SMARTEST RIGHT HAND MAN THAT I HAVE EVER HAD. YOU ARE HELL'S MANAGER. I AM JUST THE OWNER.
I AM ACCUSTOMED TO A CERTAIN LIFESTYLE. I'M TOO WEAK TO LOSE EVERYTHING! I CAN'T START FROM SCRATCH ALL OVER AGAIN!
PLEASE! PLEASE! PLEASE!
OK, OK... JUST CUT THAT OUT. I CAN'T STAND TO SEE A GROWN DEVIL CRY.
SOMEWHERE OVER SOCIETY...
WHOOSH!

POP!

Hi!

OK, LET'S SEE WHAT'S FIRST ON THE AGENDA. ASSIGNMENT NUMBER ONE, FOR CUPID... MAKE A COUPLE OF STRANGERS FALL IN LOVE BLA, BLA, BLA TIME, ADDRESS ETC. PIECE OF CAKE.

THERE IS THE LUCKY COUPLE NOW...
WAIT A SECOND...
THERE IS A MISTAKE, THE STRANGERS SHOULD BE WALKING ON THE SAME SIDE OF THE STREET SO THAT THEY CAN BUMP INTO EACH OTHER...
THOSE IDIOTS IN THE FATE DEPT!

I HAD BETTER PUT THIS THING TO THE MAXIMUM SETTING JUST TO BE SAFE.
HATE...
TOLERATE...
LIKE...
LOVE...
SUPER FREAK SEX SLAVE!!!
ZOOM!!!
ZING!
ZING!
ZING!

WHAAA?!
SUGAR LUMPS!!!
POOKIE PIE!!!
HONEY WOOKUMS!!!
I'M COMING
LAMB CHOP!!!

BAM!!!

CUP CAKE?...

I LOVE THOSE GUYS IN THE FATE DEPT.

WHAT A SENSE OF HUMOR... WELL, THIS ISN'T AS BAD AS I THOUGHT IT WOULD BE.

NEXT ON THE AGENDA...
SUBURBIA...
ALL RIGHT, THIS IS THE PLACE. I JUST HAVE TO REPLACE ONE STUPID, LITTLE TOOTH WITH SOME CHANGE AND THAT WILL TAKE CARE OF MY DUTIES AS THE TOOTH FAIRY FOR THIS EVENING.
?
HOW THE HELL AM I GOING TO GET UP TO THAT DAMN KID'S WINDOW?
POLEVAULT!

To Be Continued . . .

MURDER

REMNANTS

BY MERCEDES M. YARDLEY

The day that his eyes broke
it wasn't so hard, really. To look at him.
Not as bad as everybody says.

The puzzle of his jaw didn't fit together
right. Pieces were missing. Big pieces.
The touchable pieces.

"The doctors did their best," he said.
Their best was a disaster. Godzilla invading
Tokyo, not prettied up with
stage makeup and autograph requests.

"I love you," I said
and kissed the least ruined part of his face
I was only lying a little, but that came before this
and his newly broken eyes couldn't
produce tears, anyway.

THE SACRIFICE

ASHLEY GREEN

T he days began and ended with the creaking of a car door. A truck, maybe. Laura had been locked in an attic for roughly two weeks, give or take a day. It was easy to learn when he had gone; when it was safe to pull at the chains bound around her wrists and ankles, attached to stubborn oak beams which never gave in. It was easy to learn. Yes, but the tender flesh around her eye was a reminder that the lesson came at a price. The creak came. *One Mississippi, two Mississippi, three Mississippi.* The faint sound of gravel crunching down on itself filled the silence of the room. *Four Mississippi, five Mississippi, six Mississippi.* The soft sputtering of first gear gently swept through the boarded windows, fading away by the tenth Mississippi. She wrapped her fingers around the metal attached to her wrists and started to pull with all her might.

She remembered her first night here, head throbbing and blinded by the darkness of the attic, which she mistook for actual blindness. She had been bludgeoned in head, that much she knew, and it was probable that it had left her without sight. She had reached toward her eyes in an attempt to maybe rub away the dark, and it was then that she heard the rattle of chains, the cool sting of metal around her wrists. In what seemed to be a reflex to her fear, she pushed herself up off the ground, ready to run. As she bolted upright, the chains yanked her back towards the floor. She pushed herself forward, but the clasps around her ankles tightened, only allowing a few inches of movement. She started to scream. Her mother had told her once, as a child, that if any harm came her way, to scream as loud and as long as she could. Someone would hear, she promised. Someone would help. Laura did as her mother had told her.

It was the end of the day; the second creaking, slam of the truck door outside the attic. *One Mississippi, two Mississippi, three Mississippi.* She could feel the familiar warmth of blood trickling over her skin. She glanced down into blackness, imagining how much had pooled into the palms of her cupped hands today. Maybe she had pulled the scabs off of last week's wounds. Maybe she had new cuts from the day's escape attempt. She kept her gaze downward, narrowing her eyes, attempting to sift through the nothingness. *Thirty Mississippi, thirty-one Mississippi, thirty-two Mississippi.* The smallest sliver of red began to materialize in the dark, levitating under her eyes, bright and sparkling. Laura was in awe of it. It glittered like it was electric, rising closer to her face, growing larger and wider. Was she dead now? Had she gone crazy? Was this the Heaven she had heard about? But wasn't this light supposed to be white? Could this be the light of Hell? *Seventy Mississippi.* A soft click sounded, and the room was flooded with the orange light of a dying bulb.

"Bonjour, ma belle!" the man bellowed. The electric red was gone. Delicate streams of blood had filled the lines of her palms, gently dripping through the cracks of her fingers.

"Quelle belle soirée, non? That's French for 'what a lovely evening.' Did you know that?" His voice was charming and pleasant, almost welcoming. Laura looked up, squinting against the harshness of the light that seemed to envelope his silhouette.

"Well look at that!" He took her face in his hands, twisting her head slowly from side to side. "That shiner is going away quite nicely!"

He let out a small laugh and leaned closer to her, pulling her face towards his own. His bright, blue eyes reminded her of the sky she hadn't seen in weeks.

"You know, I hate that we got off on the wrong foot." His voice altered quickly, transitioning into a low, almost sinister whisper. "But I *really* hate that you don't seem to understand me when I tell you to behave."

He reached down, grabbed her right wrist, and shoved it in her face. The metal collided with the bruised skin around Laura's right eye, an involuntary shout of pain echoed throughout the attic.

"Look at all of this blood, Laura!" he shouted, a half-laugh mixed with the pleasance that was there before, only this time crazed. "There is so much blood!" His voice rose an octave, sweeter and higher. He smelled like buttercream, like those vanilla cupcakes Ritchie begged their mother to make every year for his birthday. Laura's stomach twisted and her eyes began to water.

"This is just a mess, just a big 'ol mess." The man wandered around, hands on his hips, kicking at the dust on the floorboards. "I thought I'd bring you dinner tonight, get you ready for the ritual tomorrow, maybe teach you a bit of French – some Bach we could listen to together!"

He was speaking fast now, wild and violent. "But then you go, and you do this and...I'm just..." his hands went to his face and he pulled at the skin of his cheeks. "To be frank, Laura, I'm just so disappointed."

An image of Laura's mother, Maryanne, flashed through her head, and she realized Maryanne was probably disappointed in Laura as well, probably let down that Laura would allow Maryanne to lose another child. She started to weep. The man groaned, shaking his head, stomping his feet. "No crying! I can't stand it! No crying! Stop!"

The tears kept coming, faster even. "I can't," she choked out, hoarse and weak. "I can't." His fist barreled forward, and the darkness had once again consumed her.

Temple, Ohio was a six-mile drive from the Newark Airport, and it was these six miles that Laura remembered best. She dreamed about them most of her life, imagining the day she would be driving the length of them to board a plane and get as far away as she could. Those same six miles were before her once again, and the thought of taking them back into the town she had so desperately wanted to leave behind made her nauseous.

"You want a lift over to your mama's place?" Harold Miller, Temple's resident cab driver, shouted from a curb near the arrival doors, beckoning towards the dumpy taxi he had bought when Laura was seven, at least twenty years ago.

Harold Miller, her first familiar face. Not a hello or how have you been. No sarcastic comments about Laura, the new New Yorker, coming back to the sticks. It was like she had always been there, just the same old Laura who needed a ride home, to the house where she and Ritchie grew up. She shook the thought from her head. She wasn't there for Ritchie. She was there for their mother.

"Did she tell you I'd be here?" Laura asked, watching as Harold pushed back the grimy fishing hat he wore and looked her up and down.

"She told me to look for little Laura Anderson, but all's I see here is a New York movie star."

Laura sighed.

The cab smelled like a tackle box and Harold was winding through the wooded streets too quickly. The odor, the speed, and the rushing of green past the passenger window made Laura dizzy.

"Look at this, a superstar in my humble little cab. I'll be damned!" Harold croaked out what may have been a laugh, but one coated in years of Marlboro Reds. Laura said nothing. "You know, your mama isn't going to recognize you with all these fancy suitcases and fancy clothes." Laura pressed her head against the window. A moment of silence passed. "Still quiet as ever, I see." Harold slowed as he reached a curve, gently turning along with the asphalt, the trees that towered either side of the road suddenly halted. A cemetery appeared around the bend. "You plan on seeing Ritchie while you're in town? I bet he'd like to see–"

Laura slammed a fist into the dashboard. "Do not talk about my brother!"

The rest of the trip was silent.

They reached the ranch style bungalow where a small, gray haired woman lingered on the stretch of porch that lined the front of the house. Laura didn't recognize her from the end of the driveway, but as the car inched forward, she realized it was, in fact, Maryanne. She watched as her mother struggled with the weight of the boot strapped to her left leg, gripping at the railing of the porch steps with her left hand, and her right arm resting in the cradle of a sling. Laura got out of the vehicle before it was in park, rushing towards the shell of her mother.

"You're home!" Maryanne chimed.

"Mom!" It was easily heard as a greeting perhaps, but Laura had been taken aback by the sight of Maryanne's slight frame, her thin hair, and bruised, withered skin. It was as though she'd aged thirty years in the ten Laura had been gone.

"I'm so glad you came back, honey."

The house was the same as it had always been, exactly what Laura feared. The same green shag rug hid the charred section of the living room carpet where her older brother taught her to light matches when she was six and he was eight. The penciled horizontal tallies that her mother made over the course of their growth still appeared along the outer ridge of the kitchen door frame. A small, solid 58 stuck out boldly next to the last line with the initials R.A. written beneath it. Photos decorated the walls; baby Ritchie, toddler Ritchie, Ritchie playing soccer, Ritchie's first day of 2nd grade, Ritchie at the school play, Ritchie at ten. There were no photos of him past that point in his life. She had been older than her older brother for a while, but it never hurt the way it did then.

"You want some coffee, honey? Let me put on a pot." Maryanne hobbled toward the kitchen.

"Mom, please. Please just sit. You're making me nervous walking around on that thing."

Maryanne looked down at the boot and laughed.

"What happened? You didn't say it was this bad when you called."

Her mother sighed. "I didn't want you to worry. I just wanted you home."

There it was again. Home. The word seemed to crawl over Laura, making her squirm. "This isn't home, Mom," she snapped. "It hasn't been home for a while."

Laura wasn't sure if she had meant to make Maryanne feel bad, but she did. She watched as her mother glanced over at the bold 58, tears clinging to the edge of a wrinkle at the corner of her eye. "Where he is, home is."

"He hasn't been here in a long time, Mom." Laura snatched the handle of her suitcase and trudged past Maryanne.

"You're wrong," Maryanne called as Laura walked away, her voice suddenly cold, wiping the tears from her face. Laura stopped; a pang of anger shot through her chest. "There's a lot of people around here who'd say you are very wrong about that."

Laura took a deep breath. She wasn't there for Ritchie. She was there for her mother.

"What are you talking about?" She heard the clunk of the boot move through the living room, a shuffle of papers on the coffee table.

"A nice young man came by a few weeks ago, gave me this pamphlet. I've been going to the meetings."

Laura turned and saw her mother standing there, holding out a pastel brochure, a family of four looking at one another, smiling. She didn't recognize Maryanne; this sad, weak, broken woman in front of her. Maryanne gave a small smile and motioned for Laura to take it. Laura's eyes welled and she shook her head. This was her mother, at the very least, the remains of the mother she had known. The force that had been Maryanne was reduced to a faint whisper dressed in a floral terry fleece robe.

She woke to the taste of blood. It caked the inside of her mouth and nose, streaking down from her left nostril and the corner of her lip where her face met the floorboard. A pool of it had dried beneath her, fastening the skin of her cheek to wood, like a ragdoll sprawled across the floor. She didn't want to move from this position. Her limbs had gone numb from the angle she had contorted herself in after The Man hit her, and for the first time since her arrival, she was comfortable. She could no longer feel the chains that bound her to this place. She couldn't feel any part of herself. It was as if she was free. Warmth crept behind her eyelids, illuminating the perpetual night she had grown used to. For a moment she thought it was the electric red light she had encountered before, back to tease her with the hope of being swallowed by the heat of its deliverance. She slowly opened her eyes and saw the tinge of soft, blue light falling into the room through a frosted window at the other end of the attic. The plywood sheet that sealed off the outside world rested beneath the wooden sill of the window. It was real light, light she hadn't seen in weeks. She stared, admiring the beauty of actual day, the beauty of total numbness.

She woke, breathing hard, blind once again. The dark had come back. "No, no, no," she muttered, pushing herself up from the ground. "No! Where is the light?!" Classical music reverberated through the floorboards, through the walls. A full orchestra shook the entire house. Laura began to scream. "Please! Please give me some light! Please give me light!"

The music stopped abruptly. A pause. Heavy, fast footfalls up and up and up the stairs. "The light of the kingdom shall warm the void, but it is the darkness that shall purge!" His muffled voice sounded through his ascent. The attic door swung open, slamming into the wall behind it.

"You're awake!" The man shouted sweetly in the dark. "It's time for your bath!" His footsteps fell hard and fast, as though he was running. Laura felt the heat from his body lingering in front of her. "And it's a good thing too," he shouted in her face. She fell backwards, surprised by his outburst, disoriented from lack of sight. "Because you smell like you've missed a few trips to the bucket! You're not two, Laura! Use the fucking bucket!"

His footsteps retreated towards the door and disappeared down the steps. Laura screamed again, feeling whatever sanity she had left slipping from her now. *One Mississippi, two Mississippi, three Mississippi.* She reached fifty by the time she heard his footsteps again, heavier sounding, slower. She could hear him grunting through the ascent, little splashes of diluted Lysol and tap water fell to the floor with every step. "Almost there!" The man called.

Laura let out a choked wail. "Why? Why are you doing this?"

The man breathed a sigh of relief as he freed himself from the weight of the buckets. "I do this, mon petit oiseau," the light switched on, "my little bird," He crouched down, cocking his head. "Because it is my duty."

Laura sobbed, holding her head in her hands. The man straightened, picked up one of the buckets, and doused Laura with its contents.

"Tell your mother that she only takes one of these a day, alright? Any more than that and she'll be on the moon." The pharmacist laughed.

Laura gave a small, polite smile and nodded. She watched as the woman pushed her large glasses up the bridge of her nose with a finely manicured finger and then placed the pills in a paper bag. She pushed it across the counter, but Laura went to grab it, but the pharmacist's hand met her own, gently stopping her. "I don't know if you remember, but I was there the day your brother... you know. I lost a child in a similar way. I just want you to know I pray for him every night."

Laura tore her hand from the pharmacist's. The woman's eyes widened behind her glasses and she pulled her own hand back as if it had been burnt.

"I don't need to know that," Laura replied in a clear, harsh tone, the bag of pills gently rattling in her clenched fist.

She stared at the stranger for a moment, wanting to say more, to climb over the counter that separated them and shove the bag of painkillers down the woman's throat. She turned instead and stomped towards the door, flushed with rage. A young man suddenly appeared at the end of the aisle Laura was storming through. Unable to stop in time to avoid him, they collided into one another. The bag of medication fell to the floor, and the young man's armful of drug store purchases clattered around their feet.

"I'm sorry," Laura said gently, pushing away the rage and now flushing with embarrassment.

"No worries, Maryanne." He smiled, offering her the paper bag and a pill bottle that rolled from it.

"Thanks." Laura offered a small smile. She continued towards the exit doors, shoving the bag into her purse and silently cursing the pharmacist, the shitty drug store, Temple, and herself.

"Hey!" His voice called. Laura walked on.

"Hey, Maryanne!" The young man was jogging from the entrance of the drug store toward her, waving her down. She looked over her shoulder, watching him cross the parking lot. He was fit, gliding along the pavement in long, graceful strides, and he was handsome too.

"My name is Laura," she shouted back at him.

His face twisted in confusion. A car backed out of its parking spot unexpectedly, almost slamming into the young man. Stomach acid rose to Laura's throat. Her heart began to beat violently. She remembered watching Ritchie twitch uncontrollably in the middle of the street, seizing and choking on his own blood. She could hear the screams of her mother.

"Watch it, man!" he yelled, slamming his fist into the trunk of the car, snapping her out of her daze. "So, Laura, huh? Are you stealing poor Maryanne's meds then?"

Laura pursed her brow, swallowing back the bile. "Did you seriously run out here to ask me if I'm a thief?" she snapped.

The young man looked surprised, raising his hands in innocence. "Jeez, no, I-I just...I thought you were cute, and I-I just wanted to say hi." He started to back away from her and the embarrassment returned.

"I'm sorry." Regret blanketed her apology. "I'm really sorry."

The young man lowered his hands. "I just got back to Ohio," Laura began, pushing strands of loose hair from her face, "and it's just...it's a lot." There was silence. Laura's cheeks burned. "Ok, well... have a nice day."

She gave a small wave and started toward her mother's car, too humiliated to try to pursue the conversation further. "Well, wait!" The young man caught her by her arm. "I'm John." He held out his hand. "Enchante." He smiled.

"Laura," a delicate voice whispered. "Laura, sweetie."

She shook her head. Her eyes were still burning, wet hair stuck to her face, the wounds on her wrists throbbed from the chemicals in the water.

"At least she doesn't smell like piss anymore," another voice sounded, this one raspy and deeper.

"It was never about her smelling like piss, Deidre," the first voice replied. "She needed to be cleansed."

Laura cracked open an eye. The light was back, except this time it was a burnt orange, and it swathed two blurred figures sitting before her.

"The sun," Laura murmured, trying to blink away the haziness the water had inflicted.

"Yes, sweetie. It's the sun. How are you feeling?" Laura tried to focus on the woman speaking. Her voice sounded familiar.

"Help me," she whispered. "Please help me." The salt of her tears stung her eyes.

"It's all part of the process, sweetie. You are being purified." Laura felt a hand stroke her cheek. "Deidre, give her some water. I'm going to go get the others."

She watched as the blurred figure of a woman walked out of the room and the other moved closer, pressing a glass to Laura's lips, tilting it just enough for cold, fresh water to fill her mouth. She coughed immediately; the liquid flew past her lips; the sharp taste of disinfectant had come alive as the water hit her tongue.

"God damn it!" the woman snarled, dropping the glass. "You spit all over me!" She stood and stormed out of the room, cursing as she left.

Laura's vision was still skewed, but she watched as the orange of the room deepened. It was maybe 6 o'clock. A guess, sure, but it was better than the sound of a squeaking hinge on a car. She was finally able to place herself in a day. It was the evening, the stink of lemon decontaminant drifted off of her skin, and she was still chained to the attic.

"You can only take one of these. I'll give you another tomorrow, ok?" Laura watched as Maryanne sipped her glass of juice slowly, swallowing the pain pill. Laura took the glass from her mother, placed it on the bedside table, and scooped her jacket up from the lounge chair in the corner of the room. She remembered the nights she and Ritchie spent sitting side by side in that same chair, how big it felt then and how small it looked now.

"Where are you going?" Maryanne asked, her voice melancholic.

Laura gave a small laugh, touching her cheek as she blushed. "I met someone today at the drug store. He's taking me out for a drink."

Maryanne didn't share the enthusiasm her daughter seemed to have about the date. Her lips formed a straight line and her eyes narrowed. "You're going out on your first night back? You can't even stay here for one night before going out and whoring around?"

Laura's smile vanished. There it was, the Maryanne that Laura had known, the Maryanne that lingered beneath the aged, fragile woman who lay in the bed before her.

"I didn't want to come back here," Laura said flatly. "I didn't want this."

"Do you think I wanted this?" Maryanne asked through half-crazed laughing. "Do you think I wanted to call you? I didn't want to call you, Laura! I didn't want you back here as much as you didn't want to be back here! But I need help! If Ritchie were still here, we wouldn't have this problem!"

It was true and Laura knew it. Ritchie had always so obviously been her mother's preferred child. It was even more evident here, in Maryanne's bedroom, where the walls were saturated with photos that weren't being showcased in the living room.

"I know that, Mom," she said quietly. "I'm just trying to make the best of this, ok?" Maryanne said nothing and leaned over, clicking the lamp on the nightstand off. Laura was left standing in the dark.

"She spit all over me!" the woman shouted from downstairs. There was more than one voice attempting to calm her. Laura tried to distinguish one from the other and how many there were, but there were too many and they were speaking too low. She was so thirsty, so desperate for the water that the woman had dropped on the ground. She leaned forward, pressing her face to the floorboards, touching her tongue to the rough, splintered wood. No water remained, just dirt and dust. She stayed there, face against the wood, her body weight pulling against the chains. She longed for the red, electric light to consume her. She longed for the numbness.

"You want more wine?" John asked, holding the bottle up.

Laura giggled, warm and lightheaded from the two full glasses before. "Just a bit." She smiled, letting John pour enough wine to fill half of her glass. They both laughed.

"How have you not landed any gigs? You're so beautiful."

Laura raised her glass to him and took a large swig from it. "New

York has many beautiful women and almost all of them want to be actresses, so...”

James rested his face on his hands and watched as Laura took another pull of wine. “I doubt any of them are as fun as you.”

She rolled her eyes. “You are, by far, the cheesiest man in all of Ohio. I want you to know that.” She slurred, pointing a finger in John’s direction.

He reached out and pushed his fingers in between hers, cradling her hand over the table. “And you are, by far, the most interesting woman in all of Ohio.”

Laura felt her cheeks get hot and wasn’t sure if it was the compliment or the wine. “I know nothing about you. Tonight, has been all about me. Tell me something!”

John looked at her, searching her face for something, it seemed. “Okay. Ohio is just a stop for me. I’m on my way up north.”

Laura looked confused. “North as in Michigan or north as in Canada?”

John smiled. “Canada. I’m driving up there with some friends.”

Laura finished the rest of her glass. “What’s in Canada?”

John poured more wine with his free hand. “Maple syrup.”

Laura scoffed, grabbing the glass mid pour. Wine spilled onto the white linen of the table, which the two of them found exceedingly funny.

“You wanna get outta here?” John’s bright, blue eyes flashed with the candlelight from the table as he waited for an answer. Laura smiled from behind her glass and nodded, taking one last full swig.

She stumbled through the restaurant, bumping into patrons, tripping over her own feet, a fit of giggles and apologies trailed behind her as she and John headed toward the exit. The fresh, brisk air whirled around the two of them as they laughed obnoxiously into the night. It was refreshing, Laura thought, to feel so...good.

“I’m gonna grab a pair of flats from my car. I’m not going to make it much further with these” She hiccupped, pointing at the heels she was standing in.

John smiled, leaned forward, and gently kissed her lips. "I parked around the corner. I'll meet you by my car."

Laura was taken aback by the kiss, but she smiled and nodded in agreement. They parted ways, John heading toward the south end of the building and Laura to the north. She stumbled through the parking lot, laughing at herself, feeling the rare warmth of happiness surge through her body. A sudden, heavy thud to the back of her head sent her toppling forward, slamming into the pavement.

The sound of what seemed to be a million footsteps flooded the space of the attic. One by one, women began to pass through the doorway, filing along the opposite ends of the room. Laura straightened herself up, the haze of the chemicals gone now, and she was able to see clearly each and every face before her. Most of them were young and pretty. Others were older, cheeks and necks etched with time, but a lingering beauty glittered around their eyes. They were all wearing robes of white, silk maybe. The threading caught the remaining light of day that shone through the window and everyone sparkled. It was beautiful, almost; these women, like angels, surrounding Laura. She thought for a moment that maybe she was saved. Then the man appeared, and Laura's stomach dropped.

"My little bird, mon petit oiseau!" He almost sang.

He walked forward, stopping a foot or so away from Laura, staring down at her with those big, blue eyes she recognized so well.

"Tonight, it begins." The softness of his whisper made Laura's skin crawl and her chest flood with terror.

He stepped to the side, turning back to the door, and shouted, "Bring in the the gift!"

Two women appeared, silently struggling with a body between them. Limp, swollen arms belonging to the body were wrapped around either of their women's necks. The body was blanketed in old sheets, a blue, silk bag around its head. The Man motioned for something near one of the women off to the side. A chair was moved to the center of the room, right in front of Laura. The two women, in unison, gently dropped the body into the seat and stepped away, taking their places in the group on either end of the attic.

"What is this?" Laura rasped. "What is happening?"

The man crouched before her and smiled, almost every one of his perfectly straight, brilliantly white teeth exposed.

"My bird, my Laura, this is the beginning. You are special. You are the reason we are all here today." He gestured to the women behind him. "You have spent the last seventeen days being purified." His eyes beamed.

Laura let out a weak, pathetic wail. "Please. One of you, please. Help me." She tried to tug at the chains, but it was useless. She was so tired.

"Stop struggling." The man spoke gently, reaching out and placing his hands on her shoulders. "You cannot stop this, Laura. Embrace it." Tears fell from her eyes.

The man walked to the blanketed, hooded body. "Sister Sarah, if you would be so kind."

A petite, young woman scurried out the door and down the steps. A moment passed and a wave of classical music swept through the room.

"Mozart," the man said, closing his eyes. "Piano Concerto no. 10 in E flat major. Andante."

His raised his hand, moving it in swift motions, following the notes of the piano. With his other, he grabbed the top of the silk bag upon the body's head and pulled it off. It was her cabbie from weeks earlier, Harold, bloodied and bruised. His eyes were swollen shut; his nose was visibly broken. Blood ran from the corners of his eyes, from his nostrils and lips, but it was where his ears had been that blood had congealed the most. He was purple and mangled, maybe not even alive. Laura screamed, throwing herself backward, away from the horrific scene before her. His head fell forward, his lips parted, and a choked sob came from behind them. Laura shut her eyes tight, pulling herself away from him. He began to cough, strings of bloodied saliva clung to the broken, bruised skin of his lips. Another choked sob came, mingling with the haunting melody of the song. Laura felt the bile rise to her throat. Harold made a gurgling noise, as if trying to speak, but the words were muddled and incomprehensible. Laura still had her eyes shut, sobbing now, trying in any way to escape the horror before her. The man rushed forward, forcing Laura's head in the direction of the scene.

"Open your eyes, my bird," he demanded, the music building. "Open your eyes, Laura! Witness this!" he shouted, his eyes bulging, his voice wild.

"No!" she screamed.

Harold made another gurgling noise.

"We've cut out his tongue, Laura." The man whispered into her ear. "He is our sacrifice, and you are our vessel. The blood of an innocent. And the soul of a murderer. You, my bird."

The music boomed throughout the room, now, blanketing the sounds of Harold's crying, blending with Laura's screams. Murderer, Laura thought. Murderer. She was a murderer. He knew. The man stood and found his position next to Harold once more.

"Open your eyes, murderer." The man yelled over the sound of the orchestra.

"No!" she screamed again.

"Sisters." The man nodded toward two of the older women. They rushed to Laura, one grasping her head tightly, the other pulling up her eyelids. Laura thrashed between them, but it was no use. Both women were large, strong, and Laura was so weak. The one pulling on her eyelids sat atop her, the other gripped Laura's head so tightly she could break her neck at any moment. Laura couldn't breathe, she couldn't move. The woman on top of her pulled her left eyelid upwards first, gently placing the top half of the wire speculum under the eyelid. She pulled on the lower eyelid, placing the bottom half in place. The woman was unphased by Laura's screams and pleads for help. There was no visible emotion on her face or the faces of any of the others. She did the same to Laura's right eye. Once finished, the woman removed herself from Laura's lap and took her place back in the group. The woman standing behind Laura continued to hold her head tightly, focusing her eyes on Harold. A lull in the song came forth, quietly winding through the packed attic. The man looked at Laura and gave a slight nod, as if thanking her for her presence. The music began to pick up once more. The man closed his eyes and held out his hands. A tall, gaunt woman pulled a carving knife from beneath her robes. She delicately placed the weapon in the man's outreached hands and his lips curled into a smile, recognizing the cool steel of the knife against his palms. The music flurried, becoming more crazed. The man took the hilt of the knife in his right hand, placing his left behind Harold's neck. He opened his eyes and focused intently on the purple, bubbled bulges where Harold's eyes should have been visible. The point of the knife rested against the tender, bloodied flesh below Harold's sternum.

"And it is with the vessel's eyes that the sacrifice is devoured." Harold gurgled helplessly. The man slowly pushed the knife upwards into Harold's body, inch by agonizing inch steadily disappearing within him.

Harold let out a shrill, cracked scream, his cries drowned by the frenzy of the music. Once the entire blade had vanished, The Man slowly removed the knife, blood spilling everywhere. Laura couldn't breathe, her sobs caught in her throat. The man plunged the knife into Harold once more, aiming higher this time, where his heart was. Harold let out a groan of pain, one that was followed by a steady stream of blood falling from his mouth. The man removed the knife quickly and watched as the ocean of red pooled around the legs of the chair. He looked toward Laura and smiled widely. The strings sounded sharply, and the man began to cut Harold in time to the rhythm.

"The vessel's eyes devour! The vessel's eyes devour!" he giggled, slicing at Harold's chest, his arms, his face.

Laura's screams were broken, hoarse. She watched as Harold's lifeless body slumped forward, blood spilling from him in soft, delicate waves. The song slowed to a melancholy finish of piano strokes which faded into silence, the faint goodbye of the strings ushered in the final notes of the song. The man handed the bloodied knife off.

The woman behind Laura freed Laura's head, and gently removed the speculum from each eye. Laura fell forward, crying softly into the floorboards.

"We pray," the man announced and bowed his head. The women followed.

Harold's body was left on the chair in the middle of the room. Laura stared at the river of blood between the two of them; the river that slowly inched its way toward her until it engulfed the area in which she sat. She didn't move. She let it collect around her, staining her legs and bare feet. Murderer, she thought between counting. She was a murderer. It had been hours since the man and the women had left. Laura longed for the darkness of the attic, but the man had flipped the light switch before he had gone, "Devour" he'd said. Harold's body swelled, death taking hold of what remained. Laura reached fourteen thousand five hundred Mississippi before she heard the familiar stirring of people downstairs. Footsteps she did not recognize crept quietly up to the attic. The pharmacist from the drug store entered the room.

"Laura?" she asked sheepishly, the voice Laura had recognized earlier. Laura didn't respond. She kept her eyes on the blood.

"Laura, I'm going to take you downstairs, okay?"

She remained silent. The click of the key into each of the metal clasps around Laura's wrists and ankles did not elicit the joy she had once imagined it would. It didn't matter now. The Laura in the attic before did not exist in the attic now.

"Murderer," she muttered as the pharmacist pulled her up from the ground. Harold's blood dripped from her legs.

"Murderer," she said again.

Laura had not known a room outside of the attic. She had not remembered the man unloading her from his truck, the same one he had parked around the corner of the restaurant where the two of them had shared too much wine. She didn't remember him carrying her through the foyer, where the women from upstairs now stood. She didn't remember traveling through the quaint, farmhouse kitchen to the secluded steps off in the corner of the room; the ones that led to the place where she would be imprisoned and tortured. Leaving the attic meant nothing now, though. The man knew she was a murderer, and if she hadn't been one before this, it would have been Harold's blood on her hands before it was her brother's. She heard the sound of the brakes squealing, the thud of Ritchie's body against the hood of the car, the crunch of the glass and his small, thin body bouncing off of the windshield, soaring through the air, and landing hard against the asphalt of the road.

There were candles throughout the kitchen, leading into the foyer and another chair, similar to the one Harold sat on upstairs. The women surrounded it, leaving a small opening for the pharmacist and Laura to enter through. They looked angelic once more, glowing under the candlelight that enveloped the room. The pharmacist helped Laura sit and disappeared quickly into the crowd of shining, white silk. A wide hand crept around Laura's shoulder, a hand she recognized immediately as the man's. His knuckles were still stained from the night's earlier slaughtering. He emerged from behind her, winding his way to the side of her chair where he crouched, eye level.

"When you were eight years old, you were outside of your mother's house playing with the chalk you saved from that Easter. Do you remember?"

Laura nodded, knowing where this story would lead.

"Your brother, Ritchie, was outside too. He was playing with the skateboard your mother got him for his birthday."

Laura nodded once more.

"Ritchie asked you to push him down the incline of the driveway. He was too scared to do it on his own, so he asked you, right?"

Laura didn't move. Tears fell from her unblinking eyes.

"You saw the car coming, didn't you? You knew it would hit Ritchie, but you pushed him anyway."

Laura shook her head. "I didn't mean to," she said quietly, the ache of guilt and shame she held in her chest all those years following the words.

The man nodded solemnly. "But you did it. You pushed him. And he rolled into the street right as the car passed your driveway." He paused briefly. "Do you remember him dying, Laura? Do you remember the sound he made as he choked on his own blood?"

Laura shook violently, reliving the moment Ritchie died in front of her.

"You killed him. You killed him, Laura, and you know that you did. You have carried this around with you for so long." The man reached up and stroked Laura's matted hair. "You were chosen, my bird. You will pay for what you've done."

The crowd tightened, gathering closer to Laura. They began to chant softly. They *were* angels, Laura decided. Angels of mercy, angels of retribution, angels of death.

Something playing from a nearby television threatened to drown out the sounds of the chanting. It sounded old, fuzzy even, like a tape being played through a VCR. Laura recognized it as soon as the familiar chimes of the Channel 3 local news music sounded. It was the news report that played the night after Ritchie was killed. Maryanne had recorded it and watched it often, crying herself into episodes of rage throughout Laura's youth. She felt the same then as she did when she was a girl. She wanted to hide from it. She wanted to run from the matter-of-fact voices that rehashed that horrific day. She wanted to lock herself away from the hate and anger Maryanne smothered her in after every viewing. *You did this!* She could hear her mother shouting. *You killed him!*

The chanting of the crowd ceased, the news report filled the silence, and the small sea of angels parted to allow Maryanne's entrance. She was swathed in a white, silk robe, holding a bloodied carving knife.

"Mom?" Laura choked out.

Maryanne's lips trembled. "I'm sorry, honey. But I need him back. I need Ritchie home."

Laura shook her head, terror and grief shaking her body uncontrollably. "I don't understand."

Maryanne stopped before her, silent tears streaming down her cheeks. "They showed me how to bring him back, honey. Those meetings I went to, and the people there, and John. John showed me how to bring him back. This is the only way. I need him home, honey."

Laura could hear the desperation in her voice, the grief that dictated her every moment after Ritchie died. She could feel her mother's heart break with every word of the news report that seemed to blare in the background.

Richard James Anderson, dead at ten years old.

Laura could imagine the older, feather haired brunette with her red tinted lips that matched her chic red blazer reciting these lines from the teleprompter. She could envision her so clearly because she had seen her deliver those same lines countless times over the course of her childhood. It was fitting she was here tonight as well.

Maryanne held out the knife and pointed it at the center of Laura's chest. The blood glittered under the light of the candles like it was electric. Laura focused on the edge of the blade, the red light she saw in the attic began materializing, almost floating from the steel.

"Mom," Laura's voice broke. "Please don't do this." She looked at her mother the way she used to, as a child, desperate for the blame and rage to dissipate.

For a split second, the length of the blade faltered in Maryanne's hand.

John stood from his position next to Laura. "No," he said sternly. "Sister, you must do it."

Maryanne let out a sob and pushed the tip of the blood against Laura's chest.

Laura whimpered, but not out of pain. Laura had suffered enough here to know that the knife against her ribs was not the reason she was afraid. It was because Maryanne stood at the end of it.

"I'm your child, too." Laura spoke the words she had hidden away since childhood, something her mother seemed to have overlooked Laura's entire life.

Maryanne's eyes raced back and forth between Laura's, both in regret and confusion.

"I can't." Maryanne let the knife fall from its position against her daughter's chest.

"No!" John shouted, sending a wave a shock through the crowd. "Summon the strength we spent weeks finding, Sister Maryanne! Your *first-born* is waiting for his vessel!"

The man's voice was uneven and savage. Laura watched Maryanne's eyes widen, as if she had never seen this side of him before, the side Laura knew too well. The man stepped forward, surprising Maryanne who dropped the knife. Panicked, she bent to reach for it, but Laura scrambled forward, watching as the red light against the blade sparkled and grew, wider and brighter. The man placed himself between Laura and the weapon, but she lunged forward too fast and too hard, falling into his legs, knocking him backward onto Maryanne.

Laura grasped the hilt of the knife and as the man sat up, reaching out and diving towards Laura, she stuck the point of the blade into his throat.

She pulled back, blood spurting from the gauged artery.

The women screamed, most rushing toward him, the rest toward Laura. There were too many outstretched arms to dodge, too many legs to outrun. Laura was so tired. She held the knife out in front of her, swiping at the space between herself and the robed women, inching toward her.

She could try to run, she thought. Just around the other side of the foyer she could see the front door. If she could just get outside, she could keep moving. It was dark now, she remembered.

Or she could go after the women; as she had, the man whose body she could no longer see. The women formed a wall of white around him, screaming and crying, no doubt trying to stifle the seeping wound. But how many could she injure? How many would it take for the group to decide she wasn't worth it?

But why go after all of them when she could go after the one responsible for this mess?

Maryanne picked herself up off of the ground, the same weak woman Laura recognized from the porch. She could tell by the use of Maryanne's good arm that the other was still in a sling beneath the robe, and the boot attached to her splintered leg was sure to be lurking underneath. She was still the fragile woman that Laura pitied when she arrived. The same, sad, old woman who had spent her life in search of a son long dead.

She thought of her weeks in the attic, she thought of Harold's gurgled cries for help. She thought of the endless darkness that consumed her. Then she imagined Ritchie, that somehow this was all for him. That somehow, he could be here instead.

The red light rose from the blade and pulsated in front of her face, readied to swallow her whole. She looked beyond it for a brief moment, catching the eyes of Maryanne who stood motionless among the flurry of chaos. Her mother's eyes flickered with tears. Tears of sorrow, remorse, and hope.

Without hesitation, she raised the knife to her neck.

Maryanne let out a brief gasp and reached for her daughter.

Laura pressed the blade against her throat and in one, swift motion, sliced the flesh open. The warm, pulsating, electric red light fell upon her. She was free.

DEATHLY PERFECT

CAROL KJAR

The sun shines down on me like a giant spotlight in the sky, making me the center of the universe. Which I am. I'm walking downtown during my workday for two reasons. Exercise. And because I'm so good at my job that it doesn't take me eight hours to do it. I've written computer programs to do everything so once I get them started, I am free to do whatever I like. My boss can't say anything about my long absences from the office because my work is exemplary. He can't touch me.

I glance into a store window and see an amazing sight. Me. I run my fingers through my immaculately trimmed hair as I stand here a moment. My reflection shows my 40-year-old perfection, neatly dressed and looking like a model. My khaki trousers are tight across my butt and my navy alligator shirt fits me like a glove. Everyone can see that I'm a bodybuilder. Muscular, lean, broad at the shoulders, narrow at the hips. I'm everything women desire. I give my image a crooked smile as I continue down Main Street. Women of all ages stare at me. The cute ones, I give a little wink. It's my gift to them.

I reach the end of my loop and return to my office. At the top of the stairs, the timid secretary always has a smile for me. I lean against her desk as we talk about what's going on in the office. The poor thing has no idea how awful our boss is so I fill her in. He's a lowlife with no redeeming qualities. I could kill him easily with only my bare hands. Breaking his neck would be too easy. He deserves pain. I'd use my full power to drive my hand up under his ribs and pull out his beating heart. He deserves it because he's a worthless, heartless piece of—I can't say the right word. Little miss innocent doesn't like cursing. I see a flicker of fear pass across her face. Her smile morphs into a grimace. She's a simpleton, but she knows who holds the power in the office.

Satisfied at having terrorized the secretary, I continue to my office. I settle into my chair and check my computer's progress on my reports. As usual, things are running smoothly. I check my desk to make sure nothing has been moved. My mechanical pencil has the clip pointed to the left. My pen exactly one-half inch to the right and totally parallel. Everything is as it should be.

I pull up results of my computer program and make sure they are accurate before I spill them into the required format. Once everything is in place and the next program started, I lean back in my chair and put my feet on my desk. I have time to make phone calls to my mom and brother. Mom loves to talk and that's no problem. I have the time.

After work, I go by the gym and lift weights with my buddies for a couple of hours. No one ever outdoes me. I'm the best. Rep after rep, I set the pace and do at least ten more than they do. Sometimes they frown, shake their heads in admiration, and mumble about how buff I am. They're envious of my body perfection. I give them something to shoot for, but will never reach. In the locker room, we joke around, tell a few stories about our wives, shower, pop a few steroids, and head home.

When I walk in the front door of my magnificent house, my wife Meagan is in the large gourmet kitchen. She greets me and tells me dinner is almost ready. My daughter and son are upstairs in their rooms, so I stop by on my way to my master bedroom. I open the door to Brandon's room, expecting him to run to greet me. My 5-year-old son is playing with his toys and says hello without looking at me. That annoys me. My kids are supposed to greet me face-to-face. They are happy to have me home. My family is perfect, but sometimes I need to remind Brandon of his duties. I close the space between us in the blink of his eye. I grab him by the shirt and lift him up next to my face.

"Get up and tell your dad hello." He looks frightened, but that means he won't forget my lesson very soon. I let him fall from my hands. He stumbles and falls backward. He needs to get better at landing on his feet. As he gets up from the floor, he comes over and hugs me around my waist. This is the way he should have greeted me the first time. The family hero expects his due allegiance and respect for his position. As I turn to leave the room, I see my 8-year-old daughter Briana peeking around the door.

"Hello, Father. How was your day?" She tiptoes to me and hugs me.

I point at her and say, "Now that's what I want to hear when I get home from work!" I reach down to pat her back, but she jumps back out of my reach. Why would she do that? I go after her. I catch her by the arm and lift her up off the floor for a bear hug. That's what she needs. I hold her very tightly and pat her back hard enough for her to feel my power. A squeal comes from her as she whines about hurting. She pushes me away. Wimp! I need to toughen her up.

Muttering something about helping her mother, she takes off downstairs. Her brother squeezes past me and follows close behind her, running as fast as he can. Going to help his mother with dinner, no doubt. Good! They should learn to help around the house and keep it perfect like I like it.

I go into our master bedroom where everything is in its place. I sit in the chair to rest a minute. My house with its manicured lawn and great neighborhood is the perfect place for me and my family. I spent a lot of time planning my life and closely followed that plan. I'd saved forty-thousand dollars, the start of my nest egg. At 23, I married an attractive woman, and we had two kids, a boy and a girl as I expected of her. My wife was a professional woman that adored me, and she was lucky to have me. We would spend our lives together, me the king of my castle and she my faithful queen. All of my plans were in place due to my diligent planning and guidance. Perfection, as planned.

Dinnertime is near. The kitchen is a mess, salad makings scattered all over the countertop and pieces of dry spaghetti on the floor. How could a nurse get so messy? Meagan knows I don't like to eat food out of a messy kitchen. "What's all this?" I ask as I get a sponge and wipe some of the lettuce scraps. I hold that sponge close to her face so she can see what's on it.

She grimaces as if she hears a loud noise. "I let the kids help make the salad, and they did a good job of it. I'll clean the kitchen later." She turns back to the stove to stir the spaghetti sauce.

I look at the kids setting the table in the dining room. "Come clean up your mess!" They turn and look at me with wide eyes. I throw the sponge at Briana and hit her square in the chest with it. I let out a chuckle as she turns away from me with a yelp.

Meagan goes to get the sponge. "I said I'll clean it up. They did the best they could and got most of it in the bowl." She wipes the countertop before draining the spaghetti in the sink. "Go sit down and I'll put dinner on the table. Briana?"

I see Briana's teary eyes peek around the corner.

Meagan gives a mewing sound that I abhor. I hear that sound when she's being too soft on the kids. They cling to her like baby monkeys cling to their mothers. I hate that. I want strong children, not soft, emotional jellyfish who go wherever the current takes them. They will not be that way. I narrow my eyes and send laser beams at them and watch them shrink back farther into their mother.

She takes a pan off the stove and pours the spaghetti onto a platter. "Briana, you want to carry the salad to the table? Brandon, why don't you take the bread."

The kids do as they're commanded as I go in and sit down at the table. An irritated anger takes over my mind. Why aren't people like computers, programmable so that they obey and do exactly what I tell them. When a problem comes up in a computer program, I change a few things, tweak it here and there, and make it run smoothly. I get the outcomes I want with no backtalk or rebellion.

I need my family to be like that. Neat, tidy, and obedient. I know what's best for them. I've got it all planned out. I am King. Supreme Leader. Semi-god. I expect my subjects to treat me as such. Obviously, they need to be tweaked so my home will run smoothly. It's for their own good.

After dinner, I sit in my recliner and wait for the family to join me. As is our usual ritual, the kids show me their school papers from the day and we discuss how they can do better. Tonight, Briana seems particularly afraid about showing me her spelling paper and once I see it, I can see why. She missed three out of twenty words. Unacceptable. There is no reason why this child shouldn't know how to spell all her words. I tell her so. "Use your brain!" I say, emphasizing the words with knuckles on the top of her head.

She cries which sets Meagan off on a rampage about how hard I am on the kids. Her constant defense of substandard children raises my ire. She doesn't know anything. Our kids must be at the top of their classes, just like I was. No second-place people are allowed in this house. They must be perfect like me.

I stand and push Meagan aside. "Briana, you failed!' My voice thunders as if coming down from Olympus. "Go to study your spelling words and come back in an hour. I expect you to know how to spell them all." My edict is reasonable. Instantaneous obedience is expected.

Instead Briana runs to her mother who tells me that it's Friday night and to let the poor girl alone. My queen's disobedience and disloyalty are all I can take.

I take Briana by the arm. Her piercing screams hurt my ears. I don't want to listen to her any longer, so I also grab her a leg and throw her up the stairs. She lands on the last step with a thud, hitting her head against the railing. Her shrill screams increase in volume and sets off Brandon and Meagan with her.

I cover my ears as I bellow above the din, "Quiet!" While the volume goes down, the crying and sobbing increase. My family is ungrateful for all my hard work on their behalf. They are my perfect family, and they will behave properly. If tweaking is what they need to behave correctly, then I will tweak them until they get it right.

I grab Brandon by his shirt and lift him from the floor. Meagan claws at my arm, begging me to release him. Tired of her interference, I shove her against the wall. She hits it hard and falls to the floor. I turn to the screaming boy in my hands and toss him up the stairs next to his sobbing sister.

"Go to bed, you losers!" I yell at them. "Tomorrow we work on spelling words and keeping the kitchen clean." Briana pulls her brother up to her and together, they make their way to their bedrooms.

The screaming is gone. All that's left is Meagan's sobbing on the floor as she rubs the back of her head. I stand in front of her, my muscular arms on my narrow hips. She looks at me with narrowed, red-rimmed eyes. "I hate you."

I blink twice, sure that I've misunderstood her mumbling. I'm sure she said she loved me. How could she not when I chose her to be my queen? I could have any woman on earth, but I chose her. No, I'm sure she said she loved me. I reach down and lift her off the floor. Pulling her to me, I kiss her hard. She squirms out of my arms and rushes upstairs.

Looking at my watch, I see my favorite television show is about to come on. With all the commotion gone, I settle into my recliner to enjoy my peaceful kingdom.

After my program is over, Meagan stands beside me with a cup of warm milk. I hadn't noticed her coming downstairs, but here she is, anticipating my needs. Good girl.

She hands me the glass. "Here's a nightcap for you, dear. It will help you relax."

I give her a smile and a wink. She's doing her job and making me comfortable. Maybe she feels bad about crossing me earlier. She leaves to go upstairs. I get it. I have another surprise when I follow her up. I let out a lusty snort and calm my rising excitement with a drink of the warm milk. As it slides down my throat, I feel its warmth and it settles me only a little. I take another big swallow. No use taking too long to drink this. I chug down the rest of the glass and set it by the chair. I try to rise, but feel a little light headed. I settled back into the recliner. Taking several deep breaths, I start to feel very drowsy. I look at my watch. It wasn't quite bedtime, but still, my eyes are getting heavy.

I try to rise again, but my legs won't support me. The last thing I remember is looking at that still-warm cup. Then sleep overwhelms me.

My eyes hurt against the bright lights. Rubbing my eyes, I yawn, then check my watch. It's 9:30 in the morning. I must have fallen asleep in my chair. I let out a yell at Meagan for letting me oversleep. I put the footrest of my recliner down and rise. The room swirls around me, and I lean against the back of the chair as I hold my head. That milk. Meagan gave me a sleeping draft! I scream out at her to come here now!

My voice echoes through the house. No sounds come back to me. I stumble into the kitchen where I find a note on the countertop. I look at it, but my eyes won't focus. I rub my eyes again, and the note comes into view. It says something about taking the kids and leaving. Says she'll report me for child abuse if I try to follow her.

I walk into the dining room and read the note again. Rage boils up inside. I slam my fist against the table, and it cracks in the middle before falling in half. So she thinks she can destroy my perfect life? A guttural laugh comes out of me. She may run, but she can't hide. No one—not her—not anyone—can mess up my carefully planned life. And when I find her, I'll—I'll... Many things come to my mind. My massive hands close into a fist around an imaginary beating heart. I file the thought away into Plan B. No, she loves me, and I'll make sure she knows that. The hard way if I need to.

It's taken me months, but I found her. Meagan is here. At her sister's house in Louisiana. Just past the door I destroyed getting inside. What's she doing here? This rathole of a trailer house. Redneck habitat. How dare she bring my kids to this trashy place. This is no place for my perfect family!

Meagan is screaming at me. Saying things I can't understand. Restraining order? I got it, but it was nothing to me. No one tells me what I can do with my family. I threw it away.

I look around for the kids. They're not here. The rage in me is burning hot. I want ALL my family. My family has had its holiday, but now it's time to take them home. Back to my perfect house in the perfect neighborhood. I grab her arm, but she pulls it away. She runs into the kitchen and grabs a skillet off the stove. She swings it at me, but I step out of reach. Enough of this. I grab her by the hair, pull her to me, my powerful hands surrounding her neck.

"I said it's time to go home!" I yell at her as I look into her frightened eyes. Or is that the look of love? That's it. She'll always love me. "I'm taking you home," I told her softly. Keeping my hands around her neck, I pull her toward the door. "Where are the kids?"

Her face is getting red and purple. Her tongue is doing funny things. She's flirting with me. She's missed me. I relax my grip a little. She gasps. "I'll let your tongue explore when we get home. Where are the kids?"

Her eyes narrow. "No," she whispers.

My hands constrict. I shake her. She must get the kids. Her eyes roll back, and she goes limp.

I hear Meagan's sister Molly behind me, growling in that annoying southern drawl. "Get outta here, you swamp scum!"

That voice is like a gnat buzzing around my ear. My blood boils at the annoyance of this worthless pest who knows where my children are. I'll swat the gnat, then come back to the spider. I let Meagan drop to the floor. I hear her take a deep gasp. I spin around and see Molly with a shotgun pointed at my chest. Her eyes moved between me and Meagan. I hear her whisper "Sister, are you okay?" It's my opening. I lunge toward her.

An explosion knocks me backward. I stumble, but stay on my feet.

I feel nothing but rage. Blinding rage. I let out a growl. I'm a lion about to take his prey. I lunge again. Another roar deafens me. I feel confused. What's this strange feeling? Weakness. I flex my muscles, but they don't respond. I hate this. I let out another growl, but it sounds weak. It takes all my breath out of me. I gasp for more air, but it's hard to pull it in. I feel myself fall to the filthy floor. I'm repulsed to be on it.

Molly stands over me, still pointing her gun at me as she pulls out the spent shells. She reaches in her pocket to pull out two more shotgun shells and puts them in the smoking gun. With a flip of her hand, the gun is readied for firing again.

I struggled to breath as I hear Meagan croak, "Is the monster still alive?"

Molly nods.

I look around, expecting to see the monster Meagan is talking about. If they needed protection, Molly should have asked me to take care of it. She's a terrible shot with the gun. She hit me instead of it. I didn't plan for wrestling monsters.

I use all my strength to raise my hand to Molly. "You missed," I whisper with what little breath I have left.

A crooked smile moves her face. "I'll try again. The gators need supper," she says as she points the gun at my head.

"Meagan!" I whisper just before everything goes black.

NIGHTSTAND

DANIEL SELLECK

A man named Wayne sits at the counter near the door of an old dive bar called Vinny's on a Saturday night. Clad in a slick black and white suit, he would like to think of himself as dashing as James Bond, but his rapidly receding hairline is making him look more like Blofield than anything. Pathetic. That's what his life had become. Forty-one, balding, and a beer gut to boot. They say it's all downhill after forty, but Wayne seems to have put himself on a fast track to the grave.

Here he sits on the fifth and final stop of his never-ending quest. His eyes locked on his glass of well whiskey swill on the rocks sitting on a damp bar napkin on top the counter as drips of condensation trickle down. It's a hot evening in August and the owner is too cheap to install an air conditioner. He frowns slightly and absentmindedly reaches over with his left hand to trace the little droplets of water up and down the glass, noticing the gold wedding band on his ring finger. He pauses and locks his weary eyes with the tiny gold circle which has been the cause of so much misery in his life.

Ten years of marriage, eighteen years with the same woman, all down the toilet because she wanted some other guy's dick. Several years, several dicks. All while his youth, money, and life were of no consequence to her. Now, he sits, an empty husk of the man he was eighteen years ago. Broke, broken, and bearing a ring that no longer symbolizes love and commitment, but hate and revenge.

The front door opens, breaking his trance as he turns, noticing this incredibly attractive creature strut inside. Blonde, curly hair draped and traced over her bare shoulders. Green eyes complimented by plump, red lips which somehow reminded him of Christmas. And that body. So fit, like she didn't even need to work out. Like she was simply designed to be this way. His eighteen-year-old self would've creamed his pants thirty seconds ago. But not now. At forty-one, he knew how to keep his composure. He hoped.

To his disbelief, the blonde pulled up a chair just one over to his left. He could smell her perfume as she sat down, sweet like honey-suckle. Subtly, he watches her out of his peripheral as the bartender approaches from the other side of the counter.

"We're closing up in fifteen. You want anything?" he says, anxious to go home.

"Vodka cranberry," she replies as she pulls a five-dollar bill out of her handbag, along with her cell phone. "It's been a shitty night."

"Sorry to hear that," the bartender says with little interest as he prepares her drink. He flings a napkin at her hand with skilled precision and places her five-dollar drink on top.

The blonde slides the five-dollar bill forward but takes no notice of the Bartender's annoyed scowl as he snatches it off the counter. Her eyes are locked on her phone screen firmly grasped in her left hand.

Wayne studies her with scrutiny. While undeniably and unbelievably beautiful, there's one piece of the puzzle still needed. One piece and he'll make her his for the night.

Her left ring finger... Just show her left ring finger...

What a catch she would be. More beautiful than any woman he's ever had in his life so far. Better than his wife the moment they met, better than the admittedly few casual flings he had in his college days, better than the girl he lost his virginity to on his best friend's basement couch all those years ago. If only she would reveal her damned finger to him.

Unbeknownst to Wayne, someone else was watching him watch her from the other side of the bar. A raven-haired woman in her late 20's, with piercing icy-blue eyes, shrouded in darkness. The bartender approaches her.

"Another sangria?"

"Yes," the woman, Lydia, replies and pushes her glass forward, briefly taking her eyes off Wayne and the blonde. "Keep it open for now," she commands, resuming her gaze on the other two patrons from the end of the bar.

"Of course," the bartender replies and walks off to fix her drink.

The blonde picks up her glass with her right hand, further frustrating Wayne as he anxiously awaits her reveal. She continues scrolling through her Facebook page through all the posts she probably finds interesting, but he couldn't care less about. All he cares about is that damn ring finger. Patience is wearing thin. Maybe he could step out for a smoke and catch a glance as he walks out? That might work. But would it be too obvious? He glances at her one more time. She's too invested in her phone to care.

Fuck it.

Wayne stands up off his seat but pauses when her phone suddenly rings.

"Hello?" the blonde answers, her phone pressed to her left ear.

He settles back in his seat and watches intently.

"Wait, you're here?" the blonde says on the phone.

He continues to watch. His foot taps on the floor impatiently.

The blonde spins in her seat, suddenly revealing the left side of her body to him. His eyes light up instantly as adrenaline strikes through his body like a bolt of lighting as the final piece of the puzzle is revealed. It's all for naught, however, as he finally catches glimpse of her ring finger and is instantly dismayed by what he sees: bare as bare could be, she is claimed by no man.

Wayne frowns sinks back in his seat and turns back to his whiskey. The blonde continues to talk on the phone, but he couldn't care less. Not even giving her a second look when she gathers her belongings, he turns away from the door. What was once an unparalleled beautiful angel has withered away to an unfathomably ugly troll in his eyes. He sighs and downs what's left of his whiskey, ready to call it a night.

"Check?" the bartender asks with the bill in hand.

"Sure."

"Give him one more," Lydia tells the bartender as she pulls up a seat next to him. "On me."

"You got it," the bartender begrudgingly replies, turning back around to prepare a drink and a new bill.

Wayne turns to see Lydia settle in her seat to his right. Her slim black dress contours to her body and slightly rides up her thigh, revealing just as much skin as she intended. Like a femme-fatale from one of those countless old film noire flicks of the past. Attractive, charismatic, and decisive? This is new to him. There's only one thing that could ruin this last chance of the night: her tiny hands, encased in black satin gloves.

"To what do I owe this?" Wayne asks as the bartender sets a fresh glass of whiskey in front of him.

"Call it an indulgence," she replies.

Wayne stares at her blankly, attempting to figure out the intent behind her words.

"I saw you with that blonde just a second ago. Got me curious."

"Curious?"

"You're not completely hideous. Probably could've made the staring a little less obvious, but I think you would've taken her home if you, you know, talked to her a little."

"She wasn't my type," he replies bitterly before taking a sip of his whiskey.

"Seems to be the common excuse when guys strike out. You didn't even try. Clearly, you've talked to at least one woman in your life before," she notes, nodding at his wedding band. "So, what is it? Cold feet? Secretly gay? Second thoughts about cheating on your wife?"

"I don't give a damn about her!" Wayne exclaims as he pulls his hand back out of view.

"I see. So, this wasn't just about some hot side action. You wanted to hurt her. That's pretty cold, even by my standards."

"You guessed it," Wayne fumes and glares at her, "We done here?"

Wayne pulls out his wallet and drops some cash on the counter as he starts to get up.

"Not so fast," Lydia exclaims and puts her hand on his shoulder to stop him. "I'm still trying to put this all together."

Wayne looks at her hand on his shoulder. He considers leaving for a moment, but decides to sits back down in his seat. "What are you, some kind of detective?"

"Avid people-watcher," she replies with a coy smirk. "Now, you're angry with your wife. You want to hurt her in the worst way possible, same as she hurt you. A golden-haired opportunity struts in and you have every chance to make this revenge fantasy a reality. But you don't. You let it slip through your fingers for her to go home and fuck some frat guy instead when it could've easily been you. *That's* what intrigues me."

Wayne sighs with frustration. "Look, lady, I've had a shitty night. I'd like to go home to my shitty apartment, climb into bed, and jerk off till I fall asleep. What's it gonna take for you to let me go and do that?"

Lydia smirks and takes a sip of her blood-red sangria. "Tell me, why you didn't make a move?"

"Because she wasn't married," Wayne groans.

Lydia cocks her head to the side, now even more curious than before.

"I'm not out looking some random bar hookup," he continues. "No, she has to be someone else's wife, belonging to another man. I need to know how those other assholes felt when they were fucking my whore of a wife behind my back. So, lady, if you're not wearing a ring on your finger under that glove, then stop wasting my time!"

Lydia smirks. She downs the rest of her sangria with her left hand and sets the glass at the end of the counter. She glances over at him, who's eyes are locked on her left hand, eagerly anticipating her next move. With full knowledge of this, she slowly, tenderly begins to remove the glove from her left hand, one finger at a time, staring at him while she does it. Finally, she slips her hand out of the satin glove revealing the porcelain-white skin of her hand and a golden wedding ring with a glimmering diamond in the middle.

His eyes widen and his heart races as he stares at the ring. Finally, months of searching, looking for that perfect woman. Slowly, he turns his gaze back up to meet Lydia's icy blue eyes and seductive smirk.

Lydia smiles back, happy to make this sad man's fantasy come true. She casually puts her left hand on his inner thigh, gently tracing her finger over, sending a jolt of adrenaline through his body.

"What do you say we make this fantasy of yours a reality?"

Wayne throws her a cocky smirk, though he's as giddy as a kid on Christmas morning, itching to unwrap his presents. He downs the rest of his whiskey and adjusts his tie.

"Let's do it."

The door to Wayne's apartment is thrown open with almost enough force to break it off its hinges as he and Lydia crash through with their lips locked together. Neither parts as they fuel each other with the ecstasy of their bliss. He kicks the door shut behind him while Lydia pulls him further inside.

Now fully inside, he slips his hand up and grasps a handful of her breast, passionately caressing it. He groans as he kisses her harder than before. His fantasy coming true before his very eyes and he can hardly contain himself any longer.

Lydia, however, breaks off from his kiss, earning a pleading look from Wayne, which she takes in delight.

"Why are you stopping?" he asks, panting.

She smirks flirtatiously, "You want this night to be memorable, right?"

Wayne nods.

Lydia glances around his bachelor pad of an apartment, almost as sad and pathetic as he is. She does, however, spy a glass decanter filled with whiskey on the counter. With a flirtatious smirk and a peck on the cheek, she pulls away from him and struts over to the counter, kicking off her heels as she does it.

Wayne leans against the door and watches her with a mix of intrigue and dismay as she leaves him alone in his living room.

"I got just the thing to make this a truly memorable night," Lydia states as she inspects the decanter. "Care for a drink?"

Wayne recounts how many drinks he had this night and starts to worry a little. "Probably shouldn't. Don't want to worry about... you know?"

Lydia laughs and walks back towards him. She leans in close and presses her lips to his ear, causing the hairs on the back of his neck stand up. She grasps his partially aroused dick causing him to jump slightly; the first woman to touch him there since his wife.

She whispers in his ear, sending him even more over the edge, "I don't think we have to worry about that."

He smiles as she pulls him into a deep kiss, letting her tongue dance around his for a few seconds before parting again.

"You don't have to worry," she says as she walks back to the counter. "My concoction has been proven to get the juices flowing like no other."

Figuring there was no harm in letting her make her little concoction, Wayne heads forward to the bedroom. He wasn't prepared to host company when he left earlier and the last thing he wants is to scare her off.

"I'll be in here when you're ready," he says a smoothly as he can with as little practice as he's gotten in the last eighteen years.

"Can't wait," Lydia winks at him as he disappears into the bedroom.

Inside the bedroom, Wayne shuts the door behind him with a cocky grin on his face. He scrambles about, frantically gathering dirty clothes and old pizza boxes to conceal the squalor he lives in. With much effort, he manages to stash every dirty piece of clothing, every old pizza box, and every empty beer can into his closet, slamming the door just in time to prevent a small avalanche of filth. He looks around his "clean" room and nods with satisfaction.

In the kitchen, Lydia instantly drops the seductress act and checks over her shoulder after the door closes to make sure he is out of sight. She places three identically sized ice cubes in two highball glasses before grabbing the decanter. She removes the top and inhales a whiff of the whiskey inside, thankful his taste in whiskey, at home anyway, is better than the swill he was drinking at the bar earlier. Slowly, and with precision, she pours the amber-colored liquid over the ice, ensuring each glass has equal amounts.

Meanwhile, Wayne proceeds to get undressed. He lets his sports coat fall off his shoulders and yanks at his tie until it becomes free. His eagerness builds with each passing second as he thumbs around the buttons on his shirt before removing it. He kicks off his shoes and then his pants along with them. Briefly, he considers removing his underpants to lie in wait nude on the bed but elects to keep them on. After taking one last look around, he flops on the bed and stares forward at that closed door, aching for it to open. However, slowly his eyes turn to the nightstand to his left beside the bed.

Lydia places her red handbag on the counter and opens it up. She reaches inside and procures the secret ingredient to her concoction: a glass vial filled with black, viscous liquid with a red hourglass sticker plastered on the front. Carefully, she unscrews the top and pulls out the dropper. She holds it over one of the glasses and gently squeezes it, releasing three drops into the drink. The perfect amount added, she securely closes up the vial and sticks it back in her handbag. Then, she grabs a small stir stick next to the decanter and gently stirs the secret ingredient into the whiskey. Satisfied, she turns now to the door, letting her small black dress drop to her feet. She grabs the two glasses and approaches the bedroom.

The bedroom door opens, much to Wayne's relief. He quickly pulls his attention from the nightstand over to the opened door. He rises but stops dead in his tracks and is stunned to see Lydia standing there, fully in the nude with two drinks in hand. She smiles as he stands there stunned, more beautiful than he possibly could've imagined. Waves of excitement flush over him as she appears to glide forward. He started the night seeking an angel, but instead discovered a goddess.

"You ready?" she asks looking deep into his eyes.

Wayne nods, almost too eagerly.

She hands him over a glass, mixed with her own secret ingredient. "Drink this."

Wayne takes the glass in his hand. She anxiously watches as he is about to take a sip, but pauses as a thought suddenly crosses his mind, prompting Lydia to frown slightly with frustration.

"One second," he says, setting his glass on the nightstand. "I got something that'll make this night memorable for you, too."

"Oh?" Lydia ponders with feigned excitement. "Maybe you should take a drink first."

He shakes his head, "I will, but first lie down on the bed."

Wayne takes the glass from her hand and sets it down next to his. Lydia sighs slightly but, again, fakes a smile to keep up her seductress act. He motions towards the bed.

"Ok," she nods as she lies on her back on top the bed.

He shakes his head again. "No. Turn over. Face down."

Lydia nods and turns over, revealing her velvety-smooth back and perfect ass to him. "Like this?"

He stares at her bare body with rekindled lust in his eyes. "Perfect."

Wayne rubs his hands together to warm them up as he gazes at her perfect body. He takes a deep breath, mentally preparing himself. Soon, there will be no going back.

"What are you going to do?" Lydia asks, growing slightly impatient.

"Close your eyes," Wayne tells her. "Just lie there and relax while I do to you what I once did to my wife."

Wayne places his hands on her back and caresses her bare flesh with his thumbs, massaging his way down her back.

Lydia, doubtful at first, begins to feel pleasure wash over her as her porcelain skin becomes flush with red under his hands. She closes her eyes and moans softly.

"This... feels good, actually," she admits.

"Just relax," he whispers as he gently makes his way down her back. "Feel good?"

"Mmm, yes."

He massages down to her lower back and stops just shy of her ass before moving back up, causing her to release a small whimper.

"You're such a tease," she mutters.

Wayne simply smirks as he massages the back of her neck. He tears his gaze from her to the nightstand. Carefully he reaches over to the drawer with one hand while still massaging her neck. The drawer opens and he reaches inside, quietly and carefully procuring an old, rusty, blood-stained hammer.

He glances at Lydia. Her face is still down, oblivious, as he pulls it towards him. His lip quivers as he stares down at her. She's helpless, fully at his mercy. His breaths become short as he raises the hammer up, moving his hand to the center of her back and pressing hard.

"You ready for it?" he trembles.

Lydia moans softly, "Yes."

"I'm going to do to you what I did to her," he growls. "And every whore of a wife I meet."

Lydia opens her eyes, pleasure rapidly turning to fear.

"Turn around. I want to see your face when I do it."

Lydia gulps and slowly turns her head back but keeps her eyes closed, terrified she may have gotten more than she bargained for.

"Open your eyes."

She obeys, slowly opening her eyes, afraid of what she may find. She screams and struggles when she sees the hammer raised up with a wild look in her lover's eyes.

It's too late. In a split-second, Wayne brings the hammer crashing down into her skull. Her body twitches uncontrollably as he struggles to hold her down in place as he caves her skull in. He releases a long-withheld roar of pure bliss and ecstasy as her screams fade away, increasingly replaced by the repeated sound of her skull cracking with each hit of the hammer.

Finally, he drops the hammer and rolls over next to her, panting and laughing uncontrollably. He shouts triumphantly and turns over to look at her once-beautiful face, now frozen in terror. Brushing aside a few loose strands of hair, he stares into her dead eyes wondering what her final thoughts could have possibly been before he ended her life. So beautiful. It'll be hard for the next one to measure up.

Out of breath and parched, he rises up and grabs one of the glasses off the nightstand, downing it in one gulp. He sets the empty glass back down and picks up the full one, walking out to the kitchen.

Wayne walks over the dress on the floor and stands in front of the counter, staring at the decanter and red handbag she left behind. He takes a large sip of his drink and grabs the handbag, emptying its contents on the counter. The usual stuff one would find in a typical woman's handbag: makeup, gum, wallet...

He takes a drink from the glass, finishing what little whiskey was left over, and spies something out of the ordinary: the glass vial filled with black liquid and a red hourglass on it. He coughs slightly and rubs his dry throat as he inspects the vial. His vision slowly gets blurry and his throat becoming increasingly dry and difficult to breath.

He coughs again, harder, and tries to clear his throat as his breathing becomes more and more difficult. His heart begins to race. He looks at the vial, then the empty glass of whiskey he just downed. His eyes widen with fear and realization that he's been poisoned. He can't believe it. It's impossible.

Pain shoots through his body and he collapses as his legs quickly grow numb and buckle under him. He groans and coughs up blood as he crawls back to the bedroom. He moves past the door, locking eyes with the corpse that did this to him. Wayne screams and gurgles up more blood, cursing her, that murderous bitch.

His final breaths pass by quick and the last thing he sees is the dead, beautiful woman lying in his bed. A sudden thought crosses his mind as he lay there dying. She did the same thing to him that he was going to do to her. The irony would be hilarious if he wasn't lying on the floor of his apartment dying.

Wayne, too weak to move any further, gives her one final look and one final thought. He now knows exactly what she felt only moments earlier…

Helpless.

MONSTERS

THE ITEMS IN MY PURSE
MERCEDES M. YARDLEY

Red lipstick, two kinds
Sequoia and Ruby Woo
pinky finger bone
one diamond earring that's missing its back
page ripped from phone book
half empty bottle of Vicodin
a silver knife that folds in on itself
and then a fixed handled skinning knife
duct tape
a small roll of barbed wire
(wrapped in cloth so it doesn't catch me)
video camera with extra batteries
hand sanitizer
grocery list (Don't forget the Yoplait)
latex gloves, three pairs, small
the napkin death threat sent by that crazy guy next door
(I'll deal with him later)
perfume
I am a lady, you know

SCALES

AME WILLIAMSON

I remember how things used to be. I used to wake up late every morning to get ready for school. I used to look in the mirror and comment on a new pimple that had decided to manifest itself on my face. Hell, I used to eat waffles, sodden with raspberry syrup, and eggs on the mornings that my mom was home and had time to make breakfast for the two of us. Things were different now. Forget it, that is the epitome of understatements. The world is dead and so is everybody on it, including me.

I stared at myself in the dirty, cracked mirror and glared at the outbreak of orange scales and purpling, bruised barnacles that had broken out on my neck. I saw that my pupils were so large that only a small sliver of my brown irises were left to be seen. Now, I was a zombie, for lack of a better term. About the only good thing I had going for me was the fact that I didn't crave human flesh, which meant that I wasn't like the others. Not yet anyway.

The heavy silence that usually laid over the valley was filled with noise as a pane of glass shattered and a car alarm followed. The noise snapped me out of my self-pity. I quickly grabbed the set of keys from the hook that protruded from the wall over one of the many useless light switches in my home. As I passed through the living room, I nearly dropped them thrice. I made a mental note to add 'lack of motor skills due to scales being uncooperative' to the growing list of the virus' symptoms.

I opened the door with little difficulty and stepped outside in my hoodie and sweats. I didn't care what I looked like because there wasn't any reason for me to care anymore. I shut and locked the door behind me, shoving the keys in my pocket. There'd be a swarm here soon; they were always attracted to the noise. Instead of hunting down the poor soul that had caused that car alarm to go off, I was headed to the gas station down the road. I needed something salty this morning and pretzels sounded fantastic.

I could hear them beginning to herd together from a mile away, their screams and howls echoed throughout the valley that I called home. There would be thousands gathered before noon, but they usually dispersed by the time the sun set. I guess it got too cold for them. Several of them ran past the entrance to my neighborhood, covered nearly head-to-toe in orange scales. Most of them were completely naked, the only thing that covered them were the scales that marked them as infected. But there were a rare few that had strips of ripped cloth that clung to their damp skin; those were the ones that had turned more recently. I understood the want to take my clothes off and rid myself from the gritty, painful chafing when they rubbed against the scales. But I refused to do it, I was still a decent human being, more or less.

I stuck to the shadows as I weaved my way through the cul-de-sac and out onto the highway. Cars were stopped haphazardly with their doors left wide open. Dried blood spattered nearly everything in sight as I walked right next to the stone fence-line that blocked the posh neighborhoods from the view of the speeding cars that once passed them in mass. Several infected streamed passed me, their acute hearing homed in on the faint whispers of the car alarm I'd left behind. I held my breath, grateful that I still had it, and smiled as they passed me one by one, glad that none of them turned to tear me apart.

The gas station came into view, as the car alarm stopped

shrieking in the distance; they must have ripped the car apart, piece by piece as they looked around for anything at all to eat. It'd been weeks since something had broken the silence that hung heavily over the town, which meant that there was no food, at least for them.

I walked through the broken glass of the station's front window as noiselessly as I could, given the circumstances. I surveyed my surroundings. A pool of dry blood surrounded a lump of rotted flesh and brittle bones in the corner of the room, and a shiver ran down my spine. Most everything else was intact, aside from the many shelves that were picked clean and the occasional splash of dried gore.

As I made my way to the back of the room, I grabbed one of the few remaining bottles of water and looked for anything that might be remotely edible for sophisticated taste buds. The remnants of perishable foods clung to the floor, just husks and random lumps that had once been fruits. Sticky substances stuck to my makeshift, slip-on tennis shoes. Tying shoelaces was a hope I couldn't even begin to harbor, so I'd just given up. I tore the laces out of my sneakers and zip-tied the tongue to a hole on either side of the top of the shoe. It saved a lot of time and effort, on my part.

I was careful to make as little noise as possible as I maneuvered my way around the mess. I didn't want them to swarm this place, I wouldn't be able to eat for a few days, and who knows what that would do to me. But keeping quiet was a lot more difficult than one would think. Those sticky things that had broken down and melted from the hundreds of unrefrigerated candies and drinks made gross, wet noises as I stepped through them; every time I lifted my foot, it was like I was ripping apart a sheet of Velcro.

I nearly jumped out of my skin as a soft bump sounded from the front of the room. Even kicking a can could bring a half-dozen zombies to my location in less than a minute. I froze rigid and awaited the gritty moan of an infected or the telltale clicking of scales as they tapped against one another. But there was nothing except a soft purr and the pitter pat of padded feet. Next thing I knew, an orange tabby cat sat in front of me. His gaze was soft as he tipped his head to the side and mewed; his yellow eyes reminded me of a kitten

I'd had, once. I couldn't remember its name, anymore, but I remembered how its eyes had contrasted with the dark speckled brown of its
fur. A smile fell over my cracked lips, and a nagging thought told me
to grab a Chapstick before I headed home.

My gaze shifted to behind the cat's head, and I saw what I was
looking for. I half-expected the beast to run from me as I scurried
toward it, but it didn't. He stayed put as I passed by and grabbed the
half-crunched yet miraculously unopened bag of pretzels. When I
looked back, I met the beast's ever-watchful gaze. My fingers groped
lazily at the bag of salty knots, and I knew it would be impossible to
get it open quietly with the outbreak that had taken over my hands.
I'd just have to wait until I got home so I could cut it open with something. I grabbed some other things before I walked out, including a
Chapstick, a six pack of those little juice boxes I know I must have
loved at some point, and a package of instant ramen. I'd probably
have to wait a while for the lukewarm water to soften the noodles, but
I doubt it would taste any different anyway. It was hard for me to
differentiate tastes anymore, but salty things gave a slight tang on my
dead taste buds. I assumed that that was the closest I'd ever get again.

I nodded toward the cat and headed out the door; the goods I'd
collected were stuffed safely in a plastic bag. Just as I stepped out of
the shadows, a bullet whizzed past my face. I barely heard a gunshot
ring out.

I knew how the virus worked. I'd seen it happen again and again.
Once you were infected, you slowly lost control of your body as it
took hold of your mind and you were eaten from the inside out. But it
was only when it killed you that you became one of them.

Then you became a sound-driven, man-eating monster.

I'd always thought I'd be the only one left standing, since the
virus hadn't taken hold of my mind just yet. As I stared down the
barrel of a shotgun, an old man with black teeth smiled coldly at me
with his finger poised on the trigger. The pit forming in my stomach
told me what I didn't want to hear. The moment he shot me, we'd
both be goners.

I met his gaze and nearly dropped my bag as I backed up a few steps toward the dilapidated store. As he surveyed me the man's eyes hardened, and I saw his finger tighten around the trigger. It was at that point of tense silence that the cat decided to join us.

It padded its way over the glass and dodged the pieces that threatened to cut into his furry paws. It finally came to a stop and sat on my right foot. I looked down quickly and saw the cultured cat lazily glance upward and then back at the man who still had his gun trained on my face.

A hearty chuckle rang out into the silence and I rattled out of my scale-stricken skin.

"The name's Willard," he said, pointing his gun to the ground and extending a hand. I looked between him and the feline sitting on my shoe for several moments before his smile widened and he took a few steps forward. I stuck my hand out, and he took it shaking it firmly before bringing it closer to his face.

"Remarkable," he breathed as he examined my scale-ridden palm. He was probably reeling to ask why, even though I was infected, I wasn't trying to eat him.

"My nay--" I furrowed my brows as I tried to pronounce the words, which was incredibly difficult for two reasons: first being I hadn't spoken to another person in years, second, the scales that covered my neck riddled the inside as well. "Name is Chance," I finished. I smiled inwardly at my successful attempt at human interaction, even if my gritty, dry tone of voice was a bit hard for the man to understand.

"You speak!" the man exclaimed before the screams of the undead echoed from down the road.

Panic set in as I lurched downward and hastily picked up the cat, who, to my surprise, didn't protest. I grabbed the man's hand and dragged them both through several windy streets that edged the hill on the west side of the valley. I couldn't do anything but hope that this attempt at losing our pursuers would be effective, if we were being pursued at all. There was no indication that the monsters that roamed the Earth had a heightened sense of smell that enabled them to locate their victims. I think I'd know, considering my circumstances, but there was really no way to know for sure.

I kept weaving my way through random streets and alleys, hauling along the now sleeping cat and a rather confused looking old man, until I had finally made my way back to my house. I dropped the man's hand as I unlocked and opened the front door, being sure to let the cat down so it could inspect the house as it pleased. The man marveled over the fact that I could open a door, not to mention the state of the house. Even though it had fallen into disrepair, it was still a livable space.

It's been eight years since this whole thing had started, but I'd only spent the last six alone. I faintly remembered what my mom looked like before she died. She had blonde hair with a matching set of bright blue eyes and an even brighter smile. I knew I had a father who was overseas fighting some war for a reason I didn't know. I could remember simple things, like how to turn on a light and twist a doorknob, but the details about my life were all a blur. It was like I had gone to a wild party and all of my memories from the night before, or in my case, my entire past, were distorted and hazy.

Maybe this is what it was like when you started to die inside from the infection. Maybe once I'd lost myself, I'd lose my sense of control and I would morph into one of those sound-hunting zombies outside. Maybe. But I'd been infected for over four years now, so I didn't think that would happen any time soon.

"Home," I uttered, the word coming surprisingly easier than the ones I'd spoken earlier.

"I can see that" he said, turning in place as he inspected every detail in awe. "You know, I haven't seen a place this intact since I spent a week in a little mansion just south of Spokane."

I didn't know how to respond, so I nodded my head and winced as the scales and barnacles on my neck clacked together sending shooting pains down my back. I remembered when I'd first figured out I was infected. Four years ago, I discovered my first scale just below my chin, and I had hastily ripped it off. I had never even left my home, since the day I buried my mom; it was easily the scariest thing I'd ever experienced. I was one of those outlying, spontaneous infection cases. Fear gripped my stomach as I ran to the bathroom to look at my dilated eyes. I cried for hours after that; I thought that I was going to die a slow, painful death and then rise up and become one of *them*. It's been years, since then. If this was what a slow painful death felt like, I envied those like my father, who'd probably died from some gunshot wound as they fought in that war with no name. That kind of quick end was a mercy I wish I'd been granted. I didn't have the courage to do the honors, myself.

I eyed the man as he wandered through the hallway, glancing into the bathroom and through the door that led to my parents' bedroom. Before he could even try the stairs, I grunted at him to stop.

"Floors are creaky, loud enough for them to hear," I choked out. I grabbed the plastic bag and opened the flip-top water bottle, and I had its contents drained in three seconds flat before I walked over and set it against the wall with the dozens and dozens of other empty bottles. The man just nodded his head; his graying hairs bobbed up and down in sync with the ones that covered his face.

The cat strutted into the main room, weaving through my feet before sitting between them. I smiled; I was surprised that the little Tom seemed to like me. The man voiced my inner thoughts.

"The little bugger seems to have taken a liking to ya," he muttered and knelt down. He extended his hand, at which the cat hissed menacingly. "Huh, feisty little bugger, ain't he?" The man glowered at the cat as it perched beneath me. My muscles tensed as the man bunched up his fist and Tom continued his silent screech, though the sound seem to resonate in my ears. The second I made a move to cover them up and ease the pain of the echoing, screaming sounds that that cat made, the man backed off.

There was a look of palpable distaste in his eyes as he retracted his hand and moved away from the two of us. The cat quit its incessant scream and my ears finally stopped ringing once the world fell silent again. I looked at the man, and his stare bore daggers into the seemingly disinterested Tom. The little tabby brought a paw to his face, licking it and proceeding to clean itself once he'd felt the danger was gone. Maybe it was a cruel, mocking gesture. I was filthy, but Willard seemed to have tripped into a vat of tar and mud and hadn't bothered to wipe away the grime and gunk.

I sighed, shifting my feet from side to side before finally giving in and sitting behind the cat, who gladly took up the chance to be petted. Who knew how long it'd been since this little critic had stumbled upon a civilized person? Anyone could tell that it had missed the pampering touch of a human. Too bad I couldn't give him the 'human' he deserved. If his owners weren't long dead and rotten somewhere, then it was highly likely they were walking amongst the scaly zombies outside.

I started when Willard cleared his throat, the noise driving daggers into my brain. And, when the cat began to purr at my touch, my skull vibrated with pain.

Be quiet. Please.

"What's wrong, kid?" The man offered his hand, but I couldn't take it, the agony having ensnared my limbs. It was like a thousand long-silent radio stations were playing in my head all at once, and the volume was continuously increasing until I felt like my ears burst. Willard fell silent, but not before kneeling closer as if to help me. It was a wrong move on his part.

The cat spat furiously, and it clawed and bat at his hand until the man's fists were bunched up once again. A vein popped out on his temple, and by the time I realized what he was doing, it was too late. The man's hand lashed out and grabbed the cat round its neck. He broke it almost effortlessly and threw Tom's corpse against the wall with an angry crack.

I let out a warbled scream and stood up in a hurry. I stumbled backward into the rows of plastic bottles that I'd collected and stacked against the wall, over the years. The disturbance sent them clattering all around us, and my scaled skin prickled with fear.

Blood and noise. That's all it would take.

Panic gripped my muscles. The man stared evilly at the cat's corpse while the sounds of the screams of the undead outside drilled into my mind, louder and more violently by the second. By that time, my eardrums felt like they were bleeding. The zombies beat feverishly at the doors, walls, and windows, which made even more noise. The rest of the herd could be here within the next few minutes; it was pointless to hope that my home wouldn't be torn apart, board by board. I managed to wrestle myself upward just as the living room window shattered and caved in under the pressure that had built up behind it.

Another cry tore through my throat as I made a mad dash for the bathroom, but a wave of panic flashed through me when something grabbed my ankle. I fell to the ground with an angry thud, but the noise was the only thing that seemed to hurt me. Dozens of scaly monsters drug themselves through the front window as I looked back at the man who'd tripped me.

"You look a lot like my boy did, two years ago. He abandoned me," Willard whispered. As the silhouettes of zombies approached us, the terror ascended into his eyes. He looked much older then, like he'd seen things that I would never understand, nor ever would. His face fell in a way that only the word 'desperate' would be able to describe. "I couldn't hide in that car when I saw them coming toward the sounding alarm. I didn't want to die alone," his eyes flew wide open as the first of the zombies stumbled through the mess of barricaded furniture, broken glass, and bottles. "I don't want to die alone," he whispered, staring behind him as the monster sprinted toward us, letting out a howl much like the one that had haunted my nightmares for years. I kicked Willard's hand with my free foot, hearing a satisfying crack. He winced in pain and drew his hand back. He frowned deeply at it, though his eyes had glossed over, and it didn't look like my assault had caused him any real pain. The man was dead meat. I wasted no time as I got back up and sprinted down the hall before quickly deciding to dodge into my parents' room rather than the bathroom.

I burst into the bedroom, slamming the door behind me. I pushed my bodyweight against the old wood just long enough for me to realize that any barricade I could make wouldn't hold those monsters back. I dropped on all fours and made my way across the bedroom.

Shadows shifted over the floor, as the zombies outside made their way toward the opening they'd already made.

I crawled into the closet and slid the door closed. Once safely inside, I found my dad's safe and typed in the numbers that would unlock it. Willard's screams died down as he was ripped to pieces in the next room, Tom's corpse probably being dealt with in a similar manner. As the little box beeped and the latch to the safe unsealed, I picked up the old 22 and shook the two remaining copper bullets out of their box, as silently as I could. Not that it really mattered, now.

The gun was sleek and black, and I remembered the last time I had to use it. Six years ago, my mom was sick with the virus. Her changing process had been nothing like mine, and the time between when we'd found her first scale to when she'd fully turned was a matter of nine days. Those nine days had been the worst days of my life; it was a sweltering hell in the cold silence.

When my mom finally turned, she found herself tied to the bed and gagged to keep her screams silent. She writhed and screamed through the cloth I'd stuffed into her mouth as she tried to get at me, but it was no use. I cried as I pulled a pillow over her scale-covered, angry face and I dragged the gun to her temple like it'd weighed as much as an army tank. The pillow muffled the sound of the gunshot that killed my mom, or at least ended the husk of the person she'd used to be. I knew all the while that it was what she wanted me to do, what she had begged me to do when we had found her first scale. It hurt just the same. I'd been alone ever since, and the occasional cry of the infected was my only company.

As I knelt, shaking, I cried just as hard as I had then. I cried, knowing that I was probably going to die, today, if I wasn't already considered dead. I heard thunderous footsteps bound upstairs, the zombies scratching at the walls and doors in search of food. I wept in remembrance of a time when all I cared about was how I looked, but now I was covered in orange scales and knobby barnacles that were far worse and more painful than any acne I'd had to deal with before it all. I remembered a time when I had been told I had bright eyes like my mom and a wonderful smile, but that was a time long passed and nearly forgotten.

Life had been simpler then, and I questioned whether this new life was even worth living. As I sobbed, I felt those memories fade away in my despair. I felt myself evaporating as my nose filled with some unknown scent, better than anything my mom had ever cooked for me. I could see her now, serving up her raspberry syrup-sodden waffles as I knelt down at the table. I didn't even bother with handling a fork, with my uncooperative immobile fingers. I shoveled fistful after fistful of the glorious substance in my mouth and savored it.

Warm and red.

Soft and rich in taste.

It was unlike anything I'd ever tasted before, and my thoughts flooded with the realization that I never wanted to eat anything else. I growled in bliss as others joined me around the table, digging into the mass that was our dinner.

And when I opened my eyes in search for that woman, that woman I couldn't seem to remember, I felt them dim slightly. I was eating Willard's body, and that last human spark within me died out. When I realized that, I didn't even care. I was already dead, and I lost myself completely to the hunger.

SHADOWS ON THE FLOOR

DAN FARREN

Alex only heard the voices as he drifted off to sleep. He didn't know where they were coming from. He thought they might be coming from inside his toy bin. For several nights he piled books on top of the container's lid to keep the voices inside. But he was wrong. The voices were not inside the bin, but they were coming from someplace in the room.

One night, Alex woke to hear a strange scurrying sound. He rubbed his eyes, peered into the dark and thought he saw a shadow running across the floor. He called to the shadow. "Who are you?"

There was no answer. Summoning up all the courage he had, Alex pulled back the covers and and placed his foot on the floor.

"Stay in bed!" said one of the shadows.

Alex rolled back into bed and pull the covers over his head. It was a long time before he fell asleep. Alex was positive he heard two voices laughing in a conspiratorial whisper. His mother noticed how tired Alex was on the way to school the next day and ask how he was doing. Alex told his mother about the voices and she tried to convince him it was just a nightmare. But to Alex, it didn't seem like a nightmare.

Alex had a plan. He would win over the mysterious shadows and make them his friends.

He had done that with a bully at school and now the bully was one of his best friends.

For several nights he set out a glass of milk and a plate of cookies. If it worked with Santa Claus it might work with the shadows.

But it didn't.

He heard the familiar scurrying in the darkness, but in the morning, the plate was untouched. He next tried putting out his favorite comic books. He heard the shadows whispering and pages turning in the night. In the morning the comics sat in a pile in the corner, ignored. Alex tried setting up his mom's phone and capture the shadows on video, but in the darkness, you couldn't see anything. Just noises and that could be anything.

Alex had just about given up communicating with the shadows when one night he fell asleep watching TV. He woke later to hear the shadows whispering among themselves. So, he left the TV on for the next week like a nightlight until one morning he woke to find the TV off and unplugged.

That was the last he heard of the shadows and their whispers for the longest time.

Greg Sisley changed all of that. Greg was a co-worker of Alex's mom at the call center.

She dated him for a while but that soon ended. Greg didn't go away. Greg and Alex's mom remained friends.

At first Alex liked being around Greg. They went to the movies, got ice cream and sometimes went to the amusement park. That all changed the day they went to the zoo.

Greg showed up smelling funny and started shouting at Alex's mother. While his mom was in the bathroom Greg got mad at Alex for taking too long in the reptile house. He yelled at Alex and grabbed him by the wrist and twisted it.

Alex tried to hide his bruise from his mom, but she saw it when they got home. She called Greg on the phone, cussed him out and told him never to contact them again. If he did, she'd tell their boss at work.

That night it was hard for Alex to sleep. Every time he'd roll over his wrist would hurt.

Then he heard a familiar whisper.

"Who hurt you?"

The voice came from under the bed. Alex answered the darkness and told the shadow about Greg and the trip to the zoo.

"Don't be afraid," said the voice under the bed.

"He won't hurt you," said a voice in the closet.

Alex heard a knocking at the front door that quickly turned to pounding. His mother opened the door and Alex heard Greg's voice. He sounded much meaner than he did at the zoo.

Alex leaped out of bed and ran in to the hallway. There he saw Greg waving his arms and screaming. Alex's mom yelled for Alex to go back to his room and lock the door.

Alex retreated or his room, locked the door and hid under the covers. He could hear his mother screaming at Greg and then, she stopped. It was quiet for a moment, then there was a pounding on his door and Greg was yelling at him.

"Don't be afraid," said the voice under the bed.

"He won't hurt you," said the voice in the closet.

Greg kicked the door open. Alex could see him standing in the doorway.

"You did this," he said in a calm voice. "You turned your mother against me."

Greg walked to the foot of Alex's bed and stood there for the longest time.

Alex was frozen. He didn't know what to do.

"Don't be afraid."

Greg looked around the room.

From under the bed Alex saw a pair of claws grab Greg by the ankles and flip him into the air. Greg landed with a crunch and howled out in pain.

"He won't hurt you," said the voice in the closet.

The closet door swung open and a tentacle grabbed Greg's twisted body and pulled it into the closet. The door slammed shut and Greg's screams fell silent. Alex climbed out of bed and slowly opened the closet door. There was nothing inside it but toys and dirty clothes. No Greg.

He ran down the hall and found his mom tied up with electrical chords. She was bruised up, but okay. Alex called 911 and the police arrived a few minutes later.

Greg was never seen again. The police figured he left town. Alex never told a soul what happened. He said something spooked Greg and he ran away. Alex knew no one would ever believe what really happened. Alex's mom was worried that Greg might return, but as the months passed by her fears went away.

Alex never heard the shadows across the floor ever again. He was never again afraid of anything that went bump in the night. There was no reason to be. They were his friends.

Greg soon realized why the shadows did what they did.

He figured they were just protecting their reputations. The monster under the bed and the creature in the closet do not like competition from the real world.

WARM, DARK PLACES ARE BEST

MIKE DUKE

Carl and Jessica walked into their new apartment, boxes in hand, knowing exactly what they were getting into.

Hell.

It was an absolute shithole, and most of the people, who hung outside and, in the hallways, looked nastier than the cockroaches crawling all over the place.

As they crested the stairs onto the second floor, a gaggle of young boys were squatted side by side, pinning a roach to the wall, before burning it to death with a lighter. Both Jessica and Carl stopped in their tracks, and looked at each other, with a "What the fuck?" look, on their faces.

Some old lady, with a walker, saw their concern, and spoke.

"Oh, it's ok, y'all," she said, looking them in the eye, then stopped and patted one of the boys on the head. "Keep it up, fellas. You know what I say. Another one dead is one less crawling in your bed."

The lady cackled lightly and started walking again. As she approached Carl and Jessica, she greeted them directly.

"Welcome to the jungle, newbies! You'll get used to it, soon enough." She extended her pale hand toward Jessica, first. It trembled and shook more violently the longer Jessica regarded it without taking it in her own hand. The lady's fingers were folded in at the root knuckles, a clear indicator her joints had been ravaged by rheumatoid arthritis. Liver spots covered the skin, and the veins were substantially visible.

"I'm Janet," she said, still waiting for Jessica to reciprocate her greeting. "Been here the last 15 years."

Jessica finally snapped out of her haze and shifted the boxes to free up her right hand.

"I'm sorry!" she exclaimed. "Thank you. I'm Jessica and this is my husband, Carl. We're moving into 2C today."

Carl nodded and extended his hand, after he sat down the stack of boxes he had been carrying.

"Pleased to meet you," Janet said, and took Carl's hand as best she could.

"Nice to meet you, too," he responded, politely, but not really feeling it. He had dreaded this day for weeks now and had made it explicitly known to Jessica just about every day, since it was finalized.

Carl looked at the boys. They had burned one roach, pinned another, and were fervently at work to set the other aflame. It seemed this was a favorite way for them to pass the time.

"Loads of fun and adult approved, as well!" the imaginary commercial for lighter and straight pin value packs targeting young boys flashed through Carl's mind and he tried not to laugh.

Instead, he spoke to Janet. "Fifteen years, huh? Wow." He looked around, momentarily counting roaches on the walls, till his eyes lifted, and took in the ceiling. Then he really wanted to get in his apartment or back outside; either one, as long as it was ASAP. Anywhere, but the hallway where those little radiation resistant germ mobiles could fall in one's hair at any moment, he thought.

He released Janet's hand, abruptly, and turned to pick up the boxes in a hurry.

"I'm going to get these in the apartment, Jess," you two can keep talking.

He scurried away, with a quick glance over his shoulder, to see Jess launch a glaring look of ill intent in his direction. He noted it, and calculated the penalty later on, but his hate for all things bugs was worse than any chastisement Jess might come up with. Instincts. Fight or flight. Hell, just good sense in Carl's book.

He pulled out the key, trying not to drop it as his adrenaline levels surged slightly and he fiddled with the lock like some teenage boy fumbling to get his rigid penis in his first lay. Finally, it slid home and clicked as he turned it to the left.

Carl was struck by a distinct moment of relief before he rushed inside, immediately looking at the ceilings. He expected more roaches that he would have to, immediately, take care of with the can of bug spray, in the box on top of his stack. To his surprise, there were no roaches, not anywhere. He walked through the entire apartment, scanning every location he thought he could spot one, or the evidence of them, but there was nothing. Absolutely not one single sign.

"Whaddaya know?" he said aloud, to himself. "Maybe management isn't as bad as they appeared. Must have set off a bug bomb, and had the placed cleaned up, good."

Carl smiled as he put the boxes in their appropriate rooms and dug out a ball cap from one of them. Pulling it on firmly, he exited the apartment, practically sprinting by Jessica and Janet, who were still talking. He didn't say a word to either woman, much less dare to look Jessica in the eye.

He grabbed three more boxes and began the trek back to the apartment. At the top of the stairs, he felt his chest tighten slightly, his breathing becoming a little more labored, even as he noted the young boys were the only ones present.

The tension wasn't full on, but his lungs were starting to complain.

"I don't have time for this bullshit today!" he silently yelled at his body. Once inside the apartment, he reached in his pocket, retrieved the inhaler, and took a hit off of it.

"Is your asthma, already, acting up?" Jessica asked, with true concern. She decided to shelve her developing plans of torture. She'd pay Carl back later for leaving her there alone with Janet.

"Yeah, a little, but I'll be alright. I'm not waiting for it to get worse." He pocketed the inhaler, smiled and turned around to head back downstairs. In the hallway, a light bulb came on in his brain, and he stopped immediately.

"Hey, fellas." He addressed the four boys.

They all turned around and looked at him, a bit of disdain in their faces for distracting them from the scheduled executions.

"Would you guys mind helping me out for a few minutes?"

They looked at each other and back at him, a confused, blank stare on their faces that seemed to say, "why would we?"

Carl wasn't the sharpest knife in the drawer, but he wasn't as dumb as he looked sometimes, either. He immediately discerned the answer he needed to give to their unspoken question.

"I'll give each of you a lighter..."

He paused to see if they would bite without offering anything else, but they knew one of the most crucial techniques in the art of haggling too well. Silence.

"And I'll show all of you how to make a little flamethrower for killing those roaches, but you'll have to catch them and take them outside to do it."

All eight eyes opened wide in unison and the leader of their little pack spoke up for them.

"You need help bringing boxes up, dontcha?"

Carl smiled big. "You're a bright boy....?"

"Derek," the lad said and stuck out his hand.

Carl took his hand, and they shook.

"I'm Carl," he said.

"Well, Carl," Derek informed him, "You got a deal."

They gave a final pump, to the deal-sealing handshake, and Derek led the boys down the stairs ahead of Carl. They made short work of the contents of the truck - including bed, couch and recliner with a little help from a man on the first floor that Carl promised to buy a beer for as payment. Jessica never had to carry another item in, which pleased her greatly, since she was always antsy to start putting things away in their proper place right away whenever they moved.

When they were done, Carl walked across the street, to the gas station and picked up a 5 pack of lighters and three beers, then returned. Derek and the boys were standing outside, patiently waiting for him to return.

"One of y'all go grab a thing of hairspray from your mom's bathroom," he said, walking up to them. "Make sure it's a metal can, aerosol, not the plastic pump hairspray containers."

Derek nodded and tapped one of the boys on the arm, who quickly bolted. In no time he was back, panting a bit, but can in hand.

"Alright..." Carl scanned the area and found a little nook where the walls dipped in a bit between buildings and had paved concrete instead of grass. "Come with me over here, out of sight," he motioned to Derek.

Carl squatted down, and the boys formed up in a semi-circle, intentionally blocking common view of their activities, with their bodies.

"OK. We did this all the time when I was a kid, screwing around. But you could definitely dispatch cockroaches like this." He smiled at them, but Derek was all business.

"So," Carl continued, "take your lighter and light it, and then get the hairspray ready." He turned off to the side, and aimed it down at the concrete, before depressing the button, and releasing the compressed contents, igniting a spout of flame two feet long or more and scorching the concrete.

The boys all exclaimed their surprise and excitement.

"Holy fuck," Derek said, with a wicked gleam in his eyes. "That is awesome! Let me try."

Derek held out his hands, desperate to give it a shot. Carl handed the lighter and hairspray to him. He followed Carl's example, and successfully made his own little flamethrower, then giggled with a glee that, it seemed to Carl, was not a typical experience for Derek.

"Here's something else cool you can do."

Carl held out his hand, took the items back, and proceeded to hose his left hand down with the hairspray, front and back, then set it down. He picked up the lighter, flicked it then lit his hand on fire, holding it up for all the boys to see. Their eyes got big, and Carl gave the old prom queen wave, twisting his hand slightly, back in forth with just a small amount of movement, on the opposite plane, to create that gentle wobble they all aimed for, while riding by in homecoming parades. When it got hot, a few seconds later, he shook his hand rapidly, and the fire went out.

"That was soooo frackin' cool!" one of the boys shouted. He grabbed Carl's hand in his own and turned it back and forth, inspecting it closely for any burns.

"How did it not hurt you?" he implored, dying to know the answer.

"It's actually pretty simple. It burns the hairspray. When it's done with that, it will burn you, too, if you don't put it out."

"Cool," the boy responded.

"Alright, that's an extra. Y'all will owe me for that one, at some point."

Carl gave a wry smile. "Now, don't burn yourselves, or do anything stupid, like putting it in your hair or on your clothes. You can't put the fire out, on flammable things, easily. Remember that."

Derek nodded, and said "You got it," then, slapped another of the boys on the chest, and issued a command.

"Ricky, go catch a few roaches in a jar, and bring 'em down here, so we can all have a go!"

Ricky nodded his head and took off.

"Alright, Derek. If anyone asks, I didn't show y'all how to do this. Comprende?" Carl looked them each in the eye.

"You bet. I'll tell 'em we learned it on YouTube. I'm sure it's on there, somewhere." Derek smiled big. "Thanks, Carl. You're cool in my book. If you need anything, let me know. K?"

Carl nodded his head, and smiled, automatically saying, "you bet," before standing to walk away. He waved 'bye', and headed for the apartment, feeling more like the kid in that exchange, than the adult, for some reason.

At the top of the stairs, Carl ran into Janet again, and almost let out an audible sigh, but caught himself, though, he couldn't hide the labored breathing.

"What's a young man, like you, breathing hard for, after just one flight of stairs? Something wrong with you?"

Old ladies, Carl thought, no sort of personal information is ever off limits. He decided to just let her have it, and not try and shuck and jive, in an effort to avoid telling the truth. She would certainly notice, soon enough, that he didn't work anywhere.

"Well, Janet, as a matter of fact, something *is* wrong with me. Has been for the last 12 years. Workplace accident. A somewhat caustic chemical gas got released, and I breathed it in. I've had very aggressive asthma ever since. I'm on disability."

"Well, at least you still look fit," she spit out, without any sense of propriety. "And you have a looker for a lady, you do. Sweet girl, that one. Count yourself lucky. We all, eventually, go through some sort of bodily hell, if we live long enough. It's who's with you that makes the difference."

Carl smiled at the little pearl of wisdom offered in Janet's, apparently, typical candid fashion, it would seem.

"Me, at my age, with hands like this," and Janet lifted both her deformed hands, "kind of hard to wipe me arse sometimes, but Bob's a loyal champ. In sickness and in health, and all that jazz. He's a keeper."

Carl's faced blanched white, and he coughed reflexively, like something had flown right in his lungs that he didn't want one bit of. Perhaps it was called TMI.

Either way, Janet just waved bye and started walking.

"See ya around, Carl," she said, a mischievous grin spreading across her face.

Carl coughed again, and thought to himself, that he truly believed, some old people just did that kind of shit because either, they had nothing better to do, and it was entertainment, or it was their little way of treading on the flowers of youth, blossoming as they themselves slowly withered to death.

Jessica was hard at work, unpacking and organizing things, when Carl walked back in. His breathing a bit heavy.

"You OK, baby?"

Carl plopped down in the recliner, shaking his head still, from Janet's personal revelation in the hallway.

"I'm fine, honey. Just give me a few minutes to sit, and catch my breath, and

I'll help you with putting stuff away."

"So, what did you give those boys, for helping out?" Jessica called, from the kitchen.

"A five pack of lighters."

Jessica stepped out, in view of him, and gave him the stare that said stop being a smartass.

"You lie," she said, bluntly.

Carl raised his right hand, and placed the left, over his heart.

"I swear to thee, dear lady, I do not."

"You're horrible," she said, and ducked back into the kitchen.

"What do you mean?" he protested. "Janet wants them to burn the roaches. And, besides, it was the predetermined agreement... along with me teaching them something."

Carl trailed off in volume, with his last few words.

Jessica reappeared.

"*What* did you teach them, Carl?" Her posture and tone said this was Detective Jess he was now speaking to, but the look on her face said she was already prepared to be utterly appalled.

"Nothing major." Carl waved his hand like 'pish, nothing of note, here, lady, just move along'.

"What?" she repeated, her teeth gritted together.

Carl exhaled and spit it out.

"I taught them how to burn the roaches with a lighter and can of hairspray."

Jessica's mouth flew wide, and he could tell she had just been uncorked, but Carl quickly cut her off, and stuck a cork back in her. He held up his finger and stood up.

"But I told them they could *only* do it outside, on the concrete. And that I never showed them. Now don't worry, that one kid, Derek, has got his act together. It'll be fine. Hell, I did it with my friends as a kid all the time. Now, leave me be on this one. You didn't have to carry a bunch of stuff. Be happy and congratulate my social engineering skills."

Carl smiled big, a smile of proportions which hadn't been seen on his face in some time, now. She sighed.

"Don't sweat the small stuff, right?" she inquired, in a rhetorical fashion, knowing it was one of his favorite things to remind her of.

"Now you're running on all cylinders, hon."

Carl cracked a beer, pulled from the plastic bag he had carried in, and smiled like a cat who had swallowed one canary, and had another waiting in its back pocket. He tipped the beer in Jessica's direction, as if inviting her to acknowledge his win in this particular conversation, then pulled the other out and extended it towards her, like some Indian peace pipe, a questioning look perched upon his face.

She gave him a look like she didn't want to admit he was right, because she never did like doing that, but then stepped forward, and grabbed the beer, her actions saying what she chose not to say with words. It was an understanding they had, and Carl knew how to work it.

Jessica opened the beer and took a sip.

"Well, I know you've dreaded coming to this place, but inside here it's not too awfully bad, is it?"

Jessica looked at him closely, as she asked the question, trying to assess what his thoughts were beneath the surface - where he either kept things hidden, or occasionally, dredged them up to throw out into the open, for all to endure. There wasn't much in between.

"Yeah, inside here isn't bad," he replied. "But I fear it's the calm before the roach storm eventually arrives. There's no way they won't be in here, with how many are outside. On the other hand, as annoying as that lady, Janet, seems, she's nice. And the boys are cool. I think they may even look out for us a little, after what I did for them. My biggest concern, besides the roaches getting in here, are the big human cock roaches around here. I saw a couple of hoodlums when I went across the street. They looked me up and down, like a prospective piece of meat, but didn't do anything. We're both going to have to take precautions, when we are coming and going. It would be easy to become a statistic around here."

Jessica gave Carl an ingratiating smile, as she walked towards him, and knelt down in between his legs.

"They didn't want to mess with you, baby, because they could smell the tiger in you. They knew a predator, when they saw one."

Carl let out a 'harrumph' sound spontaneously, a subconscious questioning of what he was now compared to years gone by, clearly hanging heavy on his brow.

"I don't know about that, honey. I feel more and more, like an old man holding onto a weapon, scared he might have to use it 'cause he's too decrepit to do anything else."

He patted his right, front pocket to indicate the small, hammer-less revolver he kept there at all times, his concealed carry permit always ready in his wallet, as well. It was a gift from his father, several years ago, when he was first injured, and his life changed forever.

His dad understood what all it meant, for a man to lose his strength, his core vitality and ability to protect himself, on his own, without looking to anyone or anything else for help. He had been in a bad motorcycle accident when Carl turned thirteen. His dad's left leg was never the same after that, and a cane was standard issue for the rest of his life.

Carl looked off into the bedroom, not wanting to look Jessica in the eye. He hated feeling weak, much less acknowledging it to her.

"Hey, baby. Remember that old saying, about being as good once as you ever were? You may not be able to train and spar, all the time like you used to do, but you can still be a badass, if you have to be. You're still dangerous in my book; no doubt about it. So, chin up. I love you."

Carl stared deadpan at her.

"Did you just use some old redneck saying, to give me life advice?" Jessica giggled, and took another sip of her beer.

"That I just did, good sir. Yes, I did. And it's true." She took another sip. "And you know it," she said, tipping the beer in his direction, a subtle demand that he not argue with her on this one.

"Hmmm. Alright," Carl said, then downed his beer, and smiled at Jessica. "Tell me, does that apply to certain *other* areas of performance, as well, good lady?"

Jessica caught his drift, but looked around the apartment, which was still predominantly unpacked, and the mattress and box springs were still leaned against the wall, with the bed frame in pieces.

"The bed's not set up yet," she said, plainly, with a hint of sadness in her voice, that they couldn't take advantage of this uncommon spontaneity.

"Excuse me, dear lady, but your protests are insignificant in stature, and easily remedied."

Carl stood, kicked off his shoes, and walked into the bedroom, where Jessica watched him lay the box springs on the floor and then simply lay the mattress on top, without worrying about setting up the frame. He walked back and extended his hand. Jessica took it, and he helped her stand, then, suddenly, scooped her over his shoulder, and headed to the bedroom, Jessica squealing in delight, even as she kicked her feet, and struggled in mock fashion.

"Me thinks the lady protesteth falsely."

Carl tossed her down on the bed, unbuckled his pants and stripped them, off along with his underwear, his excitement clearly visible.

"What do you take me for, dear sir? A mere harlot?" Jessica laid her hand, dramatically, across her heart.

"Actually, no. The lady is the rightful spoils of my warfare conducted this very day in taking over this fortress, and I will have thee, as my reward, whether thee agrees to it, or not."

Carl squinted, a provocative look, challenging Jessica to take the bait, and run with it. It had been a long time since they had done this, but from the look on her face, Carl could tell that not only did she know it was on, but she was down for the game.

"You sir, will have to take it, if thou really wanteth it. I will not go, quietly." Jessica smiled, coyly, even as her eyes flashed a lustful desire, for the delicious struggle that was about to begin.

Carl grabbed Jessica by her feet, and pulled her to the edge of the bed, lifting her so her ass dangled in the air. He quickly wrapped his arms around both legs to hold her there, while he unbuttoned her pants, and then, shook her up and down, till they peeled off, along with her underwear, and she plopped back down on the bed, naked and exposed, from the waist down, vulnerable to any attempts he would make to penetrate her.

Jessica shrimped her hips back and forth to make space between them, smiling the whole time, but still trying to play at being unwilling, to a degree. As Carl came forward, on his knees, she used her feet, to push his hips away. He snaked his arms inside, and under her legs quickly, before she could maneuver them out of his grip, and back into position. He lowered his head, and locked both arms, right at the crook of her hips, pulling her in, and burying his face in her groin.

A moan escaped Jessica's mouth, as her back arched in delight. She let him devour her for almost a minute, before she forced herself, to keep the game afoot.

She shifted her hips and pressed the back of one thigh down on his head, forcefully pushing him onto his side. She skittered back, across the bed, in a hurry, her toned leg muscles, rippling as she went. Jessica came to rest on her knees, body erect, a challenging look bearing down on Carl, as she took off her shirt and bra, and cast them aside.

"You canst not have me, wretched sir. I am strong, and can take care of myself, as you have now seen. I will resist thee to my dying breath." She shook her head, in feigned defiance.

A devious smile sprang to Carl's mouth. He was giddy, like a schoolboy.

"My lady, prepare to have your hindquarters chastised for this insolent struggle against your rightful master. Hah!"

Carl lunged forward and they tied arms up, jockeying for position, Carl not overly using his size and strength, so as to keep it sporting and fun for a bit longer. They both executed techniques they had learned in the earliest days of their relationship, when they trained Brazilian Jiu-Jitsu together, learning how to wrestle and submit people with joint locks and chokes. It had been their form of occasional play during sex, all those years ago, but had slowly disappeared over time after Carl's workplace accident.

Jessica loved the pursuit, the push and pull, the maneuvering for one end only. The sheer desire on display. The way Carl struggled to have her, it aroused every inch of skin, and caused her to become unusually wet. She truly had missed this, the challenge, the roughhousing, but especially the way it made her feel so wanted.

Carl was now overcome, with his desire for Jessica. She could tell by how he pressed forward, with no thought as to what she might do. She seized the opportunity, and hip tossed him across the bed, slapping him full on in the face, before withdrawing a couple of feet, a victorious look blazing across her whole countenance.

"You, sir, are over-confident, and unworthy of my deliciously moist nether victuals," she declared, trying desperately not to laugh. "A real man would not have made such an amateurish error."

Jessica's face was ablaze with hormones and joy, and titillating cat and mouse adrenaline rushing through her whole body all at once. Carl read her like a well-perused book, intimately familiar with each page, even if it had been some time, since he observed these specific portions of text. She longed for him to catch her, fair and square, to exert his dominance and conquer her. She knew he could, and every visibly quivering fiber in her body, told Carl she ached for him to do it *now*, without *any* further delay.

"You mistake coy restraint, and playing with my food, for the real predator's pounce, my lady. So be it! Thou has asked for it with your lips and eyes and the heady scent of your sultry pheromones" he said, then spread his arms wide, and issued his declaration of licentious war with a deep, baritone voice that boomed within the bedroom.

"Prepare thee now to see this beast in all his devouring glory!"

Carl lunged forward, dropping low at the last second, as Jessica reached out to meet him. His redirect allowed him to enter all the way inside, and place his cheek on her stomach, while wrapping his right arm around her lower back, and the other her waist. He clasped his hands together, and pulled sharply, drawing her left side tight, against his chest; a dominant position to work from, undoubtedly solidified.

Jessica was thoroughly taken by surprise, and utterly excited by Carl's skilled performance. He didn't delay either, but instantly slipped around towards Jessica's back, pulling in on her gut with one hand, as he hooked under her other arm, and cupped the back of her head with his left hand - a technique in wrestling called a half. Control of her upper body and midsection secured, he folded Jessica forward, forcing her to catch herself with the one arm that could do anything.

Carl had a plan now, and was implementing it, without any pause or delay. He reached between her legs from behind, and cupped her pubic bone, lifting her hips high enough off the bed, that her knees lost contact with the mattress, before he snatched back, roughly moving her into a more prone position. Jessica squealed in surprise, then moaned. He grabbed the wrist of the hand keeping her upper body off the bed and pulled it all the way between her thighs; another classic wrestling maneuver called a Ball and Chain.

Her head crashed into the mattress and, before she could try to struggle, he gently trapped her calves with his right shin, keeping them pinned in place to the bed. He used the wrestling half, controlling her left shoulder and head, to keep her upper body from resisting, and the other arm as a control point...and for leverage. Forcefully pulling on her right arm trapped between her thighs, enabled Carl to pull her hips to meet his rock-hard phallus.

Jessica was *so* ready for him, too. Carl slid inside her, and she released a muffled scream of pure pleasure at having been finally caught, fair and square.

The rest of their adventurous role-play was a mutually enjoyed vulgar display of power as he dominated her fully, her head pinned down, and her hips incapable of escape, as he pounded away, over and over, till they both climaxed together for the first time in years. The whole thing was a fervent commotion of rapid shouts, moans and squalls, escalating to a crescendo of howling chaos that surely gave Janet, the boys and anyone else above or below them, something to talk about concerning the newest tenants.

Breathing heavily, they collapsed, and held each other for some time in silence, except for a few glowing compliments on each other's performances. In time, they nodded off for a nap, then rose again an hour later, to continue setting up their new home together, both happy and feeling quite content.

Over the next few days, they managed to get everything put away, and hardly left the apartment except, to go buy a few groceries. Jessica filed her unemployment documents over their computer. She had tried applying to several places online. Fewer and fewer employers actually wanted someone to walk in and make a face-to-face contact, which just made it easier, to be ignored and judged, according to mere words on paper, that, she believed, could never fully represent who she was.

It was very frustrating. And the pressure was on. Her unemployment would be running out soon, and she didn't think they would qualify for welfare, in addition to Carl's disability. But his disability wasn't enough to support them financially, and they both knew it.

He hadn't been able to work long enough to generate anything in Social Security. Carl had drawn the short straw at a very young age. Just having entered the work place a couple of years prior, he was cutting his teeth on a shit job in a shit factory that didn't give a damn for their employees. Carl's father had managed to get him a job, at the same chemical plant that his father had worked at for some twenty-five years. It had been a good place to work at, but a year after Carl started, a group of investors bought out the company, and everything went to hell with great haste.

They forced people, like Carl's dad, into retirement with packages far less valuable than what they had been promised by the past owners. But there was no choice. Take it or leave with nothing – fired. A year later, the accident happened, and the company fought Carl, tooth and nail, trying to blame him, and denying him any disability, until the court finally ruled in his favor.

Only thing though, the judge ordered just a fraction of what Carl's attorney was asking for. He couldn't help but think that there was some connection between the judge and the company; a favor owed, perhaps. Either way, it was a railroad dry fuck all around, and now Carl was financially and physically locked into an unchangeable set of circumstances that only got worse as the cost of living rose, and his body aged. He was only thirty-five years old, but Jessica knew he felt like he was sixty, half the time.

She hated it and hated what it did to him; especially what it did to him, emotionally. It was like gangrene, rotting him from the inside out, but he couldn't die. Some days, it just manifested as a general malaise that zapped his sense of humanity, extracted all the color and smell out of life and turned it bland, drab, and meaningless. Other days, the anger would strike the boiling point and flash forward on anyone nearby. His tongue would flail madly, and venom would hurl from it like, some spitting cobra, enraged.

But Jessica knew that was just the reality of it. Chronic pain and suffering do that to people and the longer it goes on, the worse it is. Cycle down to crushing depression and despair and then cycle up to violent displays of hate and discontent with what life has dealt a person. That's just reality though, she thought, a vicious, inescapable circle.

But God forbid, you be around and, in its path, when the bitter upswing took place and Carl's wrath flowed. At times, it had proven formidable, indeed, though never physically directed at her. The walls, however, were a different story, and never completely safe.

And yet, Jessica empathized, and understood the struggle. Carl didn't just give in and let go. He fought the anger, the rage, and the disappointment that never stopped gnawing at his guts. He did his best to not let it reign. And like everyone, some days you fight your demons, and some days you curl up fetal, too tired to fight, and just hope they don't fuck everything up while you're gone.

Jessica surfed the net, as her mind wandered. Hunting for anywhere nearby, that might be hiring. The only thing she could find was a temp agency. She dreaded the thought but saved the page. Sometimes, you have to do things you hate for the ones you love.

"Adulting 101, but no fun," Jessica mumbled, to herself.

On the bright side, she thought, five days here, and still no roaches had trespassed upon their isle of bug-free tranquility. That had to count for something. She tried to be the 'glass half full' gal to offset Carl's 'this is damn near empty and it's not even decent beer, it tastes like piss' attitude.

The struggle was real.

Carl was sleeping on his left side, facing the wall, when he first stirred from a good sleep, something itching, or perhaps better described as prickling, across the skin of his right shoulder blade area. His brain swam into consciousness slowly, as if through a viscous fluid that struggled against him. But, finally, his lucidity surfaced, and connected the dots, which revealed something on par with a paint by numbers picture to his mind.

It looked a lot like a big ass cockroach…and it was *moving*, surely crawling across his shoulder, the sensations rising and falling, in multiplicity with each light touch of exoskeleton legs, as they traversed space in fractions of millimeters.

Instinctual reflexes triggered by a fear common unto all men engaged, and

Carl's left hand shot up to scoop at his shoulder, where he felt the unwanted contact. His fingers curled around the form, and his hand flicked, the insect sent flying across the room to hit the wall.

"Fuck!" escaped his lips in a panicked cry, without a single thought.

Carl practically, levitated, into a seated position, as if his whole body uncoiled in opposition to the bed and propelled him upwards without ever using his arms at all, as they were already actively reaching for the switch on the bedside lamp.

Light flooded the space, dispelling darkness in a small circumference. It wasn't enough, though.

Jessica jerked into a semi-upright position, both hands planted in the mattress, her upper body twisted, hips and legs still left behind, frozen to the sheets.

"What's wrong?" she sputtered, her brain automatically wanting to understand just, what had startled her awake in such rude fashion.

Carl ran around the bed, his cock shriveled with a primal fear as he scrambled to turn on the overhead light and find the offending pest. His hand stuttered back and forth, up and down, across the wall in search for a switch, that his muscle memory had not yet had the hundreds of repetitions necessary, to fully program his body to find in an instant.

His ears heard a 'click' that sounded like angels singing on high, and the room flooded with a bright, but soft white light.

Jessica stared at him, like the mad man he appeared to be. His eyes bulging, as he skittered to and fro, frantically scanning every piece of carpet, and along the edge of the wall that was visible.

"*What* in the hell is wrong, Carl?" she demanded, in a firm voice, that was trying not to panic at the unknown, or give in to Carl's own expanding fear, that seemed to be filling the room, inch by inch, with each moment he did not answer her. She was convinced, then, that his fear was seeking to get inside her as well; to infect her.

"Do you know where the flashlight is?" he yelled at Jessica.

"Ummmm, yeah. I think so. *Why*?" She pleaded for an answer.

"Go get it! Now!" he spat the response as a strict order, and then followed up, knowing her well enough to be sure another question was coming, before she did what he asked. "Just get it, Jessica! No more questions, till that light is in my fucking hand!"

Jessica scrambled out of the bed, and out into the kitchen, where she tossed the contents of a catch-all drawer all about, till she got her hand on the flashlight. She ran back to the bedroom, turning it on as she went. Carl had just finished picking up the couple of boxes that still hadn't been unpacked and tossing them on the bed to see beneath them. He snatched the flashlight from her grip without a word, and threw the closet door open, shining the light every which way, moving shoes and other items around in a flurry, a desperate frenzy of activity to find the offending little creature of God, so he could kill it.... with extreme prejudice.

But as much as he hunted and searched, he could find nothing. No roaches, or anything else for that matter. He finally gave up and sat down on the edge of the bed. His chest tightened. He hurried over to the nightstand, grabbed the inhaler, and sucked in deeply, as he depressed the button.

He measured his breaths, nice and steady. The same. Each one the same.

One, two, three, IN, HOLD for one, two, three, and EXHALE for one, two, three. Over and over, he repeated the cycle he had learned in training, to control adrenaline. Jessica gently scooted over behind him and rubbed his back with one hand, and his hair with the other, waiting silently till he had things under control again. When he was ready to talk, he let out his usual indicatory big sigh.

Jessica calmly asked him "What were you looking for, baby?"

"Some fucking bug that was crawling on my shoulder and woke me up." He took a big breath and let it out slowly.

"What kind, hon?

"I don't know. When I reached up, and felt it, I just slung it across the room without thinking. Then I couldn't find it."

Jessica continued to rub his back.

"You think the roaches finally arrived?" She gave a small, calculated laugh to try and set him more at ease.

"I don't think so. It didn't feel like a roach. It was long, three inches or more maybe…and narrow…and it felt like it had lots of legs. When I grabbed it, it felt like the little fucker curled into a ball almost as I threw him. What the hell does that sound like to you, Jess?"

Carl turned around to face her for the first time, genuine concern framing his face. She knew how much he hated bugs. Any kind of bug, just about. He didn't freak at just the sight of them, but if he thought they might get on him, that was a whole-nother circumstance. *DefCon* level ONE initiated, immediately. Jess thought about what he described.

"Well, if we were living out in the country, I'd probably say it sounds like a centipede, and a big one at that, but I didn't think you would find them here in the inner city.

More than a bit of terror filled Carl's eyes, as well as a strong sense of incredulity.

"A centipede? A fucking centipede? Are you fucking kidding me, Jess?

Seriously, don't be fucking around with me about this…"

He tapered off and waited for her to speak again. She touched his arm, a soft, intentional connection meant to help him calm down.

"Yes, baby. It really does sound like a centipede, but it could be something else. I tell you what. Let's sleep with the lights on the rest of the night. Most bugs don't want to come out in the light. They prefer the dark. Does that sound like a good plan? Hmm."

Carl looked her in the eye and dropped his head, ashamed of his fear.

"Yeah. That sounds like a rational response, babe. Thanks."

Carl laid back and pulled the sheet up and turned on his side again, facing away from Jessica. Jessica laid back down as well and rubbed Carl's back, until he could fall back asleep. The rest of the night was, thankfully, uneventful.

Carl used the daylight to prepare, in case it happened again. He put away everything in the boxes and cleared the floor. He decided he needed a beer around midday, and went to the store to grab one, but only after shaking out his shoes, vigorously. The flashlight was placed on his nightstand along with spare batteries in case the current ones failed in the midst of an emergency. He also designated a plastic lunch container to help trap the critter, because he couldn't just stomp it with no shoes on. But that made him think further, and he took a magazine, rolled it up tight, and wrapped it with some duct tape to keep it closed.

This, too, went on the nightstand.

It was like watching the kid in Fright Night, getting ready to fight the vampire in the final scene. At least that's what occurred to Jessica as she watched all Carl's preparations in silence, not saying a judgmental word to him, at all.

Carl slept through the night, not waking once, until he began to stir from his slumber, ready to get up. He was lying on his back, his whole body heavy, as he came around in stages. Jessica was already out of bed. He smelled eggs...and pancakes. She's such a doll, he thought to himself, gratitude for her, filling his heart.

The next sensation was not so pleasant. He turned his head to look at the clock and his right ear throbbed suddenly with pain. He rubbed the indentation behind that ear, trying to press in on the ear canal where it hurt.

Something pushed back...and then wriggled about inside his ear.

Carl's eyes went wide as he jumped out of bed, ignoring the pain, and ran into the kitchen screaming for Jessica.

"Jess! Jess! There's something in my ear! There's something in my ear! Oooooooooooooo!! Fuck! Fuck! Fuck! There's something in my ear!!!"

His voice was so high pitched and whiny, Jessica thought it could have been a kid.

"What are you saying, Carl? I can't understand anything but fuck and ear!"

He sat down at the computer; his right hand still pressed against the back of his ear.

"There is something…in my ear!" he spat out slower.

He used his left hand to hunt and peck and do a Google search for 'What does it feel like to have a centipede in your ear?' He hit enter and one of the first entries was about a Chinese man who woke up with a centipede in his ear.

Jess read over his shoulder, and her hand flew to her mouth.

"Holy shit! You think you have a centipede in your ear, baby?" Her stomach tilted a bit at the thought.

Carl ignored her as he read, all his focus on this poor man's tale and whatever similarities they might have. Carl's free hand covered his own mouth as he gasped.

"What is it?!? What is it?!?" Jessica was letting his panic contaminate her.

"I have the *exact* same symptoms he did. Woke up with pain in my ear and it feels like there's something wriggling in there! Fuck! Fuck! Fuck!"

Carl jumped to a standing position and began pacing.

"OOOOOOO GOD!!!! What the *fuck* am I gonna do now? I've got a *motherfucking* centipede in my ear!!!!" And again, as if he couldn't believe it himself, "I've got a *moth-er fuck-ing* centipede in my ear Jess!!!"

Carl's whole body trembled, and his knees nearly buckled, completely. He turned in circles rubbing his ear. Jess quickly read the rest of the short article.

"They said the guy went to the hospital, and a doc pulled it out with some forceps. We've got to take you to the ER. Get dressed."

"FUUUUUUUUCK!!!" Carl shouted at the top of his lungs. "We can't afford it. We don't have any fucking insurance, yet! Is there anything you can do here?"

Carl whined, as he asked for help, a trembling falsetto having overtaken his vocal cords. A tightness constricted his chest, also, as if some boa constrictor was wrapped tight around his torso, intent on killing him. He couldn't breathe.

"Hold on!" Jess exclaimed, as she pulled up YouTube, and typed into the search bar. She quickly found what she was looking for, to confirm her thoughts.

She heard the thump of Carl's body collapsing into the recliner, and the ever too familiar wheezing noises, before even turning around. She didn't even look at him, just ran to the bedroom, and returned with his inhaler, holding it to his mouth, and administering the dose.

"Breathe, baby. Just calm down and breathe. It's going to be ok. Just breathe, slow and steady. Breathe. Alright, I want you to lay down on your side, that ear up." She pointed at his right ear, as she helped him lay the recliner back, and eased him onto his left side.

"Alright, baby, just keep breathing, while I grab something." She scampered into the bathroom, grabbed tweezers then hurried into the kitchen to grab a cup of water and a dish towel. She returned, and moved about at a steady pace, implementing her plan. Jessica laid the dish towel around Carl's ear, set the tweezers down on his shoulder, pulled his ear lobe out to open up the ear canal and started pouring water into it a little at the time.

Carl startled at the water entering his ear.

"What are you doing?" he questioned her actions, trusting Jessica, but wanting her to make it make sense to him.

"I saw a video, awhile back, of a doctor getting a spider to crawl out of a kid's ear by pouring water in it, till the spider had to climb out or drown. I looked it up, and sure enough, there was a video of someone doing the same thing for a centipede. Just lay still. It'll work and quick too, I bet."

Carl lay silent as Jessica poured more, and more water in.

"I can feel it moving." Carl sounded like he was going to be sick.

"Fuck!" Jessica shouted the word, startled as the centipede, suddenly, came crawling out of Carl's ear in a hurry, speeding over his shoulder, and dropping off the side of the recliner, to the floor, before she could hardly blink much less act.

"It's out! It's out!" she shouted to Carl.

"Where is it?" he shouted in response, not feeling able to breathe right, quite yet nor sit up.

"I don't *knoooow*!" Jessica cried in frustration, as she stomped her feet, and moved about in a tizzy, a deep distress at not knowing where the centipede had disappeared to seizing her.

After a long moment of silence, she screamed again.

"FUCK!!! I lost it! I lost the fucking thing, Carl! I'm so sorry!"

Carl blindly reached for her. He touched her side, and grabbed her shirt, pulling her toward him. He was measuring his breathing in between words.

"It's ok, baby. It's ok. You did great. You got the damn thing out of my head.

That's the most important part. You're a champ. I love you."

Carl stopped talking at that point, and focused on breathing, to get the asthma attack under control.

Jessica grabbed the bottle of tequila in the cabinet, took two shots then sat down to eat pancakes while she kept a close eye on Carl.

That night the lights stayed on. Jessica had gone to the store, to buy ear plugs for them, earlier in the day, and they both said muffled goodnights, after firmly placing the foamies in each ear. Jessica, also, wore underwear to bed, something Carl knew she hated, with a passion. But she was concerned that, if it could crawl in an ear, it might be able to crawl up there, too. The mere mention caused her whole upper body to shudder in distaste and with a hostile aversion.

She got no argument from Carl. Hell, after hearing Jessica's fear he put his underwear on, afraid the centipede might bite his dick or crawl up his ass. They slid the little black eye blinders over their heads too, something else Jessica thought of, to help them sleep with the lights on.

Jessica rubbed Carl's back and tried to lighten the mood.

"Hey baby. Sleep tight..." Her voice trailed off, as she paused.

"Don't you dare do it," Carl said, bluntly.

"Don't let the bed bugs bite!" Jessica blurted it out, busting out, laughing as she did so.

Carl rolled over, and started tickling her, his fingers scratching lightly all over her, trying to simulate a centipede's legs crawling over her. Jessica's body twitched and turned and bucked and rolled.

"Stop it! Stop it!" she cried, with a limp authority Carl could never respect, but he stopped anyway, out of mercy and a desire to get to sleep and stop thinking about the heinous critter.

"You little shit," Jessica said deadpan, and giggled a bit.

"You started it," Carl responded. "Just sayin. Don't kick the hornet's nest, again."

He flashed a smile and rolled back over.

"Love you, babe." She draped an arm over his waist and drew close.

"Love you too, Jess."

The next three nights passed uneventfully. Carl actually slept ok, but Jessica couldn't stay asleep for any longer than twenty minutes, before waking up to look around. She did notice, both day and night, there still weren't any roaches in their apartment.

A search online revealed that centipedes eat roaches. But how many would there have to be, to keep out all those roaches in an infested place, like this building? That little thought did *not* help her sleep at all.

The fifth evening after removing the centipede from Carl's ear, they were sitting in the living room watching TV when Jessica saw Carl, out of the corner of her eye, jump out of the recliner and sprint into the kitchen. He started violently stomping the floor over and over, appearing to chase something across the floor as he missed, missed, missed and finally hit the target. He ground his foot back and forth, several times, before cautiously lifting it. There was a smear of innards on the linoleum, but the centipede carcass was imbedded in the tread of his shoe.

"Gotcha! You little belly, crawling fucker!!!" he yelled, in triumph.

Carl grabbed a napkin, and pulled the centipede off his shoe, and presented it for Jessica to see that he, the mighty hunter, had killed their deadly enemy, then tossed its cursed carcass in the trash.

Jessica applauded him, energetically.

"Oh my God! Yes! I can finally sleep-in peace, tonight! This deserves a toast!"

Jessica retrieved the shot glasses, and poured two shots, drank one of them, and refilled it, then toasted with Carl, and downed the other.

"I'm taking a sleeping pill tonight. I do not want to wake up for nothing. I need some quality rest."

Jessica grabbed one out of the medicine cabinet, downed it and told Carl she was laying down, naked.

"Ooo la la!" Carl said, a little sarcastically, knowing there would be no sex after a sleeping pill. "I'll be right there."

In no time, they were both out cold, content, and feeling secure, even without the lights, ear plugs and underwear.

Carl was snatched from his blissful slumber, by Jessica jumping up and down on the bed, making sounds like an alley cat squalling, before a fight or sex, or both. He sat up and opened his eyes to see Jessica going, from jumping, to bent over, as her hips cringed backwards, and gyrated about, in a way, which was not the least bit sensual. Pain and hysteria had seized her. There could be only one possible explanation, it seemed to Carl and, at that moment, he had the strangest thought intrude upon his brain, in the midst of this chaotic fervor.

"There is no possible combination of words that could possibly comfort a woman, who believes a centipede is crawling around up inside her twat."

"Nope. Not one," he told himself, out loud, "Unh, unh."

He stared on, in shock, unable to completely accept, that this situation could actually be happening. It seemed more likely to be a dream, but Jessica's next shriek hit such a high note and hurt Carl's ears.

The surreal quality, of what was happening, wore off, as if on cue, and his mental faculties began firing on all cylinders. Jessica had saved the day for him. He began thinking frantically, trying to determine what he could do, to save her from this hell that could only be exponentially worse than the centipede being inside his ear.

"She has a centipede inside her vagina," he thought again, and shivered at this terror, that no sane person would ever want to even consider, much less give voice to. But it was happening, and Carl needed to man the fuck up, and be the fucking hero, he told himself.

Jessica fell flat on the bed, and began kicking, twisting and bucking wildly. She was like some crazy woman in a possession movie, where the priest is now waist deep in the exorcism rites, locked in mortal struggle with the demon, speaking in Latin, throwing holy water and gripping his crucifix as he presses it to the creature's forehead, causing the demon to make the girl's body go completely spastic.

"That's exactly what my wife looks like, right now," he thought, mind sliding back, briefly, into a dumb morass of inaction, overcome by these traumatic and bizarre events.

"Think, Carl. Think!" he slapped himself in the face, as he continued to speak out loud, to keep himself moving forward. "Aaarrgghh! Think! Think! Think! What can you do? Ummmm...If she used water in my ear, to make it want to leave, what the fuck can I use to do the same thing to her pussy??? Dammit, man! It's not like I've got a fucking garden hose lying around! What can I do?!?!?"

Carl palmed his forehead, hard, and something, suddenly, clicked.

"A douche! A douche!" he exclaimed, an immensely exuberant look displaying his utter excitement at a possible solution.

"Fuck! Jess! Where do you keep your pack of strawberry douches?" She didn't answer. In fact, she wasn't screaming anymore. Carl looked over, and Jessica was unconscious, her body doing a little jig as some kind of mild seizure took control.

Carl let loose a startled yelp but kept his composure. He ran to the bathroom, and looked under the counter, tossing stuff out, till he found the box of douches. He quick read the directions, and prepared two of them, just in case it took more water than he thought. Scrambling back into the bedroom, he inserted it into her vagina and began squeezing it in a steady manner, pushing the fluid up inside her.

When the first one was empty, he tossed it aside, and picked up the other. He was getting ready to put it in, and start round two, when he saw a dark-colored antenna protrude from his wife's vagina; something no man should ever have to imagine, much less watch.

He waited, unconsciously holding his breath at this weird, totally alien encounter, something that, possibly, had never happened before in the history of mankind, he thought. His stomach knotted as another antenna appeared, followed by the glistening armored plates, a deep brownish-red in color, covering the head and each segment of the centipede, as it squeezed out, squirming back and forth to help free one set of legs at a time from Jessica's labia. Every limb fluttered lightly up and down, independent of one another, meticulously searching for any point of purchase to pull the body out by.

Carl felt lightheaded. The room was beginning to spin, the world flexing and relaxing with each breath he struggled to take in, the impossibility of what he was seeing, overwhelming his dire need to deny what his own eyes were telling him.

"Lying eyes! Lying eyes!" he muttered, loudly to himself, closing them hard, and rubbing them vigorously, before opening them again, only to have the traitorous bastards reveal the inconceivable reality that was this insane moment of his life; drawn out like some man dropping from the gallows in slow motion, waiting for the noose to snap tight, and end it all. The inexorable dread of that moment was his presently, only elongated and exponentially more insidious.

About seven inches of the giant centipede's body was exposed now, as it continued to flail back and forth. A pale white belly peeked out, here and there, even as the large overlapping plates that covered each segment of its back flexed, side to side, and open and closed. It used the multi-jointed yellow and red legs to pull against both Jessica's inner thighs as well as the new-found comforter.

Carl's lungs closed up tight, and the wheezing began.

The giant centipede secured sufficient traction as its legs hooked into the covers and pulled with an incredible strength, allowing it to rapidly extract the rest of itself from Jessica's flooded vaginal canal.

Life resumed normal speed for Carl as another six inches or more or appeared quickly before the centipede finally plopped out onto the bed, dual horn-like objects protruding from its rear, shaking at the ceiling in a flurry as it took off in an unpredictably snaking path, then disappeared over the edge of the bed and out of sight.

Jessica's seizures stopped about the same time Carl passed out from lack of oxygen.

Jessica came to with a gasp, sitting up and covering her groin with both hands, the instinct to protect her currently most vulnerable and sensitive area kicking in with consciousness.

The first thing she noticed was that it didn't hurt inside anymore. Not bad anyway. Just a dull ache, like the fading memory of something quite painful. The second thing she saw was Carl passed out in front of her...and she couldn't tell whether he was breathing or not.

She immediately located his inhaler, stuck it in his mouth and squeezed it, then pinched his nose, tilted his head back and blew into his mouth to try and make sure the medicine got to his lungs. After a couple of breaths Jessica listened to his chest. She could hear the heart doing its job, thump, thumping along. He was breathing too, just ultra-shallow.

After a minute of intense inspection, Carl coughed hard, and his inhalations became normal again, if somewhat labored.

Jessica let out a huge sigh. This wasn't the first time it had happened. She'd had to force the medicine into his lungs while he was unconscious a handful of times over the last 12 years of their marriage, but it always freaked her out.

She looked around, trying to figure out what had happened. She observed a large wet spot where her hips had been, when she passed out. There was a very narrow, light trail of water snaking across the covers and off the bed. She suspected that might have been a centipede running off...but to make that wide of a trail, it would have been huge. Upon scanning the room further, she observed a full douche laying on the bed, and an empty one on the floor.

She looked at Carl with nothing but love, her face softening, as she considered what he must have gone through, seeing her pass out, and then having to use a douche on her, and watch a centipede crawl out of the place that he always craved to be inside, himself.

He had surely scrambled, to come up with a way to get it out of her, while working himself up into a panic, eventually passing out, when the asthma attack put his lungs on full lockdown.

Jessica felt closer to him right then, than she had in some time. Lying down, she curled up against Carl and rubbed his chest lightly till he finally woke up.

"I swear to God, Jess! I am *not* messing with you! That thing was as long as my fucking forearm and a good inch and a half or more in width! I'm fucking scarred for life, after watching that thing crawl out of your cooch. All squirming and flailing around," Carl sat forward in the recliner, as he made twisting and flopping movements with his hands and arms to illustrate what he meant. It clearly grossed Jessica out by the contortions her face went through, after blanching at the thought of it.

Carl didn't want her to possibly puke, so he decided to pursue a little humor, to break the granite level tension.

"I'm telling you, it was having to struggle damn hard to defeat the suction power of those wonderfully soft sugar walls you got there."

Carl pointed at her crotch, to further indicate the location meant by 'there'. A smile began to creep across his face, as he tried not to laugh at his own joke. Jess stared back at him, hard, flustered by the timing of his off-color humor, but the more he smiled and giggled the closer she visibly came to laughing.

At last, unable to hold it back any longer, a snicker followed by a short burst of giggles escaped once the seal was broken. She slapped Carl on the arm, but never stopped smiling the whole time.

"The suction power of my sugar walls, huh?"

"Your wonderfully soft sugar walls," Carl corrected her, index finger held up to emphasize he was reiterating a very crucial point. Jessica's eyes sparkled, and her mouth made an 'O'. Carl suspected some memory in her cold storage, had just been thawed out.

"Dammit! I just realized you went full' Sheena Easton' on me. Sugar Walls!"

She pushed him away, playfully. "Get outta here!" She waved him off with both hands.

The shit-eating grin spreading across Carl's face beamed bright enough it caused Jessica to laugh so hard, she snorted. Carl cackled in response, and Jessica snorted again. They both busted out in unrestrained hilarity for some time, unable to stop themselves, tears rolling down their cheeks and ribs hurting.

By the time they settled back down, Jessica appeared quite relaxed, as if a load of tension had been released inside her body, all the way down to her toes and fingertips.

"I just can't believe the *size* of the centipede you're describing," she said, out of the blue. "I mean, I've heard of it; just not around here, though. You know?"

"I've never heard of it at all, but I felt like I was in that King Kong movie, with Jack Black, for a minute; watching Andy Serkis get eaten by that giant nightmare creature that should not be named."

The grin began to blossom again.

"Knock it off."

Jessica put the smack-down on any further silliness. Carl knew that look. It was time to do business and figure out just what the hell was going on.

"OK," Carl frowned slightly, and adopted a serious tone. "How do you feel...down there? And by the way, have you ever had seizures before? Because you sure as hell looked like you were having one when you passed out."

Jessica looked surprised at the mention of seizures.

"Well, down there feels fine, right now. No more serious pain and no more squirmy wiggles, just a little bit of soreness. As far as seizures, my mom used to get grand mal seizures every now and then. I had one when I was a teenager after having a panic attack."

"Alright. That explains that, pretty much, I think. I don't feel so worried now. You *seem* fine." He let his voice trail off with an interrogative tone, waiting for Jessica to confirm his assessment.

Jessica nodded her head.

"I do feel fine. A little fatigued, but that's common after a seizure. No biggie. My mom rode 'em out like a champ all the time. No doctor needed."

Carl gave her a look of pure skepticism.

"What!?" she challenged. "I'm fine, and I'm not going to needlessly burden us with any medical debt that can be avoided."

"And you're sure those sugar walls are unharmed?"

Carl winked at Jessica; a mischievous look mixed with true concern.

"I mean, you know I've invested a lot in that product." Carl placed a hand over his heart to show his sincerity and commitment. "I can't be having it ruined.

Though I don't think I'll be able to touch it till after your next period when you've shed all those corrupted skin cells. I mean, *just the thought* right now is kind of turning my stomach a little."

Carl faked a burp.

"Oh yeah. That was, uh...chunky."

Jessica picked up a couch pillow and threw it at Carl's head. His arms flinched upward just in time to cover his face.

"You little shit! Knock it off," she said, pointing her slender index finger at his face as if she wished it was stabbing him.

She stormed over to the computer and sat down, but he saw the glimpse of a smile tugging at the corner of her mouth as she turned away.

Jessica spun around for one last parting shot.

"And I'll have you know, the douche you used in me was perfectly capable of cleaning me out...but I *am* going to shower as soon as I look something up."

She faced the computer again, and her fingers began rattling away on the keys. It didn't take long before Carl heard her sharply suck in wind. He looked up to see both Jessica's hands covering her mouth.

"OH, MY FUCKING GAWD," she said loudly, then started waving frantically for Carl to come over to the computer. "You have *GOT* to see this

Carl!"

Carl quickly walked up behind Jessica, bending over her shoulder to get a good look at the screen. Jessica clicked 'Play' and everything went in motion. Some guy was holding up a giant centipede just like the one Carl had seen crawl out of Jessica. It was easily a foot long. Probably a little longer.

"*Scolopendra gigantea,*" Carl repeated what he heard the guy say on the video.

"*That's* what you saw crawl out of me?!? It was *that* big?!???" Jessica twisted her head around and looked at Carl with absolute incredulity.

"Baby, *that* is exactly what I saw crawl out of you." Carl tapped the screen for emphasis.

Jessica looked back at the monitor and just stared at it in awe. A shiver ran up her spine, causing her whole body to shudder briefly.

"Fuck me," Jessica said plainly, wiping her hands down her face. "This is just too fucking crazy. It says here these are native to South America and the Caribbean. There's also another type found in Vietnam that can get really big too."

Jessica paused for a long moment then more mumbled to herself than Carl, "What the fuck are they doing in our apartment?"

That night, at bed, the lights were on, ear plugs were in, and Jessica had even dug out some old cough masks, like they issued people to wear in ER waiting rooms when they were infectious. Those were strapped in place, covering both their mouths and noses. Jessica was freshly showered for the third time that day, her vagina thoroughly scoured with soap and a tampon soaked with more of the douche liquid inserted inside to both help further sanitize her lady parts overnight and make damn sure *nothing* could possibly crawl inside her. Underwear were added for additional shielding.

It took an hour or more, but they fell asleep.

Sometime later, it was a pulling sensation, on her underwear, that started to bring Jessica out of her slumber. She was fetal, on her side, facing Carl, when a sensation of insect legs registered on the back of her upper thighs, and there was a distinct pulling of her underwear directly over her vaginal entrance. Every one of her muscles contracted in some instinctive acrobatic maneuver that sent her body spinning towards her side of the bed, completely lifted above the mattress. She landed like a cat on all fours and immediately saw the Scolopendra.

"God, this can't be happening," her mind told her, but she knew it was. It started to scramble towards the edge of the bed, but Jessica's brain was in the fight, now. She grabbed the blanket, with both hands spread apart, lifted it, then slammed the material down over the giant insect's body. Without hesitating, Jessica tracked her hands inward, till she isolated the centipede and trapped it with the covers in a very small space. The outline of it twisting and turning was clearly visible.

Carl's hand appeared out of nowhere. He had launched into action just behind Jessica, grabbing a pocketknife, and opening it while Jessica did her part. He pressed the blade down across the hidden form, pressing in roughly till he heard, and felt, the exoskeleton cracking, then he dragged the edge across it, maintaining a strong downward pressure. The blanket opened up like a zipper as he felt the knife cut fully through the centipede's body.

He pulled the blade back and looked at it. There was a dark brown viscous smear on each side of it. He and Jess could both see the divided body parts spastically twitching and thrashing around through the slit in the cover, but it wasn't enough for Jessica. She pulled the blanket back all the way to see clearly.

It was cut into three pieces; the blade having sliced through it while it was partially curled up. Carl scanned the body till he found the segment with the large pincers, then immediately brought the edge down, bisecting it just below the chitinous plate protecting the centipede's head. The pieces continued moving for some time despite the vivisection and decapitation.

Carl retrieved a gallon size Ziploc bag. After putting all the segments inside, he sealed it and threw it down on the bed, frustration evident despite their victory.

"Tomorrow, I'm gonna ask Derek and his friends about this freakin' monster." He pointed at the bag. "As much as they roam this place, I can't believe that they haven't at least seen one of these around the complex at some point or heard rumor of some sighting. *And* I'm going to call our piece of shit landlord and demand he hire an exterminator.... fuck this shit."

"What the *fuck* do you mean you '*can't*' hire an exterminator'? I've got the corpse of a friggin' giant centipede in a *motherfucking* gallon-size Ziploc baggie....you think I'm exaggerating? I'm holding it in my god damn hand!!!"

Jessica stared at Carl, as he paused again to listen to the response of the landlord on the other end; all the while pacing like a caged animal, ready to attack anything that came near it. His neck muscles were rigid with rage. She hadn't seen him this pissed off in a very long time, but she knew his anger at life in general had been simmering for years, now. This was definitely a righteous cause for him to vent some of that pent-up hostility and frustration that he had been fighting to restrain for so long.

Carl's whole body stopped all movement at once, right before words exploded from his mouth, the rest of his torso and head shaking like volcanic earth, as the top is blown away in a pyroclastic cloud of destruction.

"*WHAAAAAAAT*?!?!?" Carl yelled, holding the phone out in front of his face, momentarily, to fully scream in it - his tone of voice ratcheted up several octaves, his face beet red. "I tell you what then, you fucking prick: if another one of these giant bastards shows up, and hurts my wife I'll be on your doorstep faster than you can call the police, and I *will* fuck you up!!!! And, as an additional bonus, you piece of shit, I'll bring the cocksucker over there, and let him crawl down your *motherfucking* throat!!!!"

Carl threw the cordless phone across the room, into the couch cushions, and screamed, head arced back.

"FUUUUUCCKKKK!!! That mother-fucking bastard said it wasn't his responsibility! Can you believe that bullshit, Jess?"

He turned to her livid with frustration, and just wanting her to acknowledge his right to feel it.

"It's ok, honey." Jessica stood and walked over to him, slipping her arms around his waist from behind him. "You tried. And you're right. He's a piece of shit landlord running a piece of shit apartment complex. We'll handle things ourselves. OK? We'll make it work. It's ok."

She rubbed his stomach and chest lightly, rhythmically, as she spoke. In a minute, his body began to relax, the tremors subsiding, till he was still. She felt him breath in deep, chest expanding, then blow it all out, at a slow, measured rate.

"How 'bout you go talk with Derek and the boys, and see what they know? I think that's a solid starting point."

Carl turned around, and kissed her on the forehead, before giving her a long hug.

"You got it, baby. I love you. I'll be back in a little bit."

Jessica kissed him on the lips once, and he walked out the door, the Ziploc bag in hand.

Carl didn't have to search far, at all. Derek and the boys were outside, burning cockroaches with their homemade flamethrowers.

"Hi fellas."

Derek and the boys turned, simultaneously, to look at him, all of them looking guilty, except for Derek. Derek had the poker face, no emotion, and nothing to indicate his activities. He might have been helping an old lady across the street, or bagging dope, or burning roaches with lighters and hairspray. You'd never know, to look at him, in that moment.

Derek gave a slight nod, in greeting, and Carl continued walking over.

"Hey, Derek. Guys." Carl nodded at Derek, and then the other boys. "I need y'all's opinion on something."

Derek cocked an eyebrow, an unconscious show of interest.

"I need to know if you've seen something around the apartment complex, and if so, what you know about them. It's pretty gnarly, actually. Can y'all take a look at it?"

Carl held out the gallon baggy, with the giant centipede pieces inside.

All the boys perked up with recognition at the sight of it but waited for Derek to speak first.

"Did you find that in your apartment?" Derek inquired, cool as a cucumber. The boy was a natural at bargaining, Carl thought.

"Yes, I did Derek. And it was quite the fucking surprise, I'll tell ya. And..." Carl caught himself getting angry again, and paused briefly, trying to reduce the emotions he visibly expressed. It would only make him appear more desperate and Derek would be keen to capitalize on that, during whatever negotiations, he could feel, were about to begin.

"And the landlord says he won't pay to have an exterminator come out to our apartment. So, Derek, I can tell you all know what this is, and it appears you know something pertinent to my current situation. What can you tell me?"

"Well, first, is this you calling in the debt for the bonus stuff you showed us, or are we going to negotiate here? 'Cause I just happen to know some important things that you don't, about your apartment..."

Derek let that last piece of info just hang in the air.

"Derek," Carl said, a big smile plastered across his face, "I thought we were friends..." Carl placed his free hand over his heart, as if the thought of them not being friends pained him.

"Well, Carl, we're friendly. This is true. Which also means we can help each other out. How 'bout that?"

Carl looked down at the Mafiosi-style kid, and smirked.

"Alright. So how can I help you out, after you help me out?" Derek spit an answer right out.

"Another pack of lighters and four cans of hairspray."

"Deal," Carl said, without hesitation.

"Alright then," Derek grabbed the gallon baggy from Carl's hand, and held it up. "This, here, is Scolopendra gigantae. Native to Peru, and other parts of South America, particularly within the Amazon Jungle. Now, as to how this big, nasty fucker ended up in your apartment, that requires a little history lesson." Derek gave a grin; the kind people give when they know something really juicy the other party has no clue about.

"They didn't tell you the last person in your apartment died, did they?"

"What?" Carl's mouth dropped open, slightly, as the single word toppled out.

"Yeah. Actually, killed, but, ultimately, that's not really important to your current dilemma. Anyway, the victim, slash tenant, was this middle-aged Asian guy, who went by the name Kenneth Wong. Weird, nerdy type and a real recluse. Hardly ever came out of the apartment. Did everything online; even had his groceries delivered. And if he needed something in a hurry, he'd pay one of us to go get it for him."

Derek indicated himself and the boys.

"Now, one day, after I went and got a couple items from the hardware store for him, he let me come inside, and *ho-ly* shit, man!" Derek's face became more expressive than Carl had seen it so far.

"That crazy dude had about twenty fish tanks, with these giant centipedes inside! Several of them had momma centipedes, with a shit ton of kids in different stages of development. Some looked like newborns, and others like decent-sized regular centipedes. If you didn't know what they were, you wouldn't realize they had a lot of growing to do. It was sick, though, man! I mean cool and interesting, but nasty as hell, at the same time. He was actually breeding them to sell. He was the supplier for some online store that sold lots of exotic insects to people for pets."

Carl felt a little nausea tickling at the bottom of his stomach.

"Anyway," Derek continued, "he must have started doing business with some shady, black market types, and screwed someone over, cause two tatted up Asian guys showed up here, late one night, and shot his ass dead. I don't think even the police know how it went down, exactly, but I was down the hallway, just come out of Ricky's place, when I saw them go in Mr. Wong's apartment. They looked sketchy as fuck, so I went down there, and listened outside the door. I heard talking, not sure whether it was Chinese, Korean or Japanese. I don't know, but I think they were going to take all his centipedes as payment for something, and not just kill him."

"What made you think that?" Carl asked.

"Well, I heard Mr. Wong scream at them, and then the fish tanks started shattering on the floor. One after another, after another. Then it sounded like they were wrestling around, and more tanks got knocked over. One of the guys screamed, and then there were two muffled shots from a handgun. Maybe a silencer, I think. I scrambled down the hall and ducked into the edge of the stairwell. Right then, Mrs. Janet peeked out her door, holding onto her walker with one hand, and her phone pressed to her ear in the other, talking to the police. Those guys busted out of Mr. Wong's door, in a hurry. One of them was holding his neck and clinching a big bag in the other hand. The other guy had a bag as well and was holding a pistol in the other. The barrel was really long, and he quick shoved it in Mrs. Janet's face, and told her 'Bitch! You ain't seen a thing!", and then took off."

"Wow. Holy shit. What happened next?"

"Well, before the police could get there, I peeked inside. Mr. Wong was stumbling around, knocking over the rest of the fish tanks. Freeing all the centipedes that the guys hadn't snatched up. After he finished crashing the last one, he collapsed and stopped breathing. I watched all those ugly bastards crawl off, out of sight, the momma ones carrying their little babies, as they went. By the time the police got there, all they found were empty tanks. They never figured out what was in them before they left or when they came back around later, asking questions. I didn't tell 'em shit."

"Holy fuck," Carl spat out, in disgust. "You mean, there's a shit-load of those monsters in my apartment, Derek?"

"Well, maybe. Hard to say where they went. Whether they all stayed in your place or went somewhere else. I mean, they like warm, dark places best...oh shit!" Derek exclaimed, an epiphany having struck him, all of a sudden.

"What?!?" Carl demanded.

"One of the big water heaters, for the complex, is in between your apartment, and the old man next to you, that's closest to the stairs. I bet those fuckers are in your walls, all around that water heater, cozy as hell."

"You know something strange?" Carl asked Derek.

"What?" Derek was genuinely interested in what Carl might have to say.

"We haven't seen any roaches in our apartment, since we moved in. Not one damn roach."

"That makes sense. I bet the centipedes are eating the hell out of them, in your walls, before they ever get to the inside of the apartment. I know Mr. Wong used to let a few of his run around the apartment, and eat any of the roaches that came in."

Carl shook his head. "That dude was sick in the head. We were dreading life for a few days, after we first saw this fucker, and knew he was roaming around the apartment." Carl jabbed his finger at the baggy, wishing he could send flames from the tip, as he said 'fucker'.

"So, then, what's the plan Carl?"

Carl looked down at Derek, lips pursed in concentration, as his brain flipped through various possibilities, then settled on the one he felt was right.

"Well, that depends. Can I get y'all to help?"

"That depends, Carl. What do you have in mind, and what's in it for us?"

Damn he's a handful, Carl thought.

"Well, my plan is to take a sledgehammer to those walls, and torch every last one of those bastards, and their young, I can find with our little makeshift flamethrowers. Jessica can stand by with a fire extinguisher, and I'll pull the batteries on the smoke alarm. You guys want to cook some centipedes?"

All the boys' eyes lit up, and they nodded their heads, vigorously.... except Derek. He had a sly look on his face.

"On one condition," he said.

"Name it," Carl answered.

"We get to keep some of them, for ourselves. I saw Mr. Wong fight them against other insects, spiders, even small snakes and lizards. It was cool as hell. I'd like to make some videos and put them on YouTube. That'd be badass."

Derek smiled big, and the other boys chimed in their agreement.

Carl shook his head, unable to understand the attraction, but willing to agree to it, for their help.

"You got it." Carl extended his hand to Derek, and he took it, sealing the deal with a shake and their personal honor.

"Alright, I'll go to the store, and buy plenty of lighters, and cans of hairspray, the ones I owe you and the ones for the job, as well as flashlights, a sledgehammer and, a good-sized fire extinguisher. Meet me at my place in two hours. I'll play some music, loud, to drown out the hammer strikes while we work. Good to go?"

"You got it, Mr. C," Derek said.

"Mr., huh?" Carl cocked an eyebrow at him.

"You've earned my respect, and then some. It takes some serious balls to do something like this."

Derek smiled and Carl smiled back, feeling kind of cool at that moment, as he turned to head for the store.

Carl walked into the apartment, arms loaded down with the supplies, and pushed the door closed with a foot.

Jessica glanced up from the kitchen sink to greet him, and stopped short, scrutinizing the items he was laying down on the couch, and trying to figure what use he intended for them.

"Ummm...honey. What's all that for?"

Carl looked up with a proud smile, and boyish anticipation covering his face.

"Extermination, baby! Extermination!" he exclaimed.

"Derek and the boys will be here soon to help us out," he further explained.

Jessica clearly looked confused, while simultaneously giving him a look that demanded a full explanation. Carl gave her the run-down in quick fashion, explaining everything Derek had told him, and what his plan was.

"So, your plan is to smash the walls in, and burn all the centipedes you find, and I'm going to put out the fires? That about it?"

"You got it, hon! Exactly!" Carl snapped his fingers and pointed both index fingers at Jessica with his thumbs cocked back, two guns ready to fire. He was obviously proud of his plan.

"Have you lost your fucking mind?" Jessica asked him, her tone incredulous.

Carl looked like she had slapped him square, his face twisting up, her blunt question a bitter pill of disrespect for all his hard work.

"No," he said bluntly. "I have *not* lost my fucking mind. I'm going to take care of this. Did you not hear me that we probably have tens of those monsters, if not hundreds, crawling within our walls? You just want to stand by and do nothing? You telling me you're gonna sleep just fine tonight, knowing that those bastards are there, in our walls, and may well end up on our bed again? You're good with that, are you?"

Carl shut up and just stared at Jessica, with a stiff neck and eyes set like flint.

He was not backing down on this one, at all.

Jessica looked at him, as she actually considered his questions, and realized she did *not* want to sleep in that apartment, and she was *not* ok with their situation.

"Fuck," she spat. "Alright, dammit. Let's do it."

Carl smiled big, walked over, grabbed Jessica by her upper arms, squeezed her, as he planted a big kiss on her lips, and then slapped one shoulder.

"Now you're talking, sidekick. Let's kick this pig."

Jessica was ready to say something about the 'sidekick' remark, but the doorbell rang, just then, right on time.

Nine Inch Nails played loudly in the background as Derek, Ricky and Rodney got their makeshift flamethrowers ready, and flanked Carl, giving wide berth for him to freely swing the hammer, and take-out portions of the wall. Another of the boys, Danny, was in charge of the flashlight, and knelt down shining it where Carl said he was first going to make a hole. His initial target was the wall directly against the water heater. If they were going to find something, the best bet was there. It also seemed likely, to him, that the greatest concentration of the critters would be there, as well. It was definitely warm and dark.

It took about four swings to open up a decent hole to see inside. Danny shined the bright light in there, and nearly cried out, as he reflexively shrunk away from what he saw.

"What is it?" Carl asked and took the flashlight to look for himself.

"A n..n..nest, I think," Danny stuttered out.

Carl knelt, and lowered his head to get a good look, gloved hands supporting his upper body. Even knowing what Danny thought, the sight of them still gave him a chill. They were all over the plywood floor, around the water heater, which appeared to be rotten, to a large degree. Carl could make out individual ones, uncurling and beginning to move around, due to the light and vibrations, while several giant centipede mothers curled more tightly around the masses of eggs, they held between their many legs.

But it was the few he spotted that had a mass of tiny newborn centipedes clutched within their circled bodies that got Carl. A shiver ran up his spine and caused his whole head and shoulders to shake briefly, as if trying to throw off some instinctive, primal fear of such things.

"Fuck me," Carl mumbled, and mentally told himself to cowboy-up, and not let his fears control him. "Alright. I'm gonna have to make a lot bigger hole for us to get to them without setting the whole place on fire. Be ready to stomp anything that comes out, while I'm clearing the plaster away."

The boys nodded in understanding. Danny looked a little nervous, as Carl handed him the flashlight back.

Carl swung the hammer, over and over, in a quick secession of strikes, breaking the dry wall and pulling it out of the way. Three of the giant centipedes came crawling out, startling Carl, causing him to jump back, briefly, which caused the boys to flinch away and yelp, as well. Carl lunged forward again without hesitation, though, swinging the sledgehammer down on one of the giant centipedes and smashing it right in the middle of its body. Derek and the boys trapped the other two with some of Jess's Tupperware to take in payment as their pets, while Danny shined the light on the hole, to see if anymore were coming.

Carl pulled the final piece of wall back, holding onto it, clearly exposing a good 4'x4' hole for the boys to work with.

"Oh, Fuck!" Danny exclaimed and pointed at Carl.

Carl had about enough time to say "huh" and, start to look around, before the giant centipede cleared his glove, and crawled up onto his forearm, clawed legs gripping his flesh. He flailed his arm hysterically, almost knocking Jess and the boys in the head, as he spun in circles, screaming 'fuck' over and over again. Then the centipede bit down on the crook of his elbow, and Carl just screamed period, pausing to see it covering the length of his forearm, the very rear legs locked onto the glove, as well.

His free hand cycled up and down rapidly, slapping at the creature in an unsophisticated flurry while shrieking like a baboon under attack. It had absolutely no affect. The giant centipede did not let go, but hung on with the poisonous mandibles, while its powerful jaws gnawed through Carl's flesh with a single-minded purpose. Carl's arm burned horribly from the venom, as well as from his flesh being sheared through, repeatedly.

"Pull it off, Mr. C!" Derek yelled. "Pull it off!"

Carl managed to hear and process Derek's words in the midst of his primitive panic, and finally gripped the body of the centipede like a vise, as close to the head as possible, then ripped back, pulling it off of his arm, though some of his flesh came along with it. Carl squeezed as tightly as he possibly could, trying to crush the monstrous bastard, but he could not overwhelm its exoskeleton.

"Spray him down, Derek, along with my glove!"

Derek gave Carl a look that said, "Are you sure?" and Carl immediately nodded. Derek hosed the centipede and the glove, thoroughly, as it thrashed about.

"Light it," said Carl.

"You got it, Mr. C," Derek responded, and flicked the lighter, sparking the flame that set Carl's whole hand on fire, along with the centipede.

Carl held his clenched fist up, for as long as he could, watching the flame-engulfed centipede crackle, before the hair spray burned off, and the glove, itself, began to catch on fire. He threw his assailant to the floor, and stomped it a couple of times, then shook the glove off, and stomped it too, putting out the flames.

Carl stumbled over and collapsed on the recliner, a combination of curses, shouts and painful groans composing a repeating cycle of noises that erupted from his mouth for some time. It was excruciating agony. He had read about it. The venom wasn't poisonous, but it could put a grown man on his ass, crying like a wimpy little bitch for a few hours.

Carl didn't have time for that, though. He didn't have time for anything, except killing these sons of bitches.

"Are you ok, honey?" Jessica asked, concerned for him.

"Do I *fucking* look alright?!?" he shouted. "It fucking hurts like thirty hells!

Motherfucker!!"

Carl's temper had climbed to a new peak. It wasn't directed at Jessica or any of the boys. It was aimed squarely at the centipedes and his piece-of-shit landlord, who wouldn't get an exterminator. It was his fault Carl was in pain. Of that, Carl was absolutely sure. Still, Jessica didn't appear to feel the difference, as her face showed the pain Carl's words had inflicted, and she backed away from him.

It took Carl a few seconds to register what he had done.

"Baby, I'm sorry. I wasn't thinking. I'm just hurting, and I reacted like an asshole. I'm sorry. Ok?"

They held eyes till Jessica believed he was serious and softened.

"I forgive you, baby," she said. "Do you want me to get something to bandage that with, and some triple-antibiotic ointment with the pain reliever in it?"

"Yes, please," he replied, "and about five extra-strength acetaminophen."

He coughed, and felt his lungs tighten, slightly. Carl knew he couldn't risk having a full-on attack right now. He retrieved the inhaler from his pocket and took a long hit off of it. Then he stood and walked back over to the large hole in the wall, closely inspecting the portion he needed to hold out of the way for the boys, as he pulled it back and used the sledgehammer to keep it from springing back to cover the hole.

Jessica returned and bandaged his arm up, wrapping everything from elbow to wrist with gauze, covering all the smaller scratches, as well as the nastier bite marks. Carl retrieved the glove and slid it back on his left hand.

"OK fellas. Spray hairspray all over them along the bottom of the water heater first. Then hose the whole area with fire. Hopefully, it will burn them good, while not immediately catching the wood on fire so quickly, I hope. Jess, stand ready with that fire extinguisher."

Derek took point, and coated the area with hairspray, watching the insects start to writhe around at the unfamiliar chemical. Then he flicked the lighter and let loose hell on the centipedes. The flames engulfed them, entirely. Carl imagined he heard little screeches, but he didn't think it was likely he could have heard them over the music.

Next, came the popping noises as the fire cooked them, and their exoskeletons crackled. Their bodies flailed all about, the mothers trying to protect their cooking young, who died first. A few of the males came crawling out of the hole, burning like pieces of kindling soaked in kerosene. They ran for some distance, then began curling and contorting as they finally felt the full effect of the flames. The boys stomped them dead, putting out the flames simultaneously as well.

Carl let the fire burn for some time, monitoring it to make sure it wasn't getting beyond their ability to put out, but making sure it burned long enough to kill these gargantuan insects, that had no place in this concrete jungle, where he lived; of that he was sure.

"Alright Jess, let it rip."

Jessica stepped up and sprayed the interior of the hole thoroughly. She waited for the white powder to settle then inspected it closely, determining that the fire was definitely out. She started to back up, then stepped forward again, spraying a little more, just for good measure.

Carl wrapped a T-shirt around his face, to prevent him from breathing in the fire extinguisher powder.

"Light, Danny," he called, and Danny stepped up, handing the flashlight to Carl, again. A lengthy inspection satisfied Carl that they had gotten everything he could see.

"Alright. Moving on," Carl declared, picking up the hammer, and shifting to another area of wall.

Over the next couple of hours, he made smaller holes every few feet, and then looked inside to see if there were any others. They spotted a few lone males scurrying around, but no more females with eggs or babies. Derek got the bright idea to use a spaghetti spoon to reach in, and drag the lone ones out, into the open. They captured three more, and burned the rest on the linoleum floor, melting it in multiple places.

By the end, Jessica and the boys were all hacking from the fire extinguisher powder and decided to wrap T-shirts around their mouths to filter it out, just like Carl had done, earlier. They went back and took a second look around the water heater. Finding nothing, Carl felt fairly happy with himself and his plan. In the next few days, he would contact a friend who could help him with repairing the drywall, thereby keeping it off the landlord's radar.

Derek looked at Carl, with a smirk on his face.

"What?" Carl asked.

"Just thought of something. Made me laugh."

Carl gave him a look that said, "Spit it out, I know you're about to be a smartass." Derek's smirk turned into a wicked grin.

"You know, you can totally expect to see roaches now, right?"

Carl dropped his head, and just shook it back and forth, mumbling curses beneath his breath.

That night, Carl and Jessica lit the one lemon 'Yankee Candle' they owned and set it in their bedroom to help mask all the nasty burnt wood and fire extinguisher chemical smells filling the apartment. Carl showered, Jessica slipping in to join him. They both breathed huge sighs of relief at finally being done with this nightmare, first hugging each other for a long time, as the hot water burned away the disgust they felt. After some time, they soaped one another down, enjoying the feel of each other's flesh.

Once out, they toweled off and Jessica dressed Carl's wound more thoroughly this time, cleansing everything with hydrogen peroxide before applying ointment. She then placed gauze pads over the deep bit marks and wrapped his whole arm with gauze and taped it down.

At last, all ready for bed, they crawled under the covers, unconsciously leaving the lights on as they snuggled up to one another and began kissing passionately. Jessica moved as if she was going to go down on Carl, but he checked her softly, his hand between her breasts, slowly pressing her to lay back and let him, instead. Pulling the sheet over his head, he disappeared, showering her abdomen with butterfly kisses as he descended to caress the gates of paradise with his mouth. He kissed her lightly, parting her lips to drink deep the intoxicating wine of her love.

Jessica groaned softly and made other soothing sounds of pleasure that dripped like a honey potion in Carl's ears, but soon grabbed his head and pulled upward.

"I want you inside me...now," she moaned and kissed him deeply, as he entered her and began slowly cycling his hips.

Carl made sure the sensations built ever higher for Jessica, enjoying every inch of friction as he moved in and out, progressively going deeper with each maddeningly controlled stroke. It drove her crazy when he moved slowly like that. She loved it, but eventually it caused her to desperately demand he give it to her with some authority and force, as she even now, commanded him.

"Harder! Harder!" she said breathlessly, hips squirming beneath him, as he obliged.

Three thrusts later, he felt a sharp pain, right on the head of his penis. It caused him to pause unexpectedly. Jessica kicked his glutes with her feet, as if spurring a horse on to run.

"Don't stop! Don't stop! I'm so close!"

Carl, despite the pain, continued, sacrificing his comfort to bring her to climax.

Another stabbing pain, struck, and another, but he didn't stop. Jessica's whole body went rigid and she slowly raked the nails of both hands from spine to ribcage, leaving a trail of welling blood. If he had been in the moment, and not already in pain, Carl would have loved it, he thought, but, as it was, it just added to discomfort he was already experiencing. As soon as Jessica shuddered and relaxed, he quickly pulled out, the pain on the head of his dick now in multiple places and not letting up.

He sat back on his haunches, pulling free of Jessica's arms and feet that were trying to keep him inside her. Then, he tossed the sheet back, so he could get a clear look at his member.

"What's wrong, baby?" she asked, sulking a little. But then, she saw his face and knew something was seriously wrong, and her stomach sank, like a ship standing on end, before sliding down into the murky depths beneath.

To his credit, Carl didn't freak out, and scramble about with no sense of purpose. Instead, despite his face indicating an absolutely terrific disgust, he sat still, and pulled the small, milky white baby centipedes off the head of his cock, one at a time, mashing their soft bodies in between thumb and forefinger, before smearing them across the sheet to clear their filth off his hands. A total of three had attached themselves to him, whether by legs or bite he did not know. He only knew it hurt.

Jessica stared at him, confused, and, mercifully unable to connect the dots, at first. But when it finally hit her, she clawed violently at the manicured patch of hair above her vagina, digging toward the opening to pull her lips back, arching her hips up desperately like some whore pretending she must have the man who has paid her for a performance, her head straining, chin to chest, in an attempt to give the eyes a better line of sight.

Right then, both Jessica and Carl observed a sight that would be burned into their minds for the rest of their lives.

"Baby centipedes are crawling out of my wife's pussy," was all Carl could think as he watched them exit her vagina and spread out in various directions; scurrying down the inside of her thighs, up into the hair covering her pubic bone, and down onto the bed.

Jessica may as well have been an animal with its tail on fire at that moment.

She flip-flopped off the bed, slapping at her groin and clawing her thighs, screeching some inhuman noises the whole time. Carl could only compare her wretched uproar to that of abused animals in fits of absolute fear, who, when approached, cry out, over and over, pitiful and helpless.

Jessica was just like that, right up until Carl held her down, and removed every one of those little bastards he could find from her body.

Then he took her to the ER. Fuck the bill.

Two days later.

Carl had called in the favor from Derek, or at least he had tried. Derek refused to charge Carl, instead volunteering the resources and aid. They wore gloves and masks completely covering their faces when they broke into the rundown flat. Derek was damn-near a master lock-picker at age twelve or thirteen, Carl still wasn't sure.

Nobody saw or heard them, except, perhaps, the crack addicts, who were high as a kite and not paying any attention, at all. They slipped through the kitchen and down the hall to the bedroom. Carl was carrying a backpack and holding a cloth he had just soaked with ether, while Derek held some type of container.

The man on the bed snored loudly, then gasped as the air was forced from his lungs by Carl plopping down on his chest. He covered the man's mouth and nose with the cloth immediately. The man tried to struggle, but his obese and muscularly weak frame couldn't accomplish much before the ether won the day.

They moved quickly, removing long, heavy duty cargo straps from the backpack and proceeding to loop them over and under the bed, then ratchet them down tightly, restraining the man across the shoulders, waist, upper thighs and knees. Once done, Carl took a pocketknife to the man's underwear, the only thing he was wearing, and ripped them off, exposing his genitals. Carl proceeded to nick the man's skin with the blade across the chest, inner thighs and even his flaccid penis.

Derek followed behind Carl, dropping a giant centipede on each location. They wasted no time, immediately biting into the bleeding flesh with their venomous pincers before beginning to chew their way inside.

Carl watched the one going to work on the man's shriveling member and remembered the pictures he had seen online of a fourteen-inch-long giant centipede that ate its way into the mouth of a snake almost twice its size...then devoured it from the inside out, exiting somewhere near the tail.

Carl looked away, after several seconds, then reached in the backpack for one last thing - an item used to keep a patient's mouth open during dental surgery. He pried the man's mouth open and shoved it into place, observing the large open hole now.

"A fucking tunnel of love," Carl thought, as he picked the last giant centipede up with the forceps, himself, and lowered it, letting it smell the man's fetid breath and feel the plastic edge of the device with its most front legs. It began to pull, its head descending into the warm, dark pit below. Carl slowly let go, watching the legs rise and fall in unison as the creature crawled into the landlord's mouth and surely began its path down the throat.

The man startled awake, trying to cough reflexively as his eyelids flew wide open, double chin quivering as his eyeballs strained to look in his own mouth.

Carl grinned with a sense of immense personal satisfaction as he stuffed a rag down inside the device hole to muffle any screams and make sure the giant centipede couldn't crawl out.

"At least not through *that* hole, anyway," he told himself, "but it'll make *a* way out when it's ready." The thought comforted Carl, scratching his vengeful desires behind the ears. His right leg damn near bounced in delight.

"Perfect," he said to Derek, a dark, menacing smile unseen beneath the mask.

"Warm, dark places are their favorite."

Carl looked at where the other centipedes were clinging to the man's body, little powerful jaws cutting through his flesh, over and over again. It was the closest thing to justice he could imagine.

"Let's go," he said to Derek.

They listened to the muffled gags and gurgling cries as they walked out the way they came in, making sure no one saw a thing.

"That's what you get for not hiring an exterminator and putting my wife through hell, you greedy, useless bastard," Carl thought to himself.

They stayed to the shadows and moved in silence, eventually taking the masks off. They'd burn them tomorrow along with the gloves. The apartment complex came into sight, and it was Carl who spoke first.

"Thank you so much, Derek. I know you wanted to keep those things."

"I've still got one, Mr. C. And one's all I need to fight against other bugs and stuff. I just wish I could get a look at that guy's body when they're done. Curious how much of him they'll eat before he gets found."

"You worry me, sometimes, Derek," Carl said flatly, cutting his eyes to give him a wink. "But I still think you're a good kid. Good to me and Jessica, that's for damn sure."

He patted Derek on the shoulders as they entered the building, then they parted ways, sharing a bond that no distance could ever break, now.

THANKS FOR READING

BYE BYE

NIGHT NIGHT

SLEEP TIGHT

HEY YOU!

First off let me say, THANK YOU FOR SUPPORTING ART. Even if you didn't "get" some of this, that's okay, that just means it wasn't meant for you, in that case go back and read my Dedication note at the beginning... if you did get our vibes, welcome to the Cult of Crazy. I'd save you a chair, but we sit on our heads. If you think you got what it takes to be in a future collection, check on the official *SpookyNinjaKitty* website for when we open for story submissions again – in the meantime please write a review online and tell a friend because we survive by word of mouth.

If you have questions about the stories, please check out our detailed appendix for answers.

APPENDIX

WAIT FOR IT ...

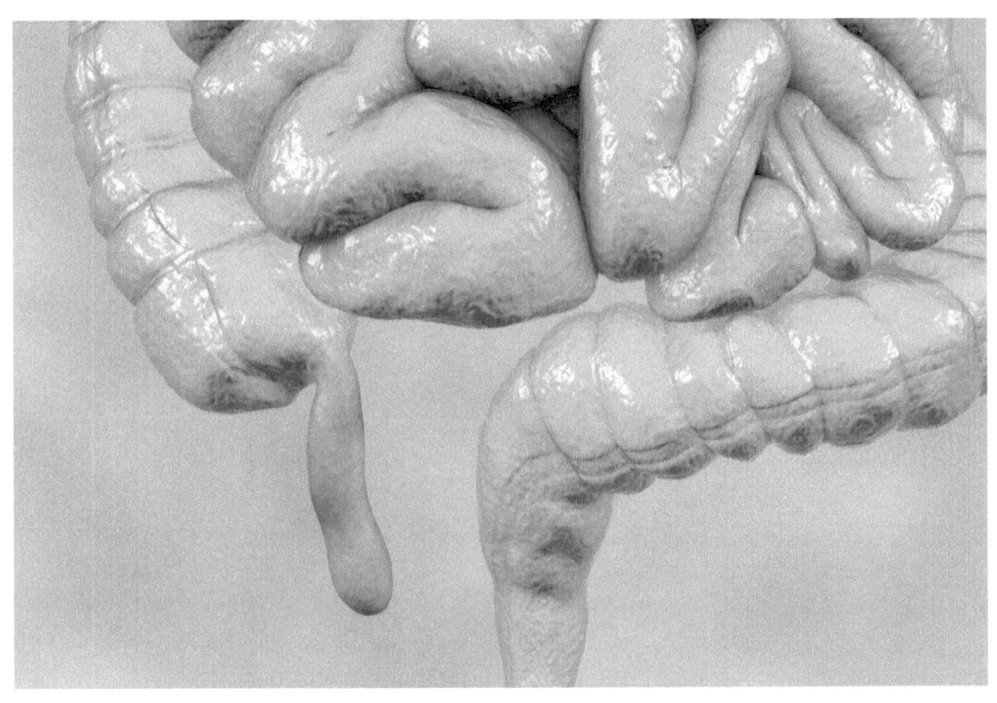

TIM CHIZMAR

After graduating from *Edinboro University of Pennsylvania* with his bachelor's degree in Communications, and obtaining his Master's Degree in Demonology from *Miskotonic University*, Tim Chizmar has written for various magazines, newspapers and websites including *Fangoria*, *First Comics News*, *Girls and Corpses*, and many others. He has sold short stories to such collections as *Chicken Soup for the Soul* and has written various screenplays for Hollywood production companies. Tim is the founder and co-chairman of the Las Vegas chapter of the prestigious *Horror Writers Association*.

Aside from the darker topics, it has not all been a career of terror as his lighter credits to date include *ABC, FOX, Showtime, Playboy, NBC, The Hallmark Channel,* and many more. He has produced various pilots including in 2010 he developed a comedy/action series for *CMT* with wrestling superstar Rob Van Dam. As a headlining comedian Tim was a favorite at The World-Famous Hollywood IMPROV, The Jon Lovitz Comedy Club, has toured all over the world playing sold-out casinos, clubs and colleges. To date he has worked with such standup legends as Jeff Foxworthy, Gabriel Iglesias, Jon Lovitz, Daniel Tosh, and many others.

When he's not inspiring fellow writers by being on various panels such as San Diego Comic-Con, WonderCon, Scare LA, or speaking at Hollywood Success events, he's constantly working on his next project. Because for Tim Chizmar... There's always a next project! After Tim had been successful enough to become a regular at red carpet premieres, he left all the glitz and glam behind in early 2017 for the mountains of Idaho as he completed this book. He always looks forward to having frank, honest, and engaging discussions on the business of the writing craft with his fellow writers. Tim's advice to young writers is this...

"Be inspired. Are you alive, or are you just breathing?"

amazon.com/author/timchizmar

instagram.com/timchizmar

twitter.com/TimChizmar